MW01133480

Sfumato *

Book One of the Harbor and Divine Series

A STORY OF LOVE, LOSS AND HOPE

by T.W. Poremba

Illustrations by Robert Capes

XULON PRESS

Xulon Press
2301 Lucien Way #415
Maitland, FL 32751
407.339.4217
www.xulonpress.com

© 2021 by T.W. Poremba

All rights reserved solely by the author. The author guarantees all contents are original and do not infringe upon the legal rights of any other person or work. No part of this book may be reproduced in any form without the permission of the author. The views expressed in this book are not necessarily those of the publisher.

Due to the changing nature of the Internet, if there are any web addresses, links, or URLs included in this manuscript, these may have been altered and may no longer be accessible. The views and opinions shared in this book belong solely to the author and do not necessarily reflect those of the publisher. The publisher therefore disclaims responsibility for the views or opinions expressed within the work.

This is a work of fiction. Unless otherwise indicated, all the names, characters, businesses, places, events and incidents in this book are either the product of the author's imagination or used in a fictitious manner. Any resemblance to actual persons, living or dead, or actual events is purely coincidental.

Unless otherwise indicated, Scripture quotations taken from the Holy Bible, New International Version (NIV). Copyright © 1973, 1978, 1984, 2011 by Biblica, Inc.™. Used by permission. All rights reserved.

Paperback ISBN-13: 978-1-6628-2473-9
eBook ISBN-13: 978-1-6628-2474-6

*Sfumato (sfoo-mah'-toe)

*Derived from the Italian word fumo, meaning "smoke." Refers to the **technique of oil painting in which colors or tones are blended in such a subtle manner that they melt into one another without perceptible transitions, lines or edges.** Leonardo da Vinci (1452-1519) himself described sfumato as a blending of colors "without lines or borders, in the manner of smoke."*

— The Art Encyclopedia

To

Cathy

with all my love,
and our sons
Joshua and Micah

twp

Table of Contents

The Chateau de Cloux, France

Home of Leonardo Da Vinci
October 26, 1517

Budding 15-year old Sicilian artist Dario could hardly believe his good fortune. There he was at the Chateau de Cloux, France, the home of his artistic hero, Leonardo da Vinci. Already Dario had met the master, toured his studio, and seen the fabled *Mona Lisa.* He was in heaven! His uncle, Antonio de Beatis, had arranged it all, however that happened, plus two weeks for Dario to study *sfumato* with Leonardo. Two weeks!

It was all part of a grand tour of Central Europe for Cardinal Luigi of Aragon and his retinue of thirty-five courtiers and servants, who were now about to leave the Chateau de Cloux to head onto the next stop on their itinerary. During their five months of touring, Dario had come to like Cardinal Luigi, as well as just about everybody else on the grand tour, so saying all his good-byes took quite a while.

But Cardinal Luigi waited patiently for his young charge and soon gave the command to head out. Off they went, leaving the Chateau de Cloux while shouting out their farewells and blessings like one of the pageants Leonardo used to create for the Medici family in Florence to lead a joyous throng to the theatre. Leonardo loved it!

After waving to his uncle and his new friends until they were out of sight, Dario eagerly found his way back to the studio near the doorway that led into the master's *studiolo*. He peeked into Leonardo's small private study and saw it lined with books, charts and monographs, filled with curious models of human anatomy and displaying frightening inventions of military weaponry. Dario had first rested his eyes upon a cutaway model of the human eye. But then he latched onto a design model for an assault vehicle propelled by two mounted horses that pushed a murderous looking machine spinning a trio of deadly scythes whirling ahead ready to mow through the human flesh of an advancing army.

That scythed chariot was quite a contrast to the tender paintings of the **Mona Lisa** and the **Virgin and Child with Saint Anne** which stood with the young **Saint John the Baptist,** all resting akimbo against easels and furniture in the main studio. Dario stared spellbound in worshipful reverie taking it all in, until the master himself interrupted.

"Dario, *figlio mio,* I am so very happy your uncle gave you permission to stay with us! You like what you see?"

"Yes, Master Leonardo. Everything. This is the studio of an artist who is also a genius."

"Thank you, Dario. But two things as we begin. Call me 'Master,' or 'Leonardo' or even 'Zio,' uncle, if you like, but only one. You choose."

"I choose 'Uncle.'"

"Excellent! Now you have two uncles!" chortled the smiling Leonardo. "Secondly," he continued, "since you want to learn *sfumato,* you must first learn the ways of light." He pointed at the *Mona Lisa,* lifted her from the floor and placed her upon an easel while he taught. "Light can make her eyes sparkle, Dario. Light can make her eyes glisten with tears that have not yet been shed. Light can make her eyes seem to follow your eyes. But to create those effects, those artistic illusions, the artist must become part scientist, part magician as well as an excellent painter," said the genius who was all three.

Dario stood, eyes wide open and mouth agape, listening enraptured as Leonardo opened up the arcane knowledge of a master artist to a fledgling, two-week apprentice yearning to learn.

"Let me demonstrate with Lisa. She is beautiful, no?"

"Yes! Very beautiful!"

"But she is locked within paint on this wood panel. We need to give her life. We need to make the light dance in her eyes, so that whoever looks into those beautiful eyes will see depth, energy, movement, even life itself. *Sfumato* plays with light in layer upon layer of very thin, lightened or darkened varnish glaze which redirects the light so that our eyes see the briefest of movements in her eyes even though it is actually our eyes that move.

"And that is *sfumato,* Uncle?" Dario asked.

"Yes. That is *sfumato,* in part. Those same layers of glaze can also cover up an artist's lines, lines that may interrupt our eyes from moving and, therefore, prevent us from seeing the sparkle, the energy, the life, and the movement in Lisa's eyes. Let me show you."

Leonardo picked up a pallet of lightly tinted, translucent glaze that matched the white of Lisa's eyes. He also picked up the smallest of all brushes and two very small knives.

"Dario, look into Lisa's right eye and tell me what you see."

"Beauty. Sparkles. Depth. Glistening joy. And life, like she is about to weep for joy or sadness. Which one I don't know."

"Exactly so. Now, look into her left eye. What do you see there?" asked Leonardo pointing to the white expanse of her eyeball near her left eyelid.

"It is different from her right eye. It is flat. Dull. Like the eye of a corpse."

Leonardo laughed heartily at Dario's crude, but accurate description.

"Precisely," he chuckled. "Do you notice anything on the edge of the white of her left eye near the lid?"

"Yes. There's a border between them. A line. Is that one of those lines you don't like?"

"It is indeed. We are going to use *sfumato* glaze to cover that edge line. We will blend the whitest part of her eye gradually into the darkest part of her eyelid with many delicate strokes of glaze that get ever so gradually darker and lighter." And with that, over the next hour, he took that tiniest of brushes, and delicately placed nearly invisible strokes of glaze first transforming the line that divides into a smokey blur, then as he continued to paint, making the line disappear altogether. Leonardo had blended the white of her eyeball into the dark of her eyelid to make it look exactly as if it were Lisa's very own eye peering out at them.

"Oh, Uncle, that is perfection!"

"Dario," Leonardo concluded, "we must always remember that exquisite art uses no lines, but only color and shading to define a nose from its cheek or a tree from the sky. Do you understand?"

"I do," Dario answered. He paused. And then in a sudden dawn of stunned realization he exclaimed, "But, Uncle, wait! WE?! Did you just say, 'we' several times?"

Uncle Leonardo smiled thoroughly enjoying this new nephew. "Yes, I did indeed say, 'we.' Several times. You and I, Dario, together, we will bring subtle, glistening glee to the remaining white of her left eye, which you said looks like the eye of a corpse. We will give Lisa's left eye the *gioia di vita*, the delight of life! To do that, you and I will first apply, with delicate strokes, slightly tinted, but mostly clear, varnish glaze embedded with nearly invisible, translucent white flecks to reflect light from deep within her eye giving sparkle to her whole face. On top of that, over the next two weeks, we will slowly build up layers of glaze to deepen that sparkle, adding fascinating dimension to the white expanse of her eye.

"It will be amazing, Uncle! But this time you said 'you and I.' Am *I* to brush your masterpiece with *sfumato* glaze?"

"Indeed, you are. With brush and palette, you will help me make Mona Lisa into a painting for the ages. And perhaps 500 years from now, when art lovers are still enchanted by the sparkle in Mona Lisa's eyes, and might think they are looking only at Leonardo's work, we will know from heaven with the Archangel Michael, that it is Dario's *sfumato* that made all the difference in Lisa's dazzling left eye."

However, nearly 500 years later it wasn't to be Dario's *sfumato* work on Mona Lisa's enchanting left eye that would have the art world abuzz. No. Instead it would be a latter day devotee of Uncle Leonardo's *sfumato:* amazing American portrait artist Gary Siciliano.

Chapter 1

Sfumato: Through a Glass Darkly

Constantly wiping away the tears, Gary steeled himself to start his life all over again. Without his wife Dianah. Without their daughter Lilyana. Oh, Lily, such a joy-energized, beautiful little girl. Long blonde hair flying every which way. "Daddy, Daddy, you're home! Hooray!" He choked back a sob. Gone. Just gone. Dianah must have tried to save her...but now both of them are dead. Gone.

"Get a grip, Gary. Deep breath," he admonished himself aloud. Then he channeled his inner baseball coach: "Come-on-now! Slow in, slow out." His cell phone rang his over-the-top ringtone, "If You're Happy and You Know It." Holy cow, that hurts. The three of them sang that old camp song over and over again on road trips sometimes at the top of their lungs with the windows open, laughing all the way. They even sang it getting breakfast together: "If you're happy and you know it, clap your hands. Clap! Clap!" So he croaked along with Dianah's and Lily's voices as he checked his caller i.d.

1

The realtor. He had contacted one in Cleveland. "Oh boy," he said aloud. "And so now it begins, leaving behind one beautiful demolished life and trying to build another in its place." Deep breath. Slow in. Slow out. There's no good time to take a next step in life when your heart is breaking. Phweww. But will it ever *stop* breaking? "Suck it up, Gar. Just suck it up."

He did and answered his cell.

"Hello, Gary here," he choked. Not bad. Maybe the realtor wouldn't notice.

"Hello!" she chirped way too cheerfully. "Mr. Siciliano? I'm Annie Dunlop from Dunlop Realty in Cleveland. You called looking for help finding some property to renovate and live in on Cleveland's Near West Side?" It irritated him that she asked a statement as a question. 'Oh, let it go.' Everything irritated him these days. Everything.

"Yes, I did. Thank you for calling me back." Choke. Choke. 'Can't even take a single breath without sobbing,' he thought. 'Just stay polite...Okay, let's do this. If you're happy and you know it...After all, she *is* helping.'

"My pleasure," Annie the realtor responded. Then she gathered herself and joyfully announced, even singing a trumpet fanfare: "A-a-and: Da-dah-da-dah!"

'Oy, trumpet fanfare and all,' Gary quietly groaned. 'Deep breath.' Surprisingly the silliness did help lighten the mood.

Annie Dunlop continued, "I have some really good news about a property on the Near West Side, an old church and parish house on the corner of Harbor and Divine. I think you'll love it!"

She was way over the top enthused. And happy. Maybe too much for Gary right now. But maybe not. He found it unexpectedly soothing to hear a joyful woman's voice. Still he swallowed hard. It would be heart-wrenching moving away from

Durango with its wonderful memories, especially of Dianah and Lily, and terrible regrets, like never having had the chance to say 'good-bye.' "Good-bye, Sweetie." "Good-bye, Lily." And then just moving "back home" to Cleveland...tough, tough, tough. But his memories from Cleveland came back and consumed him as he stood with the phone to his ear.

* * * * * * *

For Gary, it was dark irony that when the waste-polluted Cuyahoga River actually caught on fire in 1978 the whole country thought it was a terrible tragedy. Newspaper headlines all over the country told the story, even though no one died and very little property sustained damage after a monumental cleanup. But when the Durango Mountain fire storm destroyed 20,000 acres of timber reporters wrote it off as just another mountain forest fire. Never you mind that it burned up a ski resort, razed dozens of mountain homes leaving behind smoldering ash, polluting the crystal clean mountain air 10,000 feet up into a choking deadly mix of hot tar smoke and ash, and killing Dianah and Lily. "They're dead. Understand? Now *that's* a tragedy," he'd rant. These days he often ranted, mainly just to himself, but, still, it left him winded, angry and anxious. He had to tell himself, "Settle down, Gar, settle down."

Still, he felt he *should* be able to adjust to Cleveland. Right? After all, that's where he grew up. Oil refineries and steel mills poisoned the air and damaged people's lungs, but nothing like a mountain fire storm burning folks to a crisp. Right? "Adjust!" he would admonish himself again and again. But then his mind would snap leaving him angry, bitter and broken, hostile to people around him. Gary just could not see himself adjusting to anything — anything — not without Dianah and Lily.

3

True, the three of them did fly back twice a year on Frontier Airlines to visit Gary's mom and dad, get reacquainted with city bustle, urban air and empty poverty. But now, without Dianah and Lily, Gary just dreaded that move, even though it was his childhood home and where Gary's mom and dad still lived in nearby Kamm's Corners. Being near them was a good reason for him to move back. However, just thinking about moving there overwhelmed him, as if moving back to Cleveland and trying his darnedest to run away from that Durango Mountain fire storm would change anything. Anything at all. Certainly it could not bring their love back to life, nor their Durango joy.

With his wife and daughter at his side Gary had absolutely loved the Rocky Mountain Highs of Durango Mountain as well as the folksy, old hippie vibe of Durango itself. In Durango when the snow came, and the mountain slopes beckoned, store owners would hang signs on their doors: "Gone skiing! Meet you on the slopes!" And in summertime when the Animas River (which never caught on fire!) sparkled with mountain top sunshine and bass jumped after skimmer flies, they would put out signs on the front doors reading, "Gone Fishin'! See you there!" It's one of the few places you'll ever see where on any given Tuesday in August when there's one—mind you—one single fluffy cloud in an otherwise pristine azure sky, the locals would say, "I reckon we're gonna have another cloudy day!" That would be a total of three clouds all week. Cloudy? Really? Compare that to Cleveland's grey skies and polluted Cuyahoga River and declare where you would rather live. These days Gary felt like he was always on the edge of a rant.

At 7,000 plus feet high in the sky combined with the highs of legalized marijuana, every day in Durango was a Rocky Mountain High! Every day was a honeymoon for Gary and

Dianah. Then when Lilyana, their Lily, was born, every day became a happy day and they knew it, and they clapped their hands, they stomped their feet and shouted, "Amen."

It just seemed that now every minute Gary had to make choices he never, ever wanted to make, choices forced upon him by the devilish mountain fire that demolished the paradise he and Dianah built together. Instead of adjusting, he angrily rebelled, daring life to take him kicking and screaming into the next day of charred memories and lonely nights.

True, moving to his childhood home might be better than living alone in Durango where any day a stiff northwest breeze could pull the smell of fire right out of the scorched earth, and send it into Gary's nostrils taunting him with the memory of the flaming aspens that had burned away everything he loved.

Yet, Gary had to confess, Cleveland did hold lots of wonderful memories not incinerated by a hellish inferno. After all, it was on Cleveland's Near West Side where Gary started drawing and painting. It was on the Near West Side where he met Ms. Val Green, art teacher extraordinaire. It was on the Near West Side where that character-lined face of Old Tony begged to be drawn. For seven decades, life had sculpted Old Tony's face with the chisel of character, the hammer of struggle and the brush of hope into a glorious human-in-the-flesh work of art that simply begged for canvas and oils or even a sketch pad. And the best part was Gary didn't have to create that face, or imagine the depth of the creases, the length of the crow's feet, or even the leathery scales of the cheeks. All Gary had to do was draw what was there, the face of an old Slovenian man fashioned by the Hand of God the Creator, who challenged Gary to replicate Old Tony with line and life on sketch pad and canvas. It was on the Near West Side where Ms. Green introduced Gary to *sfumato*, the artist's tool to change hard pencil lines into the blurred edges of life, turning a drawing into a work of living art. It was on the Near West Side where Gary began to grow as an artist of life-breathing portraits that amazed art critics and inspired art lovers to pay ever increasing amounts of money for the right to hang Gary's paintings in their homes.

His success at Ohio art shows led him to Taos, New Mexico where at the Taos Fall Arts Festival Old Tony won Best of Show and where Gary won the heart of Dianah Springer — who one day would become his wife, his lover and his muse. Gary's success at art shows that began on Cleveland's Near West Side, eventually earned him enough money to buy and build his and Dianah's dream home on Durango Mountain in the midst of thousands of acres of aspens and overlooking fabulous canyons of the Rocky Mountains. And now that same wealth will give him the chance to flee their burned-to-the-ground dreams and carry away his broken heart filled with smoke-blurred memories of a joyous life with Dianah and Lily.

Yes, it's true, he will carry with him his painted reminders of beautiful Dianah including one of a joyful, dancing Brown Bear, arms stretched out to heaven and face graced with a beautiful, enigmatic smile. That Dancing Brown Bear painting also garnered him best of show in San Francisco and an offer from a Montana couple to buy the Dancing Bear for $350,000. He turned them down then, and he would do the same now. She was *his* Dancing Bear. And she still is. Still. No mountain fire could ever change that. She'll go with him to Cleveland. She will grace the walls of their new home with her dancing joy and arms lifted to heaven.

Thank God Dianah had gotten that painting and others out of the house and into Gary's Durango studio at the first evacuation order. If only she and Lily would have stayed put... Why in the name of heaven and earth did they go back? Even though God had gifted Gary with the ability to paint his memories of Dianah that he now can take with him, they are still only painted memories, snapshots, standing-still moments from years of joy, smoke blurred recollections of love in paints on canvas.

Now Gary would have to take the blurred edges of his two sets of life memories and somehow meld them to make one new man — Gary of Durango Mountain with Gary of Cleveland's Near West Side, no lines of separation one from the other. Life is like that, he has learned. There are no lines the human eye can see, no line that tells one moment, "You cannot escape the next moment or run back to the last." Nor can a line separate one person from another. We are boundary-less together, human beings with one another, with other living creatures, with plants, soil, mountains, air, water.

A man with a woman. Boundary-less. In art, *sfumato*.

But in life, in real life, there are moments of total chaotic confusion, mind-bending brokenness, heart-rending obfuscation that send love reeling, lost in a pit of smokey darkness.

The two most important women in his adult life had taught him the same lesson of boundarylessness from two perspectives — art and love. The first, Ms. Val Green, taught him from the artist's perspective, especially from the art and teaching of *sfumato* by Leonardo DaVinci. *Sfumato* actually means blurred by smoke. Huh. A poignant lesson now after the Durango fire. The second, and even more important to Gary, Dianah Springer Brownbear, his love, his wife, taught him those life lessons from the traditions of the nations of the Four Corners: We are all One. There is no Hopi, no Navajo, no brown man, no red woman, no white man, no slave, no free, no male, no female, no bear, no wolf, no apple, no cactus, no lines that can separate one human being from another or from the earth or from the universe or from God who creates us all.

Hopi wisdom puts it this way: We are One Person.

Leonardo's art shows it another way: *Sfumato.*

To Gary's delight, Dianah loved to demonstrate it still another way:

> We are One Flesh.
> But when the two who are one
> are rent asunder
> what then?

Can life in Cleveland heal a soul ravaged by death in Durango?

Chapter 2

Harbor and Divine

Were Gary ever to write his life's memoir, his Cleveland memories would surely include the West Side Ecumenical Ministries (WSEM), right on the corner of Harbor and Divine Streets, that hired two college students, Sandy and James, as community organizers to work with kids. When Gary was ten years old Sandy worked with little kids like Gary's six year old brother, Robert. She got the city of Cleveland to grant her money so she and neighbors could turn a vacant lot on West 45th Street, one block west of Harbor Street, from a drug dealer hangout into a little kids playground that she called "Tot-a-Lot." The neighbors had loved the idea, and they loved Sandy too, for a lot of good reasons. She was bright, energetic, and she loved the children. So when she asked for help to build Tot-a-Lot the neighbors pitched right in. In fact, even the mayor of Cleveland came out to celebrate the Tot-a-Lot dedication. In a starter-home neighborhood with old East European and new Latino immigrants, West Virginia transplants, recovering addicts plus people just down on their luck, Sandy's Tot-a-Lot was a vibrant light. Attitudes brightened, and for good reasons.

Like, one Saturday, the cops caught a five-year-old boy stealing food from the Pick-n-Pay on Lorain Ave. They turned him in to Children's Services who in turn, having heard about Sandy's neighborhood work, asked her to help the family. Of course she would do anything to help. Sandy dug into it. She found out that the boy's mother gave him a grocery list and sent him "shopping" with the list but with no money every Saturday when the store was the most crowded. In the crowd that little tyke was so short he was almost invisible. So each week he gathered groceries on his mother's list and quietly walked out the door and back home. Such a good boy! And lucky, too. He never thought he was doing anything wrong. Until one day a store clerk saw him leave without paying and reported it to the store manager. A week later they watched him do it again, innocently come in, shop and leave. Really cute, but they still notified the police, and the next week the officers nabbed him.

Understand, it was to be his food for the week. There was no money because mama used *her* money for dope. Sandy worked with the mother to help her find local churches with free food and clothing, including St. Patrick's, the Methodist Church and the West Side Community Center. Plus Sandy got mom on a rehab path so she could keep custody of her son. Sandy was a gem, and the people of the Harbor and Divine neighborhood loved her for it.

Every day Cleveland's Near West Side spawned tragic stories, some with happy endings. Many others never escaped the tragedy of their story line. Destiny some say. But love can alter destiny, change lives, proclaim second and third chances that break the enslaving chains of poverty, racism, sexism and can breathe life into "dem bones" that can rise again. The two young idealists that the West Side Ecumenical Ministries hired yearned to breathe freedom into the nostrils of the choking poor.

The other community worker, James, focused on the older kids, especially boys, like Gary. James ran a wrestling camp on Saturdays in the Methodist Church's large carpeted gathering area behind the sanctuary. Wrestling was a big deal on the Near West Side with high school wrestling powers Lincoln West, St. Ed's and St. Ignatius drawing from the neighborhood for their elite, perennially state-ranked wrestling teams. Younger boys learned takedowns, crossovers and escape moves from their older brothers and neighborhood friends, so the boys who attended James' camp already knew about competitive wrestling and were eager to learn more. James taught them about wrestling, sportsmanship and faith. Of course, he had to prove himself by wrestling (and defeating) all the young toughs to gain their respect and to keep order in a roomful of inner city boys. He also packed the W.S.E.M. van with boys for swimming trips and invited them to play baseball with him on a hardscrabble open field where dozens of train tracks once comprised the West Side switching yard. The ground was still a little rough to be sure, but they all loved it, bad bounces and all.

And then, when it got dark on the weekends, James walked bar-studded Lorain Avenue until midnight to talk with boys who were shining shoes or begging quarters outside the bars while they waited for dad or mom to stagger out and go home. Sometimes a clumsy drunk would fumble around for a quarter, get frustrated and give a dollar or even mistakenly give up a five. That made a drunken dad vigil worth it all. Unless Dad smelled the money. Gary said his dad could, you know, smell the money, the bills. How else could you explain how he absolutely knew his kid had folding money in his pocket, except to say he smelled it?

"Did you get many quarters, son?"

"Some."

"Any bills? You wouldn't be holding out on me now, would ya?"

"Ya, I got a dollar."

"Give it. Come on."

Gary could keep the quarters, but his dad got all the bills.

"Da-ad."

"Give it."

"Okay. Here." But not a word about the five in his shoe.

One of the boys whom James found "working" the bars at 11:30 that night was 11-year-old Eddie. His dad ran out on his family years ago. In fact, Eddie actually never knew his father. But James knew there was always a story, always a struggle and, therefore, always a place where he could serve, help a kid. So he asked,

"Eddie, what are you up to at this time of night?"

"Beggin' quarters. Besides I got kicked out of the house."

"What? Why? What did you do?"

"Nothin'."

"Oh, come on, you don't get kicked out of your own home for nothing. Really, what'd you do?"

"Honest, I didn't do nothing."

"So why did they kick you out?"

Eddie took a deep breath of discomfort at being pushed to answer James. "Look, it's like this — my mother and my sisters 'work' on the weekends. Up stairs in the bedrooms. They don't want me around. They kick me out so I can't be around to see their customers."

James stood stunned speechless. On Cleveland's Near West Side, he learned something new every day, every minute.

"My mother says it pays the rent."

"Every Friday and every Saturday night?"

"Yep. Even in a blizzard, dude. Sometimes the bartenders invite me in to get warm. Sometimes not, and I just freeze."

Life, especially a life of poverty in inner city Cleveland, often got played out in terms of creative immorality involving dangerous propositions that put parents and children alike at constant risk, even 'working' the bars for quarters. Those same bars where James met his boys on weekend nights, three murders took place that year. Three. All among family members or best friends — two with guns and one a stabbing.

Still disregarding the risks, James and his young wife, Lew, both just 21 years old, painted and fixed up one second floor bedroom in the parish house for their Honeymoon Suite featuring a second-hand bedroom set James' older cousin gave them.

Usually that second floor served as a retreat center for folks mostly from suburban churches to run inner-city mission trips. Adults and teens from the burbs slept on steel bunk beds nights, and during the days the organizers would take them on "And-this-is-where-the-poor-people-live" tours before they actually put them to work. It's a shock for middle class people to just drop into the 'scary inner city' to witness the dark side of poverty, so a tour helps volunteers overcome their fears — some of them, anyhow. Then with servant hearts they soldiered on to volunteer at the Tot-a-Lot or give out free clothing and food in the church next door or trek down to serve meals at

St. Herman's House of Hospitality, a Greek Orthodox monastery slash home for homeless men. Harbor and Divine was a good place to learn how to serve others. The needs of people on the Near West Side were endless, providing a myriad of opportunities for God-loving people to serve others, to make a difference in the world. That's why James loved it.

But still the risks of living there were real, even just sleeping there for a few nights on a weekend mission.

Like that one weekend when no mission groups were there, James and Lew left to visit family just 20 minutes away in Garfield Heights to stay overnight. Wouldn't you know it, thieves climbed the fire escape, broke open the door to their room and stole what meager valuables they had, like Lew's clock radio and the not-silver-silver-ware in the first floor kitchen. Lessons learned: 1. Keep vigilant. 2. Be smart. 3. Don't own what anyone else might want to steal. Every day living on the Near West Side taught James unexpected lessons.

One weekend James helped Gary pull his skunk-drunk dad out of his favorite haunt, a bar on the same stretch of Lorain that witnessed one of the three murders that year. Together they walked him home. James knew that walking those streets at night was always a risk, but he never balked, because the love in his servant heart trumped any fear. Likewise he knew that any moment could demand of him some act of kindness from his soul that might lead to life-changing hope in a young boy's life or even in his father's. Like Gary and his drunk dad.

Really. You never knew, so James just went where Goodness led him, said what Goodness placed on his heart. Especially with Gary.

One Saturday afternoon on his way to buy a filing cabinet at the used furniture store on the corner of Lorain and W 45th Street James bumped into Gary.

"Hi, Gary! Where you headed?"

"Oh, just walking around."

James noticed that Gary was nonchalantly holding a book or something so James couldn't see exactly what it was. "Whatcha got there, Gar?" he asked.

"Oh, nothing. Just some doodles."

"Doodles? Like sketches and stuff?"

"Ya."

"Can I see?" James asked gently reaching for the sketch book.

"Oh, okay. But don't laugh," warned Gary as he handed James the sketchbook of what he said were his doodles.

"Thanks," said James carefully taking Gary's thick, spiral bound sketch book already opened to pencil sketches that were so well done they made James' jaw drop. "Gary, I didn't know you could draw." He flipped though some more pages of drawings and doodles with his mouth agape and eyes wide in amazement. "Gary, Gary, these are outstanding! Where did you learn to draw like this?"

Gary shrugged and told James, "It just comes. And I draw."

And draw he did. The book was filled with hundreds of sketches — buildings, trees, trucks, flowers, even an old guy in front of a bar.

"Gary, I'm amazed. To fill up this book with drawings this good, you must draw constantly."

"I do," Gary smiled. "And I have four more sketchbooks just like this one full of my drawings. It's like everything I look at asks me to draw it. So I do."

"I guess! Hey, look, you even have a long-legged fly here. And there." James flipped through a few more pages. "This is good stuff, Gary. This is really good stuff. Even that long-legged fly is good. Different angles. There it is again. It's everywhere." They both chuckled. "What's with the fly? Is it a pet fly or something?"

Gary laughed hard. "Actually, yes."

James took a double take, "What? You're kidding, right?"

"No, no. For real. A few weeks this summer he stayed with me in the corner of my bedroom where I doodle, where I draw. He just sat there, never moved. It might sound kinda weird, but that fly became sort of a friend. I liked him. So I drew him. And when I'd get stuck on how to draw the next thing, I'd just doodle the fly and all of a sudden I'd know exactly what to draw next."

"Cool. Some artists might call that their muse. Could be a fly. Could even be a person."

Then a thought popped into James' mind. Maybe it was the fly muse, but James knew that Goodness puts thoughts in his heart, people in his path and words in his mouth. James learned never to censor Goodness. Words follow the heart. So he said,

"Hey, Gary, you ever been paid for one of your drawings?"

A smirky smile crept onto Gary's face, "You mean money?"

"Yeah, I mean money." James chuckled.

"No. Never. Who's going to pay a kid for doodles?"

"I will. Your drawings are good. I mean really good. Look," he said pointing across the street at the Methodist Church on the corner of Harbor and Divine. "I teach the Jr. High Sunday School Class in that church, and I need a big drawing. It's got to be good, though."

"How big?"

"Two feet high and three feet wide. It's a picture of the walled city of Old Jerusalem — kinda like a castle. Like this."

James showed him a small picture of Old Jerusalem from the Sunday school book he was carrying.

"How good?"

"Five dollars good. It'll be your first commission as an *artiste*." James smiled and tilted his head as he said 'arteeest'. Gary's eyes lit up. "Will you do it?" James was just as poor as everyone else. He and his wife would make $1,800 that year. Total. Plus a room in the Parish House. So even for James, five dollars was a lot of money.

"You bet, for five dollars. That'll be fun! Better than begging from drunks."

"Okay, then. It's a deal." James ripped Old Jerusalem out of the Sunday school book and passed it to Gary saying, "Go to it, man. I can't wait to see it when you're done."

Gary took the picture, "Thanks, James." And he went right at it. Got some big paper from somewhere, and in two days he was done. He rolled it up like a scroll and took it to the 1910's style brick parish house next to the church. He knew the place well, because the church people put a pool table in the dining room for the neighborhood kids to hang out right underneath the room James and Lew had turned into their Honeymoon Suite. True, it was a bit awkward for the newlyweds, but it served as a convenient destination for a cheap date for teen couples, as well as a meeting-up place for James and the neighborhood kids. Gary climbed the few steps onto a huge brick and cement porch and knocked on the heavy oak and plate glass front door. James appeared with a smile when he saw Gary waving his rolled up walled city of Jerusalem.

"I got it done! I got it done!" he chortled. "Come out and see."

"Already? You've got to be kidding me, Gary."

"Here it is!" He unrolled it. "Take a look!"

James looked and gasped. "Oh wow! You're amazing. This is great. Better than I even hoped. You did a fabulous job, Gary. Thank you very, very much!" Gary beamed. "In fact," James continued, "I think it's worth more than five dollars. Would you take seven?" he asked digging out three crinkled-up bills from his blue jeans front pocket. Never mind that it was all the money he and Lew had left for the week, James just laughed at his own poverty. Literally laughed out loud making Gary laugh.

"Sure would," he said taking the seven dollars. "Thank you, James. I never knew anybody who paid more than the asking price."

James put his arm around Gary's shoulder and said, "Let's go hang this beauty in the church so everybody can see it on Sunday."

And that was the beginning of Gary's life as a professional artist.

James asked to see all of Gary's line drawings. Gary brought the whole stack to show. James oohed and aahed until he could barely stand the joy of it any more.

"Gary, you've got such a gift. My oh my, you do. Would you mind if I show these to the high school art teacher, Ms. Green?"

"High school? I'm not that good."

"Yes, you are."

"She'll laugh."

"We won't know unless we try. How about it?"

"I don't have to be there, do I?"

"No. But," James thought ahead, "she might want to meet you. Would that be all right with you?"

"Maybe."

"All right! Deal?"

"Deal."

"Let's shake." They did, both feeling a little giddy that maybe this was the beginning of something big, unknown, unfolding, yet to come.

What a great memory that day became for Gary — his very first commission as an artist, seven dollars.

Chapter 3

Hello, Mr. Siciliano

"Hello? Hello, Mr. Siciliano? Are you still there?"

"Oh, yes. Yes, yes, I am. I got carried away in old Cleveland memories. I'm so sorry, Ms. Dunlop."

"Annie. Please."

"Annie. But Harbor and Divine? Annie, I know that house. It's next to the church, right? There's a flashing traffic light at the corner, and across the street there's a Dairy Delight. Isn't that the place?"

"Spot on. In fact, the old church building is included in the sale. That's why I'm so excited for you. On the message you left, you did say that you're an artist, didn't you?"

"I did."

"Well, there's your art studio, including a beautiful gallery in the old sanctuary, a huge gathering place to make into your working/teaching studio. A-a-and a balcony. Are you interested?"

"Absolutely! Actually I'm breathless, because I remember everything about it. You have no idea what that church and parish house have meant to me in my life. I even brought my new bride Dianah to see it before Lilyana was born to share all my marvelous experiences at Harbor and Divine. In fact, all three of us flew twice a year to visit Grandma and Grandpa for a few days in nearby Kamm's Corners. We'd visit Harbor and Divine on our way to the West Side Market, and I'd tell Lily lots of stories from when I was her age growing up in Cleveland."

Tears gushed unbidden. Gary paused to catch his breath, quiet his sudden rapid heart beat.

Annie knew better than to ask more questions about what Gary had just told her. But she did want to take the next step with him.

"When would you like to come and look at it again?"

"Right now! Teleport me." He paused to let his brain process what he had just heard to let it filter into the realities of his shattered life.

Shaking his head Gary asked, "How does God do that?"

"God do what?"

"Inject hope and possibility into the life of a broken man?"

"I don't know 'how' God does it." Annie Dunlop confessed. "But isn't that just what the preachers in 10,000 churches preach every week?"

"Yeah, I guess. And if they don't, they should."

"Amen."

Annie could sense Gary shifting mind gears, so she gave him a few beats, and then asked, "So what do you really think about looking over Harbor and Divine again with a mind to buy it?"

"I'd like that. But I have so much on my plate right now to wade through: insurance policies, funeral bills, selling a burnt hunk of mountain, sending thank you notes, and tons of phone calls to friends and family before I can get to Cleveland. Annie, our house on Durango Mountain burned to the ground in a wild fire." he started choking out his words, "I was at an art show in Columbus, and before I got home to help them, my wife and daughter died in that fire."

Annie gasped. "Oh, Gary, I'm so sorry."

"Thank you. But I don't even know why they were in the house. They had been evacuated days before the fire actually got there." Another deep breath. "Surely it will take me at least two weeks to go through all that remains, plus a minute or two to get used to the idea of starting a whole new life without my wife and daughter. Then could I call you? Can you hold the place until then?"

"I sure can. I'll stand guard night and day for you with my dogs."

"You're the best, Annie. Oh, should I send you money to hold it?"

"That would make it an official 'sale pending' for me to hold off anyone interested. But not to worry. Old church buildings, especially in the inner city, aren't the hottest sellers on the market. I'm pretty sure with your check in hand I can call off the dogs."

They laughed together. "Thank you. I'll put my check in the mail first thing in the morning. And then I'll phone you in a couple of weeks to arrange a meeting together. Okay?"

"Better than okay. And, Gary, thank you for telling me about your tragedies. It's a real motivation for me not to just sell you a property, but to help you rebuild your life and heal your heart." Annie paused, bit her lip and then asked, "Gary, okay if I pray for you?"

"Sure. Any time."

"I mean right now over the phone."

"Huh. Sure. I'd like that, Annie. I'd like that."

Tears flowed for them both, but Annie choked out a prayer that put them both in God's hands. They said their goodbyes, hung up and both of them dried their wet eyes two thousand miles apart.

Funny, as Gary ended his call with realtor Annie Dunlop his tears instantly dried up and he felt a surprising flood of vigor. "Hmm. That Annie is great," he said aloud. "More than I ever expected from a realtor in Cleveland." With that realization, he felt like he'd suddenly turned a corner on his attitude about moving to Cleveland, and was ready to tackle, one at a time, everything that had seemed so overwhelming to him since the fire. So, motivated, he made a list beginning with Durango Land and Homes real estate agent Kara Krebbs who sold Dianah and Gary the Durango Mountain property twelve years ago. Kara Krebbs was his Annie Dunlop back then. "Hmm," he said, "Kara, then Annie, now Kara. Maybe I'm on a roll here!" At last he felt he was sensing a little bit of order out of his terribly chaotic life. He caught himself smiling for the first time in six weeks. Six weeks! That long overdue smile prompted Gary to shout, "All righty then, Kara Krebbs, here I come!" He quickly found her number and tapped it in.

"Hello, Durango Land and Homes. This is Kara Krebbs."

Hot diggity dog, first try. "Hi, Kara, this is Gary Siciliano ..." He didn't get out another word.

"Oh, Gary, I am so sorry for your loss."

"Thank you, Kara." Whoa. Didn't expect that. Deep breath.

Kara jumped in while Gary collected himself. "I can't even begin to imagine how you feel. But probably you didn't call me for counseling."

"Well, you're right at that. I do need Kara the Realtor, although thank you for your empathy. I feel very empty these

days without my wife and daughter, especially making plans
for the future. However, today I am ready to get to work."

"Excellent. Plus your timing is impeccable, because we've
been talking here in the office about how we can best help you.
Since our land company still owns your mortgage I would have
called you soon anyhow, but now is the perfect time. We have
been researching your property and the comps of fire destroyed
properties in southwest Colorado, especially in LaPlata county
where you and Dianah built. In addition, we have invited con-
tractors to give us replacement value estimates to rebuild your
house and developers to give us accurate estimates about rede-
veloping the infrastructure of the East Canyon neighborhoods.
A total of seventeen homes burned to the ground; twenty-three
more are severely smoke-damaged, but not totaled. And one
other person in the neighborhood lost his life besides your
wife and daughter."

"Wow. You really have done your homework."

"We have. We want both you and our company to come to
good, solid financial decisions together."

"Thank you. So where does that leave me?"

"Depends. Here's the first question: are you planning
to rebuild?"

Gary paused. Is this the time to figure out all the finances?
Do they really matter? Or should he simply admit that his is
mostly not a financial decision, though he doesn't want to be
stupid about finances either. Another deep breath. Number
6,734. Feels like it anyhow. He already had made his decision weeks ago after the funeral, one funeral service for both
mother and daughter which lessened the heart-wrenching,
he guessed. Besides, it felt to Gary and Dianah's family like
a single funeral was most appropriate for Dianah and Lily,
because they loved each other so deeply. Anyhow, Gary knew

then, at the funeral, that he would leave them in Durango and move back to Cleveland. He would not rebuild. Whoa! Is that a decision? Hmmm. Now to say it out loud. He paused, took a deep breath and said it.

"Kara, I have made up my mind. I'm not going to rebuild."

Chapter 4

Dianah Gets a New Name

A beautiful baby girl was born to a young Dine` couple, Dine` meaning 'Of The People,' but commonly called Navajo by Anglos. Unfortunately, at birth the little infant girl had some minor breathing difficulties, so the doctors kept her one extra night in the infant intensive care unit to closely monitor her while they sent her mother and father home to get a good night's sleep. The new parents left intending to go home as the doctors instructed, but at the last minute, they decided just to go for a ride to relax, talk and settle on a name for their new baby daughter. They planned then to return to the hospital so mama could stay the night in the glassed off parents' waiting area. That way she could watch her baby and nurse her when the times came.

Unfortunately, the parents never made it back to the hospital and never named their child. On their way, a speeding drunk pickup driver crossed over the double yellow line and smashed head on into their small Corolla instantly killing both of the baby girl's birth parents.

Tribal social workers could find no grandparents or other family, so they stepped in to arrange the double funeral and find foster parents. Miraculously, within a day, they found a loving, childless, middle class Anglo couple, Bill and Della Springer of Farmington, willing to foster the baby for the next year. But during that year, the Springers fell in love with that baby girl (whom they had started calling Dianah) and they petitioned to adopt. In a few weeks, much to Bill and Della's delight, children's services approved their application. At the adoption meeting they officially named her Dianah Springer and welcomed their beautiful baby daughter into their family of love and encouragement. Dianah loved her adoptive parents and loved her life as an Anglo. She knew nothing else. But when she turned 12 Bill and Della, decided to tell her all about her birth parents, including what little they knew of her Dine` heritage. Dianah was surprised, but not stricken by the news. Bill and Della were still her mom and dad. However, as she grew older she became ever more curious about the Navajo people and the Dine` culture, especially now that she realized that she was full-blooded Navajo. Plus, over the next few years, she sought out Navajo friends in school who helped her learn more about her Dine` heritage, especially her friends Hannah and Lina.

Throughout her teen years Dianah became so fascinated with her native ancestry that when she graduated from high school she talked with her parents and her school guidance counselor about going to the two-year Dine` Studies program with Hannah and Lina right there in Farmington at what was the first ever tribal two-year college established in America. She told her parents and the guidance counselors that since she was raised Anglo, the common reference to any American not of First People origins, she wanted to learn more about being native American.

Bill and Della thought that was a great idea, so Dianah enrolled along with her two best friends. Over the course of her two years of Dine` studies Dianah learned a great deal about traditional Dine` values of thinking, planning, learning and faith. She also studied traditional arts such as dyeing the wool of Navajo raised goats and sheep with natural dyes to weave rugs, blankets and make clothing. She also learned the traditional arts of sand painting and pottery making. Everything she made was beautiful.

In the college's main entry was a student run gift shop which sold traditional hand-crafted Navajo/Dine` art created by students and faculty. Hannah and Lina, both on work/study programs, had jobs in the gift shop, so one day they invited Dianah to sell some of her art there.

"Your work is so beautiful, Dianah," Lina gushed. "You just have to let us sell some of your work."

"AND," Hannah added, "You get to keep the profits, you know."

"What a great idea! I could use the money, for sure. Plus it will light a fire under me to refine my skills and make even more items to sell in the store. Girls, that sounds like so much fun, especially since you are the ones who will sell what I make! Hannah and Lina, you are such good friends! Thank you for your wonderful idea!"

"Our pleasure," they said.

"Oh," Dianah suddenly thought. "Would you both help me pick out a few items you think people would like to buy? I have no clue what people like, and every day you see what folks purchase."

"We'd love to!" Hannah answered.

"Besides," Lina added, "your work is so gorgeous people will buy anything you make! You're amazingly talented!"

Dianah blushed and said, "Thank you, what a sweet thing to say."

"We mean it, Dianah, we both love your work."

Dianah bobbed her head, smiled, said another quiet "thanks" and then added, "But one more thing."

"Anything," Lina replied.

"Well, I think 'Dianah Springer' doesn't sound much like a traditional Dine` name or even an anglicized Navajo name. What if I took an artist's name, a *nome de plume*, to sign my native art?"

Her friends giggled with enthusiasm, as Hannah exclaimed, "What fun! Can we help you decide on that too?"

"Absolutely, that's why I asked. I'd love your help. Here's what I've been thinking." And the three friends huddled together.

Dianah told them how much she loved the idea of having a bear as her spirit guide. They had all learned about how the Dine', 'The People,' revered bears. They thought of bears as nearly human and called them the Mountain People because, for one reason, bears stood up on two legs like human beings. They also believed that bears possessed supernatural powers of healing and wisdom, and that by their strength they guarded The West (one of four sacred boundaries) to keep The People safe. For those reasons, the Dine` believed that bears could be a person's spirit guide, leading a person to become decisive, deliberate, strong and wise, like bears.

Two species of bears still live in the high desert and mountains of the 27,400 square miles of the Navajo Nation which stretches south and west from the Four Corners Region in the four corner states, New Mexico, Arizona, Utah and a small bit of Colorado.

One is the American black bear, the smaller and more plentiful of the two. The other is the massive, American brown bear, a subspecies of which is the grizzly bear, 'grizzly' meaning 'fearsome' or 'with grey tipped hair.' Dianah told her friends how much she loved the great brown grizzly bear because the grizzly was ready to take on all comers, often standing on two legs to a full height of seven feet of fearsome, menacing muscle as the Dine` Guardian of the West, the protector of the people. Unfortunately, big game hunters had decimated the grizzly bear population, so that even sighting a grizzly was a rare, nearly spiritual event for the Dine`. And it sure was spiritual for Dianah the one day she got to see one up close and personal. She could barely wait to tell Hannah and Lina:

"Yesterday, I was climbing the rocks leading into the mountains, and suddenly came upon a great brown grizzly bear in the rocks about a hundred feet below me. I stopped still and just stared at him. I know you're not supposed to do that — stare into the face of a bear. But guess what happened?"

"What?" they asked with bated breath, knowing the fearsome reputation of grizzly bears. "Weren't you scared?"

"A little scared, but he stared right back at me. Neither of us moved a muscle, yet I felt this intense connection with him, almost love, if you can love a huge brown grizzly bear."

"That does it!" exclaimed Hannah. "You should be Dianah Brownbear!"

Lina agreed. "Hannah, that is perfect! Dianah Brownbear. What do you think Dianah? Do you love it or what?"

"I love it," she told them laughing at first, and then straight away melting into tears. Since she was twelve Dianah had struggled with her mixed identity. Now, after two years of study and research, with the help of her closest friends, Hannah and Lina, she now had a new name that celebrated both her Anglo and her Dine` identity, combining her two selves into one woman: Dianah Brownbear.

"We'll tell everybody that's your new name!" her friends rejoiced.

"Awesome!" she said at first, but then Dianah had a second thought. "Oh. Could we wait until I run that by my mom and dad. I'm sure both of them will love the idea, because it honors them as my mom and dad who named me and raised me, but it also honors my Dine` birth parents and my Navajo cultural heritage! Still, I want to respect my parents and get their approval first. Is that okay with you? After all, you thought up my name."

"That's perfect, Dianah," Hannah told her. "I respect you more because you are honoring all four of your parents."

"And you know what else?" Lina added, "for two years the three of us have learned how, as Dine`, we must give great honor to our ancestors. And you are doing that by your new name, living in a way that honors our ancestors and would certainly make them proud."

"Thank you. I love you both so much. You have given me a very special gift, a new name. Dianah Brownbear. I am Dianah Brownbear."

When Dianah talked with her mom and dad, they also loved the idea and the name every bit as much their daughter, the artist, did. Her legal name would still remain Dianah Springer; but her artist's name, and her Dine` name, would be Dianah Brownbear. All three of them wept together at the idea of two names — legal and art, Anglo and Dine`, Springer and Brownbear. It was exactly what Dianah needed to blend together her love for her mom and dad with her honor for her birth parents. She no longer felt the need to separate the two; she could hold them both within her heart and soul. No boundaries. Just a peaceful co-mingling that made her into a very unique, beautiful young woman.

That decision to accept the two fountains of life within her energized her as if she had become a new creation. She felt more bounce in her step, more brightness in her outlook, less confusion in her spirit. She walked straighter, taller, prouder and with new found elegance. Even her art became more glorious than ever before, a mountain of work that she sold at Division Headquarters in Farmington, at Chapter Headquarters in Shiprock as well as at the student center gift store. People loved her art and snatched it up as soon Hannah and Lina put it on display.

Chapter 5

Kinliah Lahcheen

A few weeks later, Dianah got a telephone call from a surprise admirer of her art.

"Hello, this is Dianah Brownbear. How may I help you?"

"Hello, Dianah. I am Kinliah Lahcheen, president of the Shiprock Chapter of the Navajo Nation. How are you today?"

"I am doing very well, thank you Ms. Lahcheen. And are you well?"

"Very well, thank you. I am calling you today because last week I bought one of your blankets."

"Oh, I hope it was all right."

"For sure. It was a beautiful brown bear motif that I believe is an original of yours, traditional, yet very beautifully updated. It reflects well your personal heritage and your fine character. And you charged me $75.00."

"Oh, was that too much? I can make it right."

"On the contrary. It's worth much more than that. May I meet you somewhere to talk with you about your beautiful work of art? This afternoon, perhaps?"

"Yes. Yes. I would like that very much. How about 2:00 in the Division Center cafeteria here in Farmington?"

"That would be perfect. I'll see you at 2:00 in the cafeteria."

'What a wonderful surprise,' Dianah whispered to herself after she hung up. 'I wonder what she has on her mind. I guess I'll find out at 2:00.'

As it turned out, Dianah Brownbear and Kinliah Lahcheen arrived simultaneously at the cafeteria.

Dianah immediately recognized her from the day Kinliah had bought the Brown Bear Blanket. "Oh, yes, I remember you. I was there when you bought the blanket. A blanket such as that is like a child to me that I carry within me until the spirit within me gives it life. When someone purchases it, I feel like it is an adoption, just as I am an adoption. And I will remember you always with love in my heart, especially now that I know your name."

"What a beautiful sentiment, Dianah. It makes my Brown Bear Blanket even more special than it already is."

"How can I help you today, Ms. Lahcheen?"

"Please call me Kinliah."

"Thank you. Kinliah it is."

"First, I want to give you this check for $225. When added to my original purchase price of $75 it makes $300 which is a much more appropriate price both for your wonderful work of art and for my conscience."

"That is too much money, Kinliah."

"Dianah, it is a fair price for such an exquisite work of art. At first when I bought your Brown Bear Blanket for $75, I walked away gloating that I had gotten such a work of art for a steal. When I got home I realized it indeed was a steal, and I could not live with myself having cheated a sister out of a fair price."

"Kinliah, if all the people who buy my art are as gracious as you are, I will live a very happy and blessed life."

"Thank you, Dianah. But there is one more thing. You, with your art and your traditional character, add a wonderful dimension to our Shiprock community."

"Thank you."

"You're welcome. But saying that is not all I have in mind. Someone mentioned to me that you might enroll in nursing school and pursue an appropriate "Bear Career" in healing. And a fine choice that would be. However, I would like you to consider making traditional art your full time vocation in our Shiprock Chapter. I hope you will open a studio to teach the children of all ages the beauty of our Dine` culture. In fact, some friends of mine and I would like to help you establish yourself in an available building. I believe we also have some community funds that we can designate for your work. Our college here in Farmington is eager to lend a hand as well. They said they know you well, and that your art is already so well-known in Farmington as well as in Shiprock that people I know want to hang on to you as part of our chapter family."

"What an awesome invitation, Kinliah. I feel honored. I have also thought I would love to open a teaching studio and teach traditional Dine` art. Your invitation comes at a perfect time in my life for me to make a life choice and to pick up a new challenge. We can teach the children, bring honor to the Navajo Nation and introduce many tourists to the beauty of Dine` art and culture. Perhaps, right from the beginning. we can even invite community people to be involved with us in shaping this "Shiprock Community Art Studio" that you envision. It sounds exciting to me, and I would love to further explore your vision. In addition, your invitation for me to become part of the Shiprock Chapter family touches my spirit.

I already have one beautiful adoptive family, my mom and dad. But I would love to have another family of Dine` friends to grow with."

"Wonderful! I'll call you in a day or two and we can set up the meeting you suggested after I talk with my friends who will be very excited to meet with you. Would that be all right with you?"

"Yes, thank you, Kinliah, I would love to meet them. My head is spinning from the amazing opportunities you have opened up for me. I can hardly wait to get started!"

Over the next six months, with lots of help, especially from women leaders in the chapter and the college who champion women-owned businesses, Dianah Brownbear opened the Shiprock Community Art Studio. Within a year Dianah, her art collaborators and students were producing beautiful traditional art with ancient Dine` techniques and colors plus some updated patterns. Their art drew new patrons to Shiprock to purchase beautiful blankets, rugs, scarves, pots and permanently sealed sand paintings, about which the tribal leaders had considerable debate as to whether sealed sand paintings could actually be considered traditional Dine` art. Traditionally, sand painting is done in the open air as a gift back to the Creator. They finally agreed that Dianah should teach both types of sand painting, traditional and sealed, and still call it Traditional Dine` Art. The sealed sand paintings sold like hot cakes and for hundreds of dollars each, much more money than any of them had ever imagined.

In time Dianah and members of her Shiprock Community Art Studio entered local art shows with a lot of success. When people learned that the Shiprock artists would be showing their art, the crowds grew larger, and honors and profits for the Shiprock Studio grew as well.

One day, after business hours, when everyone else had gone home for the day, Dianah explored the Shiprock Community Art Studio's building, meandering through the open cubicles of the artists so she could enjoy admiring their current projects. Her students and collaborators had learned traditional Dine` techniques of weaving and pot making so well that to gaze upon their works made her heart swell with pride, satisfaction and thanksgiving.

Even to look around the building itself, formerly an auto body shop, caused her to celebrate the hard work of students and community volunteers. Their tireless efforts transformed old garage space into a first class art studio complete with kick wheels, kilns, drying racks, hundreds of feet of shelving, easels, copious storage areas, hanging racks, spacious work benches and extra large windows to let in glorious floods of light. Plus they kept all six see-through garage doors so they could open them wide for fresh air on calm, dust-free days.

The art studio board also decided to keep the auto spray booth with its up-to-code safety features as well as two large bead blaster units. Originally Dianah had no clue how they would use such equipment, but she soon found out that community metal artists and car enthusiasts were eager to rent those facilities for their projects. To figure out the details of how best to use the paint facilities, she and the art studio board met together with interested artists and the studio's insurance representatives to come up with fair rental rates, regulations and contracts to protect all parties as well as the machinery. What they came up with pleased everyone, and the Shiprock

Paint Bay became a marvelous, unexpected asset for Shiprock as well as other surrounding Navajo Chapters.

As Dianah continued admiring the art within the building, she got to one particularly gorgeous weaving still on the loom after four months of painstaking work. She got lost in admiring the artistry and realizing what an incredible success the Shiprock Community Art Studio already was after less than two years since she first spoke with Kinliah Lahcheen. Her cell phone startled her out of her reverie, and she fumbled to find it in her purse and answer it.

"Hello, Shiprock Community Art Studio, this is Dianah Brownbear."

"Hello, Ms. Brownbear. My name is Tony Patroni."

Dianah could not stifle her giggle at his musical name. "I'm terribly sorry for my rudeness, Mr. Patroni, but I love your name."

"My wonderful Italian family gave me a musical Italian name. The whole thing actually is Antonio Francisco Leonardo Patroni, after my Grandpa, St. Francis and Leonardo DaVinci."

"What a wonderful group of men as spirit guides."

"Yes, that's true. But another way to look at it is that I have a lot of living up to do in character, saintliness and artistry. It's quite a burden, but it also means I will always have stars to shoot for and right paths to walk upon."

Dianah thought this Tony Patroni sounded fascinating.

"But to keep me humble, I just go by Tony."

Still giggling, Dianah said, "Thank you, Tony. Now how can I help you?"

"I am the curator of three art studios in Taos."

"Wow. And I think I'm busy with one!"

Tony chuckled. "They're small, and I don't create any of the art. My job is to recognize good art when I see it and then sell it. That's what I learned in my art history and business studies in college. And I have seen your Shiprock Studio's art, and, Dianah Brownbear, I'm calling to tell you that your studio's art is more than good. It is fantastic. So, I have two business propositions for you."

Dianah was still smiling at this Tony's patter. She decided she'd keep on listening to see where it would lead, and said, "Oh?"

"Proposition number one is this: We have 80 art studios in Taos. Can you believe that? In that small town? Each studio has art from its own stable of local artists as well as factory reproductions. I would like my three studios to be your points of sale in Taos for your art, with an agreement that your studio will sell your original only in my three studios, and not any of the other 77 remaining studios in town. This, of course, would not limit any sales that you could make at any of our community art shows or anywhere else in the world outside of Taos. But with such an agreement I will gain customers who are looking for Shiprock Studio Traditional Navajo Art, and you will gain customers who know exactly where to find your Shiprock Studio Traditional Navajo Art. There will be no other Taos studio trying to undercut the value of your work. We will agree ahead of time on the prices and the share of the profits for each piece of art. What do you think?"

"That's an intriguing proposition, and thank you for the compliment. Of course we would need to see your proposal in writing, and I will need to get the approval of all of our artists as well as our board. Besides, I would like to visit your studios and talk with you face to face as well as, perhaps, with some of your client artists if you can arrange that."

"Those sound like very good, level-headed next steps."

Dianah agreed, and said, "Now, after that surprising proposal, I am eager to hear proposition number two."

"Actually, my second proposition is much less complicated as you will soon see." Then he said with the flair of circus barker, "Proposition Number 2 i-i-i-i-is:" Then with more reserve, "Would you consider entering your studio's art in the Taos Fall Art Festival this year?" And he punctuated it with a disarming grin, that had she seen it would have sent Dianah off the rails devolving into girly giggles. As it was, over the phone, she smiled at his patter. Tony continued. "It's a four-day event starting on September 24. If you go on line you can get all the details, plenty of video of the events plus names, e-mails and phone numbers of the directors of the Festival. You'll see my name there, because I love the event and I eagerly work as hard as I can to promote both art and my hometown. Because we run such a good show and offer cash prizes we attract artists from around the country, especially the western states. But this year I'm really excited to have nabbed Gary Siciliano, a well-known young portrait artist from Cleveland, Ohio. He has a website with some of his work you may want to see. Anyhow, have I interested you in the Taos Fall Art Festival?" Their smiles somehow connected over the phone, even without seeing one another.

Dianah was enchanted, and responded, "Definitely. I'll be sure to bring it up at our next studio meeting. We still have a few months to sign up, right?"

"Right. But sooner is better so that I can get the best space for your studio. Oh, yeah, one important item is this festival is an indoor/outdoor show with the indoor space costing a little more but with a discount if you rent a spot in both venues. Please let me know what you, your board and your artists think about my proposals. I hope to hear from you soon with two affirmative answers."

"You're quite a salesman, Mr. Antonio Francisco Leonardo Patroni! I have enjoyed talking with you and I look forward to the possibilities. I'll be in touch within two weeks. Is that soon enough?"

"You bet, Ms. Dianah Brownbear. So long until then."

"Bye."

Dianah went right to her computer to search Tony etc. Patroni, the Taos Fall Art Festival and maybe this Gary Siciliano too. What an interesting phone call, she thought. As it turned out, things went nowhere with Tony Patroni of the fascinating name; however, the Shiprock Studio did enter the Taos Art Festival. Plus things did sparkle when she finally met the subject of her other computer search — Gary Siciliano.

Chapter 6

Sfumato: Smoke and Mirrors

Kara Krebbs did not disappoint, even after Gary told her he was not going to rebuild upon the charred building site, all that was left of his and Dianah's dream home. Even though it was, twelve years earlier, the very same Durango Land and Homes realtor Kara Krebbs who had helped make Gary and Dianah's dream home on Durango Mountain become an elegant reality.

Back then, Kara began by taking them to the perfect East Canyon wall building site including a flat two acre shelf cut by nature into the mountain face creating a stunning alpine meadow of columbine, primrose, orchids and coneflowers stunningly framed by a golden cascade of aspens, all connected by their roots holding the mountain side in place. A stand of aspen trees is nature's web to hold soil and plants fastened to the rocky mountain sides, preventing erosion and giving golden beauty to Colorado mountain lovers. Gary and Dianah instantly fell in love with the site.

Dianah gushed, "Will you look at this meadow, Gar. I love this place. Let's build our log cabin dream home right here."

Gary, speechlessly entranced by the mountains all around just nodded at first and then said, "I am one hundred per cent with you, Sweetie. This place is perfect. Kara, you hit a home run, for sure."

Kara beamed at their enthusiasm. "And I know a builder who loves to build log houses on the mountain. In fact, on our way back down I can lead you past several of his builds that I think you'll love. Fred is a master builder, who does quality work always a couple steps above 'builders grade' and charges a fair price for both himself and the home owner. How does that sound?"

Gary and Dianah eagerly responded together, "That sounds great."

As they walked back to Kara's 4x4 Gary and Dianah peppered her with excited questions from Dianah's "How long will it take to design and build?" and "Can we outfit it with solar panels?" to Gary's "What about all the other utilities like water, heat and sewer systems?"

Kara responded to their questions in order. "The first answer is, about a year. Second, yes, solar panels are a great idea up here. And third, water and sewer are already in place. Years ago the former Purgatory Resort complex built the Mountain Water Purification System for the Purgatory Ski Resort's needs. Fortunately that meant hundreds of resort condos and private homes were able to tap into Purgatory's city style water and sewer as well as power. Now it's called Durango Mountain Resort instead of the dark sounding Purgatory. Fred will work out all those details with you. You'll love working with him. He's laid back, hard working, honest, prompt and kind. Ready to go see some of his work?"

Gary and Dianah were more than ready. "You betcha!" "Let's go!" "This is so exciting." "Let's get to it!" And off they went.

That was twelve years ago, but now for Gary it was like looking agonizingly into a smoke obscured rear view mirror. Fred did indeed build their dream home in a year with beautiful logs, soaring ceilings, a mammoth fire place that could heat the whole house, and an enormous front porch that gave gorgeous panoramic views of the entire East Canyon with tens of thousands of aspen trees. Unfortunately it was those very same beautiful aspens, dried from successive hot, dry years, along with the East Canyon updrafts that propelled soaring eagles, it was those very same aspens that fueled the firestorm that blew so rapidly up the canyon wall taking Dianah and Lily by surprise and turning their dream home into their funeral pyre.

This phone call from Gary to Kara Krebbs was about that charred dream on the mountain side that could better be called Purgatory now, or hell itself. After Gary told Kara he would not rebuild, he promised Kara a phone call in two weeks when he had taken care of the difficult business at hand. Two weeks later he kept his promise.

"Hello, Durango Land and Homes. This is Kara Krebbs."

"Hello, Kara. This is Gary Siciliano."

"Hi, Gary. Did you get your work finished?"

"I did. Sadly, so many moments of closure caught me off guard. But something got me through it."

"And we both know what."

"Yes. Faith and Trust. Right?"

"Right." Kara waited a beat. She was good at reminding Gary of their shared faith in God. It gave Gary another moment to collect himself, something he was getting better at doing these days. He shifted his thoughts back to Kara.

"Have you sold the property?" he asked.

"Yes, I have, and I'm happy to say that we got more than double your original price for the land and utilities. Plus your insurance company paid off one hundred per cent of the remaining mortgage as well as all of your equity and furnishings. Since your automobiles were not damaged, they are now fully released to you."

"Yes, I'm actually driving the Jeep now, and I sold the other one."

"Good." Kara thought for a sec. "I have meant to ask you, where have you been staying since the fire?"

"The General Palmer Hotel in town. I have always loved the well-cared-for character of that century old building including the art work on the walls not to mention the home-made chocolate chip cookies they serve hot and mushy with late morning coffee. And, besides, that's where Dianah and Lily were staying. Their stuff is still here."

"That must be very tough."

"It's all of that, for sure. But the cookies are good."

"A small consolation." Kara waited a few beats to see what Gary would say. Nothing, so she asked, "So will you be flying to Cleveland soon?"

"Well, no. Actually, I've rented a U-Haul for everything Dianah saved, mostly personal items, plus small studio furniture and art I had in Durango. As I went through it all again, I may have discovered the reasons she and Lily went back into the house. Missing from the art we had in the house, her art and mine, were several small pieces as well as a large portrait of her standing on the front porch with a panorama of the East Canyon behind her. She looked so beautiful when I was painting her, and she loved that painting. I'm afraid they may have run in for it, figuring they could grab it quickly and hustle out. A strong canyon updraft must have taken them by surprise. But to be honest, I'm actually glad I don't have that panorama of the aspens that fed the firestorm that took their lives. Any thoughts I have of those terrifying moments send shivers of sorrow through my heart." He couldn't say anything more.

Kara quietly respected Gary's silence. Then she said, "Gary, I am so very sorry."

"Thank you, Kara. Over the last twelve years you and I have done both joyful and mournful business together. Through it all you have become more of a friend than just a business partner. Thank you."

"You're welcome, Gary." Tears did not flow for either of them. Still, the sadness was thick. "Will I see you before you leave?"

"I think not. Sorry, but that might pull me right back down into the pit of darkness I've been climbing out of. I'm making slow progress, and looking forward to seeing light and hope at the top. But thank you. Thank you for all your help, Kara. I wish you well. And God bless."

"God bless you too, Gary. Be safe. Get happy. Good-bye."

"Good-bye, Kara."

The next morning Gary woke excitedly anticipating the long trip to Cleveland. He used to love those road trips to Cleveland with Dianah and Lily, all the singing, laughing, making plans starting with "When we get there..." Their plans to ride all the coasters at Cedar Point, talk with every animal in the Cleveland Metroparks Zoo, and cheer the Cleveland Indians onto victory usually topped the list after visiting Grandma and Grandpa Siciliano. Without Dianah and Lily, planning his schedule in Cleveland this trip was, unfortunately, bound to be much more subdued, less silly and more worrisome.

Right now, as he drove the U-Haul truck out of Durango onto US Route 160 east toward Interstate 25 he was remembering the first time he and his dad drove to Colorado from Cleveland. He had just bought a late model, used truck, and the two of them took turns driving. The two-year-old Dodge 1500 pickup drove like a dream, so much so that they often found themselves far exceeding the speed limit. Gary was the first one to get a ticket: $110! His dad offered to pay half, but Gary insisted on paying it all himself. His dad felt bad he hadn't helped.

He felt bad, that is, until he got his own speeding ticket. This time it was a set-up, designated as a work zone with double the fine rate signs posted, and then double that because he was, supposedly, going more than 20 mph over the posted speed, a 40 mph work zone speed. He was going the normal 65 mph, clocked by the State Patrol at 72 mph. Since they clocked him at 32 mph over the 40 mph work zone speed, it jacked up the fine even more and meant an automatic court appearance within a week or pay it on the spot to the patrolman: $1,090! Yep. Dad called that 'highway robbery,' —hah, hah — and he refused to pay on the spot taking the court date instead. After all, he had a plane to catch later that day. But by the time he got back to Cleveland, and had plenty of time to think through his problem, adding up the cost of a return roundtrip flight to Durango, plus a hotel for a night not to mention lawyers fees and a probable fine, he decided to call a lawyer friend who called a lawyer friend in the county on the citation to handle it long distance. Guy made a deal with the lawyer that she would appear in court on his behalf. She did and got the fine reduced to $90. Hooray! But then she billed his dad $1,000 for her efforts. Total: $1,090 — the very same amount he could have paid to the patrolman on the road. He paid it, of course, and the whole family has been laughing about it ever since. In fact, Gary was chuckling out loud as he drove on US Rt 160, the very same road on which his dad had been bamboozled. Everyone they told that true story laughed and said they instantly gained a renewed understanding of the term "Speed Trap."

Memories came fast and furious as Gary let his mental guard down with a thousand miles still left to drive, people memories especially. Like when James the community worker took Gary's pencil sketches to show high school art teacher Ms. Val Green. How terrified Gary had been that she would laugh at his drawings. She didn't. No. She was so impressed with his 10-year-old's doodles and sketches that she wanted to talk with him about his "work." That's what she called it, his "work," like it was laborious drudgery. It wasn't that at all. Not then at age 10 and not now at age 44.

So they met. And he was nervous. But she smiled, welcomed him, and said, "This is a wonderful folio of art, Gary."

'Art? Really?' Gary marveled to himself. 'Is she pulling my leg?'

"Simply wonderful. How about we look at each one together."

"Okay," he squeaked out. Then together they leafed through every single picture Gary had drawn. Every single one. And for every picture, must have been 70 or 100 of them, for every one she had a compliment, a word of praise, or an encouragement — or, amazingly sometimes all three. On that day, Gary, for the first and only time in his life, fell in love with his teacher. Plus she was pretty to boot.

After she had gone through every single drawing with him, including the two foot by three foot Old Jerusalem, which she said, "just blew me away!" yes, she said that, she did, she picked out two drawings, well, one drawing and one doodle. She laid them on the table where they were 'working,' she looked him square in the eye, and she said, "I love these two, Gary. Just love them." Gary chuckled in the U-Haul remembering how he melted at her words, especially how she drew out the word "love" each time she said it. Swooned he did. He knew then and there that he would follow Ms. Green to the very ends of the earth.

First she picked one of his scores of doodles of the long-legged fly, which he drew next to nearly every other drawing. In fact, he still draws them, paints them, scratches them into the corners of his art. The long-legged fly helped him then, helps him still, to refocus so that he would know just how to draw the next thing, no matter what it was. James had called the long-legged fly his muse. So did Ms. Val Green.

"Gary, the long-legged fly that you have drawn in all its variations, from dozens of perspectives, you draw with the same 28 lines." And then she counted them out loud. "One, two, three, etc. 28 in this one. In the next one, 28. In the one after that, 28. See? 28, 28, 28. And in each doodle the lines slant just a little differently to give the long-legged fly a sense of motion or readiness for motion. You show him head on, then 3/4 left, then from the back, then with wings ready, then with wings at rest. Your variations on the long-legged fly make a fabulous study in what your eye sees when the fly is near you. What you have done with that fly by drawing him from all different directions, from different perspectives, you can do with anything. A rock. A man. A tree. A hat. A nose. Anything. And when you can do that with everything, you will create great art. That long-legged fly is your first step to great art."

Then Ms. Green pulled out Gary's sketch of Old Tony. And she said, "Like Old Tony."

Chapter 7

Old Tony

"Like Old Tony," Gary said to himself in the U-Haul truck. "Great art like Old Tony? How did she know way back then? Great art?" Sure, Gary remembered Old Tony. The stinky, old Slovenian. Boy, he smelled. It was a six-foot body odor. You had to be more than six feet away not to smell it. More if the wind was behind him blowing at you. But what a face. My goodness. Old Tony's face was carved by the hand of God. Gary knew, even at age 10, that drawing Old Tony's face was a divine command for him, like to Moses out of the burning bush: "Gary! Draw this face!" So Gary felt an urgency that compelled him. Like an obsessive-compulsive hand washer. Wash! Wash! Wash! Thus compelled and undeterred, Gary sliced through the haze of stink, took a breath (whoa!) and introduced himself right there in front of the Cleveland Public Library branch on Divine Street.

"Hello, sir. My name is Gary."

"Hello, Gary," Tony said in his still strong Slovenian/ Cleveland accent, "My name's Tony. What can I do for ya?"

"I draw — things, people. Would you let me draw your face? Please?"

Tony had laughed, "This ugly, old mug?"

"Old, yes. But ugly? No way, sir. Your face has been carved by the hand of God, and I want to draw it." Even then Gary recognized art's divine call.

"By the hand of God, huh?" Tony marveled at the kid's intense desire to draw him. "Okay. Sure. When do you want to draw me?"

"Any time you say, Tony."

"Hows 'bout now? I have a break in my busy schedule." Tony laughed and heaven shined from his face like Moses coming down the mountain with the tablets. Gary stared at the sight, caught himself lost in wonder, and knew that he would forever remember that look and that laugh. Even though Tony's offer caught him off guard, Gary remembered his determination not to let the moment pass him by.

"Now? Sure. That'd be great. Yeah, that'd be great."

Gary still remembered, now 34 years later while driving a U-Haul east on I-25, he remembered the excitement he felt at the privilege to draw the face of Tony, which he entitled "Old Tony." Old Tony had given him a gift that blessed Gary the Artist, Gary the Boy and Gary the Man yet to be. At age ten, Gary could not articulate it, but he already could feel the enormity of the gift that the old Slovenian Tony had given him.

It was Old Tony the pencil portrait that paved the way for Gary to get Ms. Val Green to mentor him in all things art. It was Old Tony that Ms. Green used to teach Gary facial proportions and how the shapes of facial features change from a front elevation to 3/4 to profile. It was Old Tony who Ms. Val Green used to teach Gary how to use shading in pencil and then in paints instead of lines to express boundaries. It was Old Tony who Ms. Green used to teach Gary *sfumato*, Leonardo da Vinci's techniques of using shading and light to blur the artificial boundaries of line art and in the process give depth and movement to the painting, as well as life to the person being painted. Gary drew, redrew; chalked, rechalked; painted, repainted Old Tony so many times that Gary began to believe that he was actually giving birth to Old Tony years after Tony's demise.

And then once Gary finally had painted Old Tony beautifully, he read and reread Leonardo DaVinci's notes on mixing and applying ultra thin layers of shaded or lightened glaze to build depth on facial features, turn tiny wrinkles into canyons of character and flat facial expanses into bold plateaus to draw the viewer's eyes to rest. Some of the smallest wrinkles required twenty or thirty micro layers of glaze to create the topographic map of character that God had created in the living Old Tony. And when the viewer would move to the left or to the right, the topography, the layers of glaze actually gave movement to Old Tony's face, especially the wrinkles of his soft, sweet smile.

In the first few pencil or charcoal cartoons Gary drew, Old Tony told him how he had immigrated from Slovenia with his family; how he had come to love America, gotten a job in the steel mills in Cleveland's flats, become a U.S. citizen, then lost his job when Jones and Laughlin shut down its Cleveland mills and built new ones in Birmingham; how he had lost his wife to cancer, lived on welfare in a two-room apartment on W. 25th Street, marched in the Poor People's March and loved and trusted God. Every conversation motivated Gary to imbue Old Tony's portrait with the joy, the hard work, the struggles, the sorrow, the faith and the hopes that God used to carve character into the face of the original, living Tony.

In fact, it took eight years for Gary to paint Old Tony.

Nearly every one of those years Gary entered what he thought of as an unfinished painting into art shows, first in high school, then at the Cleveland Institute of Art, the Columbus Arts Festival in the Ohio Expo Center, the Taos Fall Arts Festival, the San Francisco Academy of Arts Show and a dozen more, and each time he won Best in Show with an unfinished Old Tony. After several years of entering the unfinished Old Tony, art lovers began to understand that Old Tony was in process, and so they began following Gary and his painting from show to show, standing in long lines each year to see the next iteration of Gary's fabulous portrait. For them it was like watching Leonardo paint Mona Lisa step by step.

Gary's celebrity grew, but before his second trip to Taos for the Fall Art Festival, Gary decided that when he got to Taos he would auction off the completed Old Tony as well as eight framed and signed partially completed Old Tony portraits displaying stages of Gary's artistry, especially *sfumato*. At auction the fully completed, framed Old Tony brought in $1.2M. from a private collector in Minnesota. The other eight signed portraits unfinished and at various stages of completion were all bought as a lot by the Cleveland Museum of Art for $1.4M. The museum curators figured this Cleveland-born artist's masterpieces would surely draw to the museum Cleveland fans who cheered every hometown hero.

In fact, the Art Museum immediately scheduled a show for the unfinished portraits for artists, teachers and fans, hoping they would come. And come they did. They came not just from Cleveland, but from around the State of Ohio and from around the country to pay homage to Old Tony. And they willingly spent hours in line to pay handsome prices for advanced sale tickets, only to spend more hours studying Gary's artistic techniques, especially his steps in *sfumato*.

Art critics proclaimed Gary the greatest disciple of Leonardo da Vinci's *sfumato* in the history of art. A bit much, Gary thought, even then. But as he drove toward Cleveland he smiled broadly at the memory.

Now, twelve years later, it was Gary that famed artist, who drove a U-Haul truck from Durango to Cleveland to purchase the church and parish house at Harbor and Divine for his new home and studio. Although the weight of fame had lightened considerably since that Taos auction of Old Tony twelve years earlier, he still returned to Cleveland a favorite son, especially in the Cleveland art world. Gary had already called his realtor Annie to tell her of his decision which made her ecstatic. She actually squealed with joy like a teenager over the phone when he told her the news, making Gary chuckle and wonder if she squealed every time she made a sale. Or was this sale somehow a little more special to her? Hmm. A smile crept across his face at how much he enjoyed the squeal, and liked the prospect of meeting her in person.

Chapter 8

Sfumato: Never Quite There

N ot quite half way to Cleveland, Gary pulled into the
Comfort Inn and Suites in Topeka, Kansas for the night.
It broke the trip roughly in half, but more importantly it was
the same hotel where Gary and Dianah had stayed on their
first trip together to Cleveland to meet Gary's parents. Gary
had already met Dianah's family in Farmington the weekend
he proposed. They were an up-to-date, middle-age, Anglo
couple with a middle class Anglo lifestyle who were very proud
of Dianah's decision to embrace her Dine` heritage in her col-
lege education and her art. They had always felt that Dianah
would need to adopt her native heritage if she were ever to feel
at peace with her dual identity. Her mom and dad impressed
Gary with their love for Dianah and their encouragement for
Dianah to explore her birth parents' beautiful heritage.

That night in Topeka Gary fell asleep remembering Dianah
and the American cultural mix of her life. He loved that about
her. Not only did he love her cultural and racial mix, but he

loved how she had blended the hard edges that typically separate Dine` people from Anglo people into one woman. She became like a *sfumato* painting: seamless contradictions, full of life and very beautiful. As he was falling asleep Gary realized how blessed Dianah made him feel, even now. For the umpteenth time he thanked God for Dianah. Her impact upon his life had always filled him with gratitude and peace in the past, but now in that very moment, Gary could feel her love from God healing his broken heart. Truly healing him. Like the Brown Bear Dianah took as her spirit guide, her spirit was healing him — her lover, her best friend — and releasing him from his brokenness. That's when, with a smile on his face, Gary fell asleep into a deep, beautiful, peaceful sleep.

Next morning he woke up late. That was the plan. He had not set his alarm hoping that he would sleep in and begin the day refreshed. It worked. He woke up with that same smile on his face filled with excitement for the day at hand. But the woman on his mind was not Dianah Brownbear from last night. To his wonderment, he woke up in Topeka, Kansas, half way between Durango and Cleveland, thinking about Annie Dunlop.

"What craziness is this?" Gary said out loud. As recently as just three weeks ago Gary had still felt as though Dianah's and Lily's tragic deaths had broken his life irreparably in two with a tectonic rift in the earth, leaving a chasm over which there could be no crossing ever from then to now.

And now this morning he wakes thinking about Annie Dunlop? He felt like a guilty betrayer. All that was missing was the 30 pieces of silver. Yes, it was true they were both still gone, but the chasm between that beautiful life with Dianah and some sketchy new life yet to come that just last night had seemed impossible to bridge, today somehow had become a blurred, softer separation. Like real life *sfumato*, the line between Gary's past and his future had nearly disappeared under layers of glaze of healing, hope and love. Perhaps, if Leonardo could take real life dissections of eyes and lips and skin and muscle, along with studies of optics about what the human eye actually sees and does not see, and with all that knowledge put life into the two-dimensional painting of Lisa by using tens of thousands of tiny brush strokes of translucent glaze of light and dark, up to thirty layers thick, could not the inverse apply? What if real life is more like the DaVinci portrait of that 24-year-old Italian woman with the beautiful, enigmatic smile? What if Gary's human eye sees no hard lines between nose and cheek? What if his human spirit apprehends no division between the woman in the painting, the natural world of the Arno River in the background or even the art lover in the gallery? What if Leonardo's blurred lines and layers of glaze portray life as it really is: no hard lines, no divisions? Instead of the chasms, divisions, separations which our human weakness invents, real life is made of smokey, misty connections from moment to moment, person to person, past to future. Gary who had spent his adult life emulating Leonardo's artistry to create art that looks like life, now realized that his life looks like Leonard's art with no hard lines separating love passed from love yet to be; no chasms separating joys now gone from surprises of happiness in that new day. But, and here's the rub, is it then ever possible on one's life journey to actually get to where you're going, arrive at the hoped for destination? Are wounds of the soul ever truly healed? Or are they just covered up with glaze?

Gary thought out loud, "Will I always be not quite there, forever on the road running from fire and smoke, dreaming of a new heaven and a new earth without the old love? Or am I being healed in a motel half way to Cleveland?"

He stopped talking and just thought in silence. Why should he marvel that somehow Dianah's love has become the agent of healing his heart, setting him free for a new day, maybe even for a new woman? After all, Paul of Tarsus wrote, "So faith, hope, love abide, these three; but the greatest of these is love." Each of those divine gifts blurs divisions, conquers what seems to divide person from person and yesterday's joys from today's possibilities and tomorrow's hopes. Love even leaps over the flames of death and through the smokey haze of destruction to give a new hope, a new joy, a new heaven and a new earth. Gary's heart soared at the thought that while love may not be transferrable from Dianah to any other woman, it is abiding still. Love beckons a broken man to leap over the wreckage, through the smokey haze from a moment of loss to a new day, a new promise.

Gary showered, packed up, got a bagel and some coffee to go at the breakfast bar, and walked toward the woman at the front desk to turn in his key card. "Am I good to go?"

"Yes, you are. But didn't you get your statement that we slipped under your door?"

"Oh. I must have walked right over it. Never even saw it."

"No problem. You must be excited to get on the road."

Gary took a beat and thought as he said, "Mmm. I guess I am. I'm half way there."

"Half way? That's good. But where's there?"

"Cleveland. Started out in Durango."

"Someone special there?"

"In Durango there was. But she died in a mountain fire along with our daughter." Tears gathered but didn't fall.

"Oh, I'm so sorry."

"Thank you. Me too." Gary marveled that once again he didn't get snagged by his grief. Instead he smiled. "But in

Cleveland? Just possibilities, maybes and hopes. Nothing for sure, but for the first time since that terrible day, I'm looking forward to them, whatever they be."

"Well, good luck to you."

"Thank you."

"And have a safe trip."

"Thanks again. So long."

He walked outside and started whistling. Stopped short. Really? Shook his head and started singing instead, "If you're happy and you know it clap your hands: clap, clap..."

Road trip!

Chapter 9

Sfumato: Smoke and Hope

Gary climbed into the U-Haul happy. Holy cow, who woulda thunk it? Remembering all the old camp songs that he and Lily and Dianah used to sing on road trips, he sang his way out of Topeka and onto I-70 toward Columbus, Ohio. Happy songs filled the cab of the U-Haul for the first hour, and then happy memories filled up his mind to overflowing for miles after that.

Like when he first met Dianah in Taos at the Taos Fall Arts Festival. Wow. Did he fall heavy for her or what! He remembered having the same lost little boy crush on Dianah that he had on Ms. Green way back when. Goodness. How he stared at her long raven black hair and gorgeous eyes, not to mention her fabulous figure. And when she came up to speak to him, his legs got a little wobbly.

"Hi!" Just that did him in, but then she held out her hand. Oy. "I'm Dianah Brownbear."

"Hi. I'm Gary Siciliano."

"I know. I was hoping that would be you."

"Oh?"

"Tony Patroni, one of the directors of the festival and an art dealer in Taos, mentioned that you would be coming. He was very excited that you would be here. Said you had a growing reputation as an excellent portrait artist. So I Googled you and was very impressed. Since then, I have been waiting eagerly to meet you and see your work."

Gary smiled and said to himself, 'So that's how she knew me, and that I would be showing and selling my artwork in the galleries.' Out loud he said, "Thank you. I'm flattered." And that was the truth!

When they shook hands he felt a buzz shock right through him from head to toe. From how wide her eyes opened, she must have felt the same thing. Goodness, goodness, goodness. He asked her to lunch (fair food on a picnic table), and she invited him to her studio's display. (Oh?) Somehow they forgot to talk about art. By the end of the day he was holding her hand and singing that old Beatles tune in his head. And for four days they were an item that her friends and art students couldn't help notice. In fact, they pelted her with questions the moment she returned to the tent to close up for the night. She blushed and admitted it was a fun day.

On the third night the judges announced awards with a dozen of them going to Shiprock Community Art Studio and Best of Show going to Gary Siciliano's Old Tony. As they stood together holding hands, they were so excited for each other's success that they flew into one another's arms and jumped up and down like little kids. At the sight, her friends laughed like crazy, but she didn't notice anything except that she was in Gary Siciliano's arms and she loved it.

For the next year they e-mailed, texted and planned trips so they could be together. Gary flew back to Farmington four times for extended stays. On the third trip he asked Dianah

Springer Brownbear to be his wife. She shouted a huge "Yes" and flew into his arms. Gary put a ring on her finger, kissed her like crazy and carried her out to her car. She didn't know an artist could be that strong! They drove crosstown to share the news with her mom and dad, who were elated but not surprised, since Gary had asked them for her hand the day before. Then for the fourth trip Gary flew to Farmington for a week, then they drove Dianah's car to Kamm's Corners in Cleveland to visit with Gary's parents, Guy and Phyllis, who were thrilled to finally meet their future daughter-in-law. They all embraced, and Phyllis served a lunch made straight from West Side Market food she had bought fresh that morning: pastrami, hard salami, chip-chop ham, havarti cheese all from the Greek meat and cheese stall, freshly baked Jewish rye, five inch kosher dill crock pickles, hickory smoked salmon plus baklava for dessert. Dianah raved about how delicious and fresh the food was.

"And you bought it where?" she asked.

"The West Side Market," Phyllis told her. "It's been a Cleveland institution for generations. My father and mother took me shopping there when I was a little girl and let me pick out my favorite fruits, cookies and candy. I always chose windmill cookies, freshly baked, but slightly broken. They were the best dunked in milk for an after school snack! It was at the West Side Market that I first heard people speaking foreign languages, some dressed in long robes, some with red dots on their foreheads and some that looked just like us except they talked funny. Gary tells us that you speak a Native American language."

"Just a bit. I was born Dine` — Navajo is the common Anglo name — but my parents died in a car crash the day after I was born. So my wonderful mom and dad adopted me.

They are Anglo, so I grew up as an average all-American girl. I learned about my heritage in the Dine` Community College in Farmington. Language was one part of it, so I know a few words. My real interest became learning traditional Navajo art forms. I had such fun making baskets, weaving blankets and creating sand art, that it surprised me that people actually started buying my work at the college craft store. Eventually some of my Dine` mentors and colleagues got me to start up and run The Shiprock Community Art Studio. We ended up displaying some of our studio's art at the Taos Fall Arts Festival, and that's where I met Gary. Lucky me."

"Lucky ME," Gary chimed in.

"So you are both artists with different skills."

"Exactly. And we cheer for one another, complement one another and love one another. Right, Gary?"

"Exactly right, sweetie."

They talked a little bit about wedding arrangements and then Gary said, "Hey, Dianah, since you loved the lunch food from the West Side Market so much, how 'bout I take you on a tour of it? We could be there in 15 minutes or so. Want to?"

"Sure, if it's all right with your mom and dad."

"Perfectly fine with us," Phyllis said, speaking for Guy.

Guy nodded and smiled. "You two have fun and we'll catch you later."

"Good deal," Gary said. "See you later!"

And off they went to shop at Cleveland's famous West Side Market with its 65 open air produce stalls and an indoor arcade with 30 more stalls including a large, very smelly fresh fish market, several cheese mongers, many fresh baked goods stalls, a half dozen butchers with everything from homemade sausage to whole passover lambs hanging on hooks for the holy days, plus booths selling nationality specialties from Greek stuffed grape leaves to Latino whole sugar cane to Polish pierogies. Gary loved the whole old world market vibe with it's varied languages and everything from fresh caught lake chub to freshly roasted cashews from the Nut House, a Public Square landmark for generations in downtown Cleveland. Even more, he loved sharing it with Dianah.

They bought two of Gary's market favorites: smokies to munch on while they shopped and a huge Lady Finger pastry with delicious cream filling to share for a treat.

Dianah felt like she was in heaven. "Gary, let's come here every time we visit your mom and dad. Okay?"

"You've got a deal. And I'm glad you like it. It's one of my all time favorite places not only in Cleveland, but anywhere I've been in the whole country.'

"I can see why," Dianah said as she suddenly kissed Gary on the lips with a very messy, very sweet and very sticky Lady Finger kiss laughing as she did. Gary got right into the moment and kissed her right back rubbing the goo all over both their faces giggling like two little kids.

"Dianah Springer Brownbear, I love you more than all the Lady Fingers in Cleveland."

"Gary Siciliano, I love you right back double!"

They walked outside arm in arm and sang, "If you're happy and you know it, clap your hands." He clapped his sticky hand with hers. "If you're happy and you know it clap your hands. Clap. Clap. If you're happy and you know it then your face–get it? *your face*–will surely show it. If you're happy and you know it clap your hands. Clap. Clap."

They laughed and hugged some more, and together they sang it again. So much in love. Such marvelous memories.

And right there on I-70 East in his rented U-Haul truck cab Gary found himself singing at the top of his lungs, laughing for the joy of the memory, and weeping at the tenderness of falling in love with Dianah. He had to pull off at the next rest stop to gather himself from the flood of emotions. What a blessed life he had lived. What an odd thought by a man who lost his wife and daughter in a mountain fire, not to mention their dream home and most of their belongings. He took a breath as he pulled into the rest area. And in a flash he realized that blessing and loss have no lines separating them in his life. Real life blends it all together in one man, one woman. Like Leonardo's *sfumato*, he thought, no hard lines. You can't get rid of the deep sadness, the grief, no. But together with memories of Rocky Mountain Highs of love and life with Dianah, Gary still felt whole, confident, blessed. Trust, faith and hope cover the sharp edges with ten thousand tiny strokes of shaded life glaze. An enigmatic smile grew on his face. Like Mona Lisa's in the painting. It was a smile that knows heartbreak mitigated by joyful songs already sung and new songs yet to be. "Watch out now! I will make all things new," promised the Lord. That Mona Lisa smile crept through his whole being like a lover's kiss, and Gary drove right past that next rest area. No need. Love's next level healing had done its work. Step on the gas, Gar. You've got miles to go before you sleep, miles to go before you sleep.

You're gonna be just fine.

Chapter 10

Cowboy Music

G ary found some cowboy music on the radio. He liked that it's different from country western. More yearning than sadness. More overcoming than failing. Just what he needed, and he was surprised to find some in the middle of Illinois. He sang along with the ones he learned out west and found himself learning some new ones as well. So he turned up the volume and the miles flew by. Then suddenly, for whatever the reason, he stared straight down at the gas gauge bouncing on E.

"Holy cow! Would you look at that. Good thing you looked down, Gar." Then he looked up and read the road sign: "'Next Rest Area two miles.' Wow. Thank you, Lord." He'd been saying "Thank you" a lot lately. Maybe it was part of the soul healing he was experiencing. Maybe you only get truly thankful when you've truly lost. Hmm.

This time he got off and felt a little like a cowboy trucker as he slid out of his cab. He liked the new songs he'd learned. He wondered if there was cowboy music in Cleveland. Had to be. There's cowboy music everywhere. "If not I'll get Sirius in my car. Gotta have my cowboy music." He had started dressing in cowboy gear years ago, even before he and Dianah built their Durango Mountain home. He loved the tight, western plaids in shirts studded with silver and white horn buttons, fancy trimmed shirt seams, matched with trimmed out, boot cut, cowboy jeans over comfy cowboy work boots and topped with an off-white ranch work hat. It made him look a little taller than his slim, five foot ten inch frame and made him want to saunter a bit.

The sauntering always made Dianah laugh, mainly because he wasn't very good at it, but also because it was good enough to stir her hormones. She knew he had even taken to horseback riding with her in order to get some bowleggedness to improve his cowboy gait. All of it made her smile in love, knowing that here was Gary, a world famous artist, acting like a cowboy to get the girl. And it worked every time. When she said, "Come here, cowboy," he sauntered over to her and said, "Yes, ma'am?" in the best cowboy drawl he could muster, and her heart would go pitter-pat. She would take off his hat and smooth his hair and sigh. Dianah loved the look and feel of his soft, used-to-be-blonde-but-now-it's-brown hair. Once Dianah had met Gary's parents, especially his fair-skinned, light-haired mother, she fully understood how a guy could be swarthy in skin color but have such soft, straight, smooth light-colored hair at the same time, like Gary's.

After he pumped more than $100 of gas into the truck and onto his credit card he headed toward Columbus, turned the cowboy music way down and suddenly felt like cowboy shirts might be a little out of place back in the inner city. After all, Ohio was coming up fast, and he started thinking about Ohio things, Cleveland things, Harbor and Divine things. And–fwoohf–Annie things. "Gary Siciliano, for goodness sake, just get a hold of yourself. Just 'cause she giggled once doesn't mean she's all about you. Cool your jets, Mr. Big Shot." Still…Then a road sign interrupted his self-chastisement.

"Okay, here you go. One hundred and forty miles to Indianapolis, and then onto Columbus." His plan was to hop on I-270 toward Worthington, then zip onto I-71 North to Cleveland, Believeland, Never-gonna-leave-land. He chuckled at his cleverness, turned back on the cowboy music. "I know Indianapolis and Columbus have cowboy music. So easy does it, cowboy. It's all good. You're gonna be all right. Yeee-Haw!"

Now thoughts of Columbus snagged him, because the first time that Ms. Val Green had convinced him to enter Old Tony in an art show competition outside of Cleveland it was in Columbus. It was one thing to enter competitions in art shows in Lakewood, or the Jewish Community Center on the East Side, or Case Western Reserve, or the Cleveland Institute of Art where he earned his Master of Fine Arts degree in portraiture. Even the Cleveland Museum of Art with its high powered artistic staff and world-wide reputation still seemed like his home field. He and Old Tony, at various stages of completion, had won best of show at all of them. Still, in Columbus he would be on foreign turf with judges not familiar with his work — or so he thought. And this was a big one with 260 acclaimed artists from around the country, a huge staging area covering both sides of the Scioto River, with numerous indoor venues, free shuttle buses, musical entertainment, dance competitions, and food all over the place. Old Tony looked his best ever. Gary had spent countless hours studying Leonardo's journals about *sfumato* (in English, of course) and following his instruction. He had heard that some Old Tony fans from Cleveland, knowing how meticulously Gary was applying glaze ala` Leonardo to Old Tony, were making the more than two-hour trip to Columbus just to see his progress on Old Tony. That felt like a big deal to Gary. Creeped him out a bit, like he was some kind of celebrity or something, but he still loved Old Tony's fans.

By that time in June Ms. Green had been hospitalized again with cancer. She had beaten it once decades earlier when she was a junior in high school, but it had come back, and so she was admitted to the Ohio State James Cancer Center for treatments just like last time when she beat the odds. She said she was trying to get a doctor's pass for a quick trip with medical staff to see Gary and Old Tony. She'd let him know.

They had talked on the phone, and Ms. Green calmed him each time with her sweet voice and sensible encouragement. Gary really appreciated her support as well as his dad's. Gary's dad, Guy, who had stopped drinking and been sober for five years by that time, was driving down with Gary. They had grown to love and admire one another deeply in the last five years, so Gary was thrilled Guy would be there with him. Since it was a three-day festival, Guy had gotten a room at the Holiday Inn near the OSU campus. They would have some "buddy time" together, and Gary was really looking forward to that. His dad had learned what he could about Leonardo and *sfumato* and had become Gary's best cheerleader.

When they arrived for the set-up day, Guy and Gary carried Old Tony, like the treasured old friend he had become, wrapped and crated for safety, to his numbered display spot. Two women on the festival staff welcomed them and then helped them to set up.

Sandy, one of the women, unexpectedly told Gary, "I have, in fact a lot of us on staff have, really been looking forward to seeing Old Tony and meeting you. We have many friends

69

in the Cleveland art world, and they rave about both you and Old Tony."

"Whoa," is all Gary could say at first, but his megawatt smile said it all for him. Then he added, "That's great. It'll be wonderful seeing some familiar faces and having friends here."

"You may have more friends here than you think. We love to cheer on our Ohio artists. Can we unwrap Old Tony? I truly am dying to see him in person."

"Of course. Want to help my dad and me do it?"

"I sure do!"

Together they carefully decrated and unwrapped the two by three foot framed painting, and when they did Sandy gasped. "Oh, Gary. He is magnificent. I thought my Cleveland friends were exaggerating, but I can see they certainly were not. Gary, it's the nearest I have ever seen an artist replicate Leonardo's *sfumato*." At that tears streamed down her cheeks. "I'll make sure we have double rope barriers around Old Tony. We don't want any accidents to happen. And let me get two step ladders so the two of you can lift him up and hang him right in that spot. See where I mean?"

"Yes. You ready, Dad?"

"I am. But first let me just look at him. I haven't seen him for a couple of weeks. And Mom helped you pack him." Guy stepped back in awe. "Gary, I'm so proud of you. This is one more moment for which I thank God that I am sober." He stood there and wept. And Sandy started crying all over again.

"Gary," Guy said back in control. "Let's get him on the wall."

And when they did Old Tony seemed to jump off the two dimensional canvas with life. His eyes sparkled and followed them around the room.

Sandy witnessed for herself how Old Tony, once he was displayed, burst to life, just like her Cleveland friends told her. "We'll definitely set up barriers," Sandy confirmed. "Want to help?"

Gary and Guy responded simultaneously, "Absolutely!"

"What do we do?" Gary asked.

"I'll call maintenance to bring us hard and soft barriers, and then we'll help them set up. Hard barriers keep careless people out and the soft ropes look elegant. I want both kinds of barriers, because lots of people who come to this show each year don't yet know art etiquette, mainly, 'Don't get too close' and 'Don't touch.' Ooooo! And now I can smell your paint, so it's not even fully cured yet. I remember reading about some supposed expert art restorers who tried to clean the Mona Lisa in the 1800's, and they rubbed off her eye brows and lashes that Leonardo had added on top of and underneath layers of sfumato glaze even after hundreds of years. Experts too can get carried away. Just a sec, and I'll call."

A few minutes later the maintenance men arrived with what seemed to be enough material to build a second story. But they knew what they were doing and Gary, Guy and Sandy gladly did what they were told. Sandy thanked the men, turned to Gary and asked, "Are you happy with that?"

"More than happy. I truly was concerned about leaving Old Tony here overnight or even for Dad and me to get some dinner. This is great, and I want to thank you from the bottom of my heart that you 'get it,' that you understand the immense effort that goes into such a painting."

"You're welcome, Gary. Thank you for sharing Old Tony with us."

"My pleasure. See you tomorrow."

"See you tomorrow."

Crowds did come. Some cheered. Others wept just like Sandy and Guy had. Gary stood forty or fifty feet off to the side, and he was simply amazed, humbled, and plainly overwhelmed by people's reactions to Old Tony.

The original flesh-and-blood old Tony, that sweet, smelly, character-filled old Slovenian man on the Near West Side, had given Gary an incredible gift to allow a ten-year-old boy to sketch his beautiful, character-lined face. Then Gary asked Tony four more times to sit for him; first, to draw a much larger cartoon for painting; second, to refine the cartoon and begin to paint it with color, which took forever; third, to make corrections; and fourth, to paint it all again. Tony happily obliged. Each time Gary used a new canvas so that he could memorize every line, every shadow, every tint of color in Old Tony's character-carved face. They became friends, old Tony and young Gary before Tony passed on. And as Gary stood in the art gallery with the crowds gathering to see Old Tony the painting, Gary felt humbled that Tony's blessings to Gary multiplied exponentially year after year. So much so, that as Gary stood there in the exhibition hall he felt as though he was introducing an old friend of his to all the people who came to visit.

He wanted to grab a microphone and tell them all about the man they were staring at. "Hey, everybody! Thanks for coming. This is not just a painting. This is my friend, Tony from the Near West Side of Cleveland. Listen up, he immigrated with his mother and father from Slovenia 87 years ago. They raised him to work hard, make his own way, pay his own bills. In the steel mills he worked right there in Cleveland, and he loved his new city. Even more, he loved his new country so much that he learned English and became an actual United States of America citizen. Tony was so incredibly proud of becoming an American citizen that he marched in the Poor

People's March in the 70's, as a poor, but proud American. In addition, let me tell you, not only was Tony hard working and proud, but he was kind, gentle, honest and loving. Yes, he was poor, but Tony was still a man of high character. You can see all that in his face, can't you?"

Gary never did say all of that. But he felt it. For eight years he had painted the character of a man that shone out from that God-carved, beautiful face. And now to stand in the presence of his old friend and watch people weep humbled him. And made him proud...of Old Tony. Very proud.

Nobody in the crowd there really knew that the young guy in the corner was the artist. Not yet, anyhow. That would come down the road, not that Gary ever craved the notoriety that eventually came. No. What Gary did covet was this added blessing of anonymity, so that he could humbly watch and see the faces of people relating to the Old Tony Gary loved.

His dad walked next to Gary, put his arm around his son. "Gary, this is amazing, remarkable, isn't it?"

"Dad, this is more than I ever imagined. They love Old Tony, don't they."

"They sure do. And you don't even want them to know you painted that portrait, do you, that you're the artist?"

"No. Old Tony draws them in, draws them to himself. I'm just totally amazed at the power of a painting done in love, in respect. That was my goal, that people would come to know Old Tony like I did, and experience sitting not in front of a painting but in the presence of the man. I'm so proud of Tony."

Guy put his arm around his son, "Gary, I'm so proud of you."

The hours passed, the crowds thinned and Sandy walked up to Gary and Guy. "Well, it's about time to close up. What do you think?"

Gary stumbled with his words. "I never imagined. Never ever imagined what people would do when they stood in front of Old Tony."

"They fell in love with him," Sandy whispered.

"Yes. Yes, that's exactly what happened. You hit the nail right on the head. Standing here I felt like a voyeur watching person after person fall in love with Old Tony."

"I have only seen such an overwhelming response to a piece of art a few times in my life, because that only happens in the presence of a masterpiece. This is a masterpiece, truly a masterpiece." Sandy's eyes teared up once again as she put her arm around Gary's shoulder and told him, "I'm really proud of you, Gary, you and Old Tony." Then she paused and looked around as if she were worried that she might miss even one little sparkle in this glittering day. Satisfied that she had not missed a single glint, Sandy just stood there smiling, basking in the afterglow. Very satisfied, she said, "But now it's time to close up shop. Let's get some sleep. We've got two more days. Ready?"

"Can I sit with him alone for a while first?" asked Gary, also enjoying the gloaming close up with Old Tony.

"Sure, for a little while. I'll let you know when time's up, okay?"

"Thank you." Then Gary and Old Tony looked into one another's eyes until it was time while Guy waited nearby.

The next two days were much the same, except the Saturday and Sunday crowds were larger. Gary got exhausted standing to the side watching people. Their weeping especially took its toll on him. He had never expected such an emotional response from so many people. "This is like watching back to back to back to back Hallmark movies," Gary whispered to himself.

"What was that?" Guy asked him. Even though Guy had heard the weeping, he could not comprehend people weeping in front of a painting, even though Guy himself had done that at first. He figured he wept because his son was the artist. But it was more than that — Old Tony had power to tug upon the emotional depths, the very soul of one who gazed upon his God-carved face.

"No, really, what did you just say."

"Oh, nothing really. It's all just so much more emotion than I ever expected from the crowd. And so much more crowd."

"Well, how's about we tear ourselves away, take a little break and walk to the Starbucks concession for a coffee and a muffin?"

"Good idea, Dad. I'm emotionally drained, and I think I could use coffee and fifty deep breaths of fresh air." Guy chuckled, put his arm around this son, and arm in arm they headed for the mobile Starbucks set up for the fair. Guy marveled that he was actually walking arm in arm with his son after all those drunk years of selling time with his son for hours on a bar stool. Those first two days had already overwhelmed Guy with an amazing bonding with Gary that he never saw coming, especially at an art show for crying out loud. 'Another blessing from Old Tony,' he told himself smiling, picking up Gary's way of counting all the good things happening to both of them because of Gary's Old Tony masterpiece. Then Guy, as he had learned from his AA friends, offered a silent prayer, 'Thank you, God, for Old Tony and for Gary and for being sober.'

They spent the next two hours together not saying much. They just enjoyed being together like never before. Guy finally broke the quiet and said, "Gary, I never imagined having a grown son could be this good. I love you for who you are and for the man you have become."

They leaned in for a shoulder bump, and Gary replied, "I love you too, Dad. And I'm more proud of you every day for what you have accomplished in the last five years. You have put our family back together, and it's wonderful."

They both got misty, and Guy said, "Maybe we better get back for the judging. I'm excited to see what they're going to do with Old Tony. How 'bout you?"

"Yeah, me too. But, Dad, I've got to tell you, no award can top either the responses of the people to Old Tony, or the closeness you and I have right now."

Guy almost lost it again, but instead of blubbering he asked, "Yeah, but a blue ribbon would nice too, no?"

"Sure would," Gary said as they both laughed. "Very nice."

As it turned out when they got to Old Tony, they found him already bedecked with three blue ribbons for oils, portrait and novice categories, and one Gold for Best in Show. Guy whooped, jumped, cheered, grabbed his son in a huge bear hug, kissed him on the cheek and choked out, "Gar, this is awesome! This is a big f-in' deal!" Gary laughed at his dad, and as they embraced he told him, "Dad, you're embarrassing."

"Sorry," Guy said, 'but I am over the top happy and proud. And I don't care who knows it. You're tops in my book, kiddo." And they laughed even more.

People nearby caught their joy together and started cheering. They cheered loud and strong, and someone began chanting, "Tony! Tony! Tony!" and everybody around joined in, including Gary and Guy creating one of those forever father and son moments.

When the celebrating died down and some people moved on, others made their way to give their personal congratulations to Gary. Among them was a wizened old woman moving with a cane.

"Hello," she said with a thick German accent. "My name is Trudy. My sister Erna and I knew Tony. He would have been proud of you, young man. Very proud."

"Thank you, Trudy," was all he had time to say, because the kind old woman turned and walked away wiping tears from her eyes.

More blessings from Old Tony.

The organizers invited all the artists to a reception just for them to honor the ribbon winners. And for the next two hours Gary received the congratulations of nearly all 260 artists and hundreds more Old Tony enthusiasts. The most special congrats of all came from Ms. Green who arrived accompanied by medical staff from the James Cancer Center. Show organizers escorted her to the front of the line, and Gary just lost it. He wept, cautiously embraced his mentor, and said through his tears, "Thank you so much for coming."

"I wouldn't have missed this for all the art in France!" she told him. "I'm just sorry I can't stay longer, but I have to go or else my carriage will turn into a pumpkin."

They laughed, embraced again and waved, and Gary felt twelve feet tall as he watched his fabulous artistic mentor slowly make her way through the crowd, cheering her in his heart.

Blessings from Old Tony fell like *manna* from heaven.

Chapter 11

The Church at Harbor and Divine

Wonderful memories made driving time fly by for Gary. He stopped to fill up on gas at the last Springfield, Ohio exit. He got a couple rest area hot dogs, a cup of coffee, a can of Arizona energy tea and a bag of chips. He checked the oil, cleaned the windshield and got on the road again. He decided to bypass downtown Columbus on I-270 and head up I-71 to be in Cleveland in about three and a half hours. He was tired, but thought his excitement would carry him through just fine. He called his dad to let him know he would pull in to their home right about supper time just as they had planned. They had invited Gary to stay in the spare bedroom as long as he needed to, which Gary appreciated immensely, even though he felt awkward imposing on them. And when he got there, after hugs and kisses, Gary thanked them for opening their home. "But I just don't want to be imposing on you."

"What? Imposing?" his dad scoffed. "You could stay in our house for a month of Sundays and you would still not be imposing." Gary laughed at his dad's straight-to-the-point Cleveland talk.

"I won't stay that long, but I sure appreciate you keeping your invitation open-ended for a while. I think Annie the realtor has been working hard to expedite the sale, so it may not take more than a couple of weeks to get renovations started. She even has had the City of Cleveland building inspector out a couple of times to help her make a punch list of important improvements needed to bring everything up to code including the structure and utilities of both buildings. I told her that to begin, I am more interested in the house, so I could move in."

"That makes sense," said Guy.

"Let me call Annie, and see if all of us can get to see it after supper. How does that sound?"

Both his mom and dad lit up, "We'd love that!"

"Good."

He dialed Annie's office number and she picked up right away. "Hello, Dunlop Realty. This is Annie Dunlop."

"Annie, this is Gary again."

"Of course. I didn't look at the caller id."

"No *problemo*. Hey, Mom and Dad would like to come with me. Would that be all right with you?"

"All right? That would be awesome," Annie cheered.

"Great. But let me ask you something first, because I'd like to tell them just how long they're going to have to put up with me in their house. So tell me this: How soon before I would be able to move into a bedroom upstairs there? In a week? Two? What do you think?"

"I think two weeks or less is doable, Gary. In fact, the building inspector told me he would declare the house habitable as soon as the utilities get turned on and there were no big problems."

"That sounds awesome, Annie," Gary chortled, "but is that likely?"

"I think so, because the pastor of the most recent Latino congregation made upgrades over the years to keep the house up to code for him and his family. And they moved out less than two years ago when the church closed up shop. The inspector assured me that the house is in good shape and that he was fairly certain any future repairs would be minor. What do you think?"

"I think I'm excited. So can we still see it tonight?"

"Right now if you want to."

"Really? Goodness. Annie, you are either the best realtor on earth or just a top notch person. Or both."

Silence on Annie's end. Not that Annie didn't like hearing what Gary had said. She loved it, but it caught her up short, surprised her, especially since she remembered Gary Siciliano from high school at Lincoln-West when he was a senior and she was only a freshman. She was pretty sure he would not remember her, especially since Dunlop is her married-now-divorced name. But she certainly did remember him, had a crush on him in fact. He was just a really nice, cute guy, medium build, wavy light brown hair and eyes to get lost in. She had always regretted that she never had a chance with Gary. All the other guys she dated, even Phil Dunlop whom she married, came in second place to Gary Siciliano. Of course, Phil introduced her to real estate, and that was good. But then, after they were married for a childless 16 years — his fault on the childless part — he ran off with a flashy, younger real estate broker from Atlanta whom he met at big motivation seminar in downtown Cleveland. Annie never suspected a thing until Phil told her "Good-bye, Annie," and moved to Atlanta. The fact that Phil signed over the business to her in the divorce settlement eased her pain, subdued her anger — but still, what a jerk.

Oh well, that was years ago, and now, here was Gary Siciliano, coming off a tragedy of his own. At least she was pretty sure it's the same Gary — 99.7% sure. She'd know for sure when they meet. Even without it being the same Gary — oh, get out, it's HIM — Annie was way over the top too excited for an ordinary home sale. Could she help it that her imagination was running away with her? It *had* to be him. So for Gary to say such nice things over the phone just made her breathless, a little light-headed and unable to utter a single word.

Gary intuitively understood what he had just said. 'Oy, what a lumpkin am I,' he told himself and quickly waded back into the conversation trying to save the awkward moment.

"So how about in an hour and a half. Mom is just about ready to feed us a dinner I don't want to miss. So, what, say seven-ish?"

Annie found her voice, "Sounds good to me." It was like a fairy tale coming true right before her eyes.

"Wow. This is going so fast. Is that good? Is that usual?"

"Better than good, Gary. See you soon."

"Okay. Bye."

"Bye."

"Hokey smoke," Gary said aloud after he hung up. "Real estate is not the only thing here that's going so fast. Get a grip, Gar. You've got to get a grip, man."

Dinner was great. Ninety minutes flew by. Gary was as nervous as a long-tailed cat in a room full of rocking chairs, and he knew it wasn't just about the Harbor and Divine real estate either. 'Just take it slow, Gar,' he told himself.

Annie Dunlop waited for them in the Parish House, which once served as the parsonage for Methodist pastors for more than 100 years. Built in 1910, the 1,728 square foot brick house still stood as a solid anchor in an ever-changing neighborhood. Founded by German speaking Church of the Brethren folks, the church served as the spiritual home for a parade of immigrant families including German, Polish, Slovenian, Irish and most recently Latino. In fact, in the 1950's and 60's job hungry American-born men migrated to Cleveland to find work in the steel mills and oil refineries, some living in flop houses so they could earn enough to send back money home to their West Virginia families who stayed put in the home towns and hollers they loved.

Church folks had taken really good care of the house through two world wars, the Great Depression, urban flight as well as the inner city twin plagues of drugs and guns. Wide planked woodwork maintained its deep-stained luster, updated bathrooms witnessed to money well spent on improvements plus refinished original yellow pine floors that gleamed with loving care. "Gary will love this place," Annie said aloud to herself. "At least I hope so."

Footsteps on the porch interrupted her reverie as Gary and his parents knocked on the front door. Annie broke into a big smile as she walked to the front door to let them in.

"Come in. Welcome to Harbor and Divine. I'm Annie Dunlop."

"Hi Annie, I'm Gary Siciliano and this is my mom and dad Phyllis and Guy. Thank you for inviting them to join in on the tour."

"Hello, Gary!" (This is absolutely him. Absolutely!) "Mr. and Mrs. Siciliano, nice to meet you."

"Annie," Phyllis said, "thank you for including us. This house and this church hold incredible stories about our old neighborhood here, especially Gary's life. It's a miracle that it's available. And that it is still beautiful. Look at this place."

"So you used to live on the Near West Side?"

"We sure did. And this was our church." Phyllis answered. "Those were happy, yet tough years for our family, right Guy?"

"Right. And I was the author of the 'tough' years part," he confessed. "I was a drunk, and my wife and sons were saints. Why, do you know, Gary and some church community worker —name of James, I think — even pulled me out of my favorite drinking hole one night when I was drunk as a skunk."

"Were you ever in this house?"

"A few times. AA meetings mainly. Gary was 10 or 11 years old."

Gary jumped in. "Dad, those days are long gone. You turned your life around, all our lives around, and Mom and I are still really proud of you." Everybody took a beat. Gary continued, "So how 'bout we take that tour and let Realtor Annie tell us what's going on?"

They all agreed, so Annie gave them a good realtor's pitch of the house and then of the church building, and an hour later they gathered on the front porch of the house which still had two old green steel gliding porch chairs on it from another era long past. Guy and Phyllis sat in the two chairs, Gary sat on the brick and stone porch rail and Annie stood as she wrapped up her sales proposal, including a price for both buildings that Gary said he could easily afford including adding in all the renovations.

"So, Annie, when do we sit down and sign papers?"

"Maybe next week some time. How does Wednesday sound?"

"Perfect. At your office?"

"Yes, maybe late morning, say ten o'clock?"

"Ten o'clock it is. I'll be there at ten sharp. Just one thing. Where is your office?"

"Oh," she chuckled, "small detail. It's actually still in Cleveland on Lorain, about half way between here and Kamm's Corners." Annie asked if they knew the way, and they did, so they said their good-byes made their way back to their cars.

All business, Gary thought. No goofiness. Good.

Chapter 12

A Wrinkle and a Confession

Wednesday morning Gary drove to Annie's office, and walked into a cheery "Good morning, Gary!" Made him smile, really smile. 'Easy, boy!' he scolded himself.

"Good morning, Annie."

"Are you always this prompt?"

"I think so. At least I try to be. I think it has a lot to do with the self-discipline of being an artist. If I'm going to accomplish anything at all, I have to glue my butt to the stool at 9:00 sharp and get to work."

"Totally makes sense. And not just for an artist. Even real estate. Sit, pick up the phone and make the calls.. Yep. You're right."

"So are we ready to do business?"

"Maybe."

"Maybe? What's that mean?"

"It means we have a wrinkle, and I have a confession."

"Uh-oh. A wrinkle and confession sounds bad," Gary told her.

"Maybe not all that bad. First, the wrinkle is this: the listing agent made a mistake thinking that the First Hispanic Congregation owned the property. In fact, First Hispanic trustees *thought* they owned the property. As it turns out the United Methodist denomination owns both of these church buildings, and every other United Methodist building in christendom. We could maybe separate the house from the church—maybe—and sell you the house. But for sure we can't sell you the church building until the United Methodist District and Conference approve the sale."

"Whoa. That's a punch in the gut."

"Yeah. I'm sorry. Do I lose my status as World's Best Realtor?"

"Hmmm. Let's see how you do under pressure," Gary grinned.

Annie returned the grin, "Challenge accepted. Already on it!"

"Well, let's get to it then."

"I did some fast footwork this morning with the United Methodist District Superintendent. He supervises about 75 churches in Metro Cleveland. He told me that the Harbor and Divine church has been a mission church for generations, and just because First Hispanic moved out, doesn't mean the Methodists plan to give up the mission."

"Makes sense. Sounds like my kind of guy."

"Mine too. So, Gary, here's the deal. Mission for them can take on countless forms as long it it serves people in need, loving them where they are in their lives."

"So mission could be art maybe? That's like way too close to how it happened to me thirty-four years ago."

"Just what I was thinking. So I actually ran that by him, saying 'I've got a client who is a nationally acclaimed artist who grew up at Harbor and Divine and is moving back to Cleveland to 'give back' what that church gave him.' And, Gary, he got it. Immediately. Without any explanation. Didn't miss a beat. He asked me, 'You mean like an art mission? He could work with the Cleveland Institute of Art and the Cleveland Museum of Art as an urban art outreach?' Can you believe it? That is exactly what he asked!"

Eyes as wide as saucers, Gary's face lit up, "Like we'd be partners right from the get-go?"

"Exactly. The Methodists would take care of the buildings, plus they already have a mission pastor slated to assign there, like that James guy you told me helped you. You might have to share the church building with the food pantry and clothing center in the basement, as well as a Sudanese adult education program, and A.A...."

Gary interrupted, "But that's exactly my vision of giving back to the community that gave so much to me."

"Just what I was thinking, and the Methodist guy is right there with you. Are you ready to explore it?"

"You betcha. I'm amazed that whenever I'm looking for some way to help out people in need, things just fall into place one after another after another. Just one small thing though: where do I live?"

"Funny you should ask," Annie teased. "I found a two-story century home, fully renovated inside and out, no work for you at all. It is gorgeous! And not yet listed. Interested?"

"You bet. Where is it?"

"Right across the street."

"What? You've got to be kidding!"

"Totally serious. And for a lot less money than it would have cost you to buy and renovate these two huge properties. In fact, you could buy it and probably move in a few weeks."

"A few weeks?"

"Yep."

"A lot less money?"

"Less than a third."

"And no work?"

"No work at all."

"Annie, that sounds sweet. I do believe you are on your way to reclaiming your World's Best title," he said with a grin. "Let's go look."

"I hoped you would say that. But before we hop in our cars for another house tour, we have to deal with my confession. Okay?"

"Sure. It can't be too serious, can it?"

"You tell me. Gary, did you graduate from Lincoln-West?"

"Yep. Twenty-six years ago."

"I thought so. Well, when you were a senior I was a freshman, Annie Rogalsky."

"No way! Cute little Annie Rogalsky? I remember you. If you had been a year older I might have asked you out. But seniors didn't date freshmen back in those days. Annie, this is so cool!"

"I'm glad you think so. I didn't want to hide anything, especially when I'm trying to sell you a house."

Gary grinned from ear to ear, shook his head in modest disbelief and said, "Thanks for being up front, but no apology necessary. Let's go look at the house."

"Let's."

They parked their cars on Harbor Street across from the mission, met on the sidewalk and walked toward 1965 Harbor Street, the most beautiful house in sight, north, east, south or west.

"That house?" Gary sputtered.

"That house," Annie proudly confirmed.

"It's beautiful, Annie. Gor-ge-ous!"

"I told you so. Want to go explore?"

"Yes, I do."

Annie opened up the realtor's lock, got the key, unlocked the front door and they walked in.

"Oh, my goodness. Oh, my goodness. Would you look at that. Oh, my goodness. Annie, you're the best. This is magnificent. Can I just stay here starting right now? It looks like a brand new old house, know what I mean."

"I sure do. They nailed it on the renovations and the decor. And I'm glad you like it."

"Like it? Love it! Where do I sign?"

"Whoa, pardner. Hold your horses, cowboy, until we look around some first."

Gary did a double-take and thought, 'Does she actually know I like cowboy music? Oh, Gar, that's stupid.'

Annie kept talking, "We need to check the wiring, plumbing, foundation, rafters, joists, windows to make sure they didn't skimp on essentials. After all this still is an old house."

"You're right. I guess I'm easily distracted by new and shiny. Look at that kitchen! And that bathroom! And these floors! Shiny, shiny, shiny!" He looked at her sideways grinning and jumping his eyebrows. Annie laughed.

"You're incorrigible. But let's get down and dirty starting with the basement."

"Yes, ma'am!" he said, and not one word more. Such a good boy.

An hour later they had explored wire, pipe, nook and cranny. Annie was impressed with the building, and Gary was impressed with Annie, so he asked, "Annie, you're good at this. How do you know so much about houses?"

"Gary, I do home inspections as part of my job, and as far as I can see, they did a good job everywhere. What do you think?"

"I think you were very thorough, and I am impressed ...with the house. What's next?"

"Let me express some interest on your behalf to the seller while you explore ideas with the Methodist super. Here's his phone number. His office is in the University Circle United Methodist Church, often called the Holy Oil Can."

"Oh, that church that looks like one?"

"The very same. And get this. That church, the Holy Oil Can, already has an art outreach on the East Side started by the Methodist superintendent you will be calling. But the building is not in a neighborhood like Harbor and Divine. Still, there could be a lot to learn from them plus, I think, they are just good people to contact."

"Good ideas." He didn't tell Annie that they already had his paintings hanging in the Cleveland Museum of Art, and he knew a bunch of people who were already looking forward to talking with him. There was no sense telling her that. After all, "Pride goeth before the fall," and he wanted no prat falls with Annie. Everything about her intrigued him. Not that he was over his love for Dianah. No, no. Not in the least. But still... cute little Annie Rogalsky?

Chapter 13

Sfumato: In France

"First things first," Gary told himself aloud. "I've got to call the Art Museum and explore things with them before I make up things I can or can't do or even talk with the Methodists." He had lots to talk about with Dr. Zurkos, like how could Gary teach *sfumato* techniques without Old Tony there to serve as a model.

Since Gary was living on investments from the sale of Old Tony to the folks up in Minnesota, he really could not move Old Tony to Cleveland in order to touch him up. Of course, he could paint a duplicate of Old Tony, but that would take forever, like eight more years. Or he could let his studio study Leonardo on their own to learn *sfumato*, leaving him free to paint a new kind of original, an idea he had had ever since that day he auctioned off Old Tony for a gazillion dollars, like selling off his best friend. He had worked on Old Tony for eight years. Wow. Doggone it, Old Tony was like his grandfather, for crying out loud. The day Gary had left the auction house in Taos he had an emptiness, a hole in his soul that was still there, actually, though not even close in size to the cavernous longing he felt for Dianah. But still, he would like another painting of Old Tony hanging in his house. He was thinking that maybe the museum folks would work with him on studio space near the restoration labs, right in the same room they had already displayed his eight unfinished Old Tonys. It could be another large glassed in room outside of which art teachers and students could hold sessions on technique, particularly *sfumato*.

Gary's idea was that he could set up shop inside the glassed area and repaint Old Tony as an exhibition to be watched by ticket-buying art lovers. It could be an oil painting with *sfumato*, but clearly different enough from the original so as not to diminish the value of Old Tony the first. Then maybe along side that traditional painting he could paint an impressionist acrylic of a joyful, laughing Old Tony No. 2 from his other two boyhood sketches.

Gary had already stretched and sized a canvas, ready to paint years ago; however, Laughing Old Tony number two never did get painted. The idea wasn't new for him. But serious impressionism? That was new. True, Gary painted countless other oil, water color and acrylic impressionist portraits from photographs for patrons over the years, and his customers all had raved about his work, especially his portraits of children and families at the beach. Almost every single patron paid him more than the agreed price just like James had all those years ago. Gary surprised himself at how proud he was of those non-*sfumato* portraits, and even more pleased that they paid the bills without him touching his investments. Of course, none of them were Old Tony quality masterpieces, for sure. Gary knew all along that classical oils, *sfumato* in particular, were his consummate strengths, not acrylic or water color impressionism. Still, even back when Old Tony number one moved to Minnesota with his new owners, Gary knew that if he were ever going to paint an impressionistic Old Tony, he would have to up his game and study impressionism. And what better place to study impressionism but in the ancestral home of French Impressionism, Paris!

So he ran a plan past Dianah for them to go to Paris for six weeks so he could study with current impressionist master artists in the environs of the great French Impressionists at the French Academy of Fine Arts (*Academie des Beaux-Arts*). The *Academie* had long been the top institute of fine arts in France and surely the best place in the world to learn to paint *ala* French Impressionists. Plus the *Academie* sits right across the Seine River from the Louvre.

Dianah loved the idea.

"It could be like a second honeymoon!" she cheered.

When Gary asked his long-distance colleagues at the French *Academie* what they thought about his ideas they loved them, if, they said, Gary would teach some master classes in *sfumato*. Gary eagerly accepted their invitation, and relished the opportunity to teach internationally. True, he had taught at the Cleveland Institute of Art and the Cleveland Museum of Art as well as in Columbus while he was working on his MFA, so master classes did not intimidate him. Yet the *Academie* was number one in the whole world in classic, 19th century French Impressionism. Those were some serious artists. Hmmm. Actually, he thought, that would make the master classes be even more fun. When Gary told Dianah that his French colleagues offered one of the *Academie's* guest apartments facing the beautiful gardens on the grounds of the *Academie*, she actually jumped up and down and flapped her hands for joy like a little girl. Little did Dianah and Gary know just how very well French Impressionism and an over-the-top French garden apartment would bless their lives. Ahh! *Sfumato* in France! She couldn't wait!

As the time to leave for Paris drew near, Dianah eagerly took charge of the travel arrangements, the packing as well as generating the excitement. "France! Gary, we're going to France!"

"We are indeed, Dianah Springer Brownbear! Next week!"

"I'm so excited I can barely sit still for a minute," she said as she ran to Gary, threw her arms around his neck, kissed him mercilessly and kicked her feet for joy.

And before they knew it they were in the air and on their way.

Pierre met them at the airport. "Pierre," of course. He later confessed that wasn't his real name. "But I thought that two Americans in France for the very first time would love being picked up at the airport by a Pierre!" Gary and Dianah laughed at his kindness.

Gary confessed, "It's funny, but we have to admit that you were absolutely right. We loved being welcomed to France by a Pierre."

They chatted on the way to the *Academie* in the sixth a*rrondisement* and in no time at all they arrived at their stunning French garden apartment with a river view.

"Oh, my goodness," Gary marveled. "Would you look at that! Oh, my goodness. Pierre, this is out of a fairy tale. Thank you for inviting us to stay here for our six weeks. This is simply splendid!"

"You're welcome. Both of you. We hope you enjoy your stay. All of us in the *Academie* are excited to work together with you for the next six weeks. We will all grow as artists, no?"

"Oui! That is my hope."

Dianah noticed that the arched door into the apartment was open, so she left Gary and Pierre to chat, ran inside and in a flash started calling out, "Gary, Gary. Come on already. Come see! You've got to see! This apartment is simply beautiful!"

Gary and Pierre followed, and, by golly, she was right. The interior was as stunning as the exterior. Dianah, mouth agape, tears streaming, said, "I can't believe we get to stay here. I'm not going to want to leave!"

"I'm glad you approve, madame," Pierre said with a courtly flourish. "The apartment is stocked with food, toiletries, towels and linens. Please explore. Gary, I'll return for you tomorrow morning at 8:00. And Babbette, my wife — also not her name, but it goes with 'Pierre' — she will arrive at 9:00 for Madame Dianah, if that would be convenient."

"Very convenient, Pierre," said Dianah, "and wonderful. Thank you. And may we continue to call you Pierre? Or shall we call you by your given name?"

"Pierre and Babbette for two days for the joy of it," he answered with a grin. "After that, I'll let you know. *C'est bien?*"

"Very good. And thank you again very much. Good night."

"You're very welcome. Good night." Smiling, Pierre left them alone and full of delight for the night.

In the morning Pierre introduced Gary to *Academie* teachers, staff and resident artists, and the week began. Babbette gathered up Dianah for an all-day tour of Paris. They bonded instantly and spent a glorious day together, aided in particular by Babbette's flawless American English and her patient help with Dianah's French.

Right from the start the artists at the *Academie* eagerly shared all they could about French Impressionism with Gary in such a short stay; and Gary demonstrated for them the laborious layering techniques of *sfumato*, which of course they knew, but had never seen demonstrated with the left-handed skill that was uniquely Gary's. Every day at the *Academie* was like two master classes in painting: impressionism for Gary and *sfumato* for his new French colleagues. Gary soaked it all up like an eager college exchange student.

On the flip side of their French adventure Gary and Dianah loved their cozy, very Parisian apartment on the grounds of the *Academie* across the Seine on a walking bridge from the Louvre. Every day they explored one or two of the galleries in the Louvre, and every day Dianah blossomed more and more as Gary's muse, his model and his lover as Gary's exquisite paintings fully displayed! Their Parisian adventure exploded into the kind of second honeymoon that couples yearn for to re-cement their love. It was while they were in France that Dianah and Gary discovered the *sfumato* of love: one heart, one flesh, one person.

"We are one person," she told Gary in the midst of their love making. "It's an old Hopi teaching, but now I really understand it." And they melted once again into one another's arms. It was also there in France, as they later discovered much to their delight, that they had conceived Lilyana.

Every day Gary and Dianah cloistered themselves for hours as Dianah became Gary's model. At first she was a bit shy, but with Gary's encouraging, smiling "Ooo-lah-lah's" Dianah got into it, and thoroughly surprised herself at how much fun she had modeling and, yes, showing off for Gary. She loved looking at him look at her, and then seeing herself through Gary's eyes as he drew and painted her sensuality and her readiness to pounce upon her beloved with either the graceful power of a lioness or the ferocious strength of a dancing brown bear. It never took long, though, for Gary to totally succumb to

Dianah's beauty. He could watch and paint for only so long before he would throw down his brush and chase her around the apartment, both of them laughing themselves silly until they fell passionately into one another's arms.

Gary filled his paintings with the intimate, unbridled joy they both felt in their cozy, very French apartment. However, since art education is a show-and-tell endeavor, Gary's French mentors and collaborators asked him to bring in some of his work for a master class. Dianah wasn't sure she was ready to share.

"Gary," she said as they sat in bed and looked at dozens of water colors, acrylics, charcoals and oils, "you're holding the brush, but that's me, all me, *au naturale* that people will look at, gawk at."

Gary laughed. "You do have a point there; however, I confess, you are gorgeous to gawk at. But think of it this way: at the end of six weeks you'll never see them again. And besides you're not modeling for them, only for me."

"That's true. But *all* of the pictures? Definitely not this one. No way anybody sees this one but you and me." She paused. Grinned. "I do love it though. Just not ready to share. Can I eliminate some of them from the stack that are just for us?"

"Of course. That's a good idea. How about after you cull through them, I get to pick three from what's left that demonstrate that I have actually learned a bit about impressionist painting." He smiled. "Then you get to pick the one I show."

Dianah quickly picked out Gary's favorites, and hers, gave them to him and said, "These, my love, are for your eyes only." She smiled that smile that she knew turned Gary into mush, "Okay?"

"Okay." From the remaining work Gary easily picked three that demonstrated his improving skills. He laid them out for Dianah to see. "How about these?"

"Those are perfect. And Gary, I love you."

"I love you. You want to pick one?"

"I pick all three."

Gary grinned. "Thanks. I'll take them. I don't want the class to think I've been loafing." Dianah smacked him with a pillow.

"And they'll think what instead?"

"Hmm. Good point. They'll think we've become very French."

The next day when Gary put his paintings on the wall the whole class broke out into a chorus of whistles, cheers and "Ooo-lah-lah's," even the women. After class, when he returned to the apartment, he just simply smiled and said, "They liked my work." And when he told her about the details, Dianah turned beet-red and then, much to Gary's delight, smiled that smile he couldn't resist. She then replayed the scene that Gary had captured in line and color in one of the three, ending work for the day. Who could have guessed that art classes would become a fantasy of romance and delight that they hoped would never end?

C'est la vie.

Unfortunately, those six weeks passed by much too quickly for both of them, and before they knew it they were air bound for the USA with the art work packed and shipped to arrive a few days after they got home. Totally exhausted they slept all the way to Houston where they got on a Frontier Air Lines turbo prop for Albuquerque.

Back home in Farmington, in the condo they bought right after they got married, Gary and Dianah relived their experiences and made love for two full days. And when Gary's paintings of Dianah arrived they studied them all again and extended the two days into four.

"I guess we brought a little Paris home with us, huh, Gar?"

"More than a little, holy smoke. I'm so glad we went together. How else would I have learned the *sfumato* of love — or how to paint impressionism of my beautiful Dancing Bear? Dianah, you make my heart sing songs I never knew were there to sing. I love you more than ever."

She answered by throwing herself into his arms and knocking him backward off his feet and into bed. Gary laughed, grabbed on and told her, "Congratulations, Dianah Brownbear, you have just earned your Parisian Purple Belt in the art of *sfumato* tackling to be worn when, and only when, employing the *sfumato* of love — with me." Dianah giggled softly and Gary presented her with a purple ribbon lying under them on the bed, the one that Dianah had used to wrap up their art.

"Thank you, Master Gary-san." She bowed her head. "I will cherish this always."

More giggles, more wrestling, more *sfumato* of love.

By their fifth day home from Paris Gary and Diana began feeling a certain urgency to get more mundane things in order. Dianah made phone calls to the Shiprock studio, and Gary began constructing a 30x42 inch stretcher with canvas for Old Tony No. 2. He mixed and applied his sizing just before lunch and set it on the drying rack. The whole house smelled like an art studio again as Dianah walked into the kitchen. Lunch was on the schedule, but they couldn't keep their hands off one another even for two minutes. The smell of Paris, perhaps.

A half an hour later they finally got to lunch sitting commando at the table, eating sandwiches and grinning at each other.

"I hope Paris never wears off," she said.

"I second that," Gary grinned.

Chapter 14

The Empty Canvas

The canvas Gary had stretched, now twelve years back when he and Dianah had returned from Paris, was still blank except for the sizing. Who knows why. For 12 years Gary had stored it first in their home in Farmington and then when they moved, in his studio in Durango unfinished while he finished hundreds of portraits for patrons. With each painting he perfected his learned-in-France impressionist strokes to be lighter, brighter and bubbling with a living joy, springing from within his soul first at being Dianah's husband and Lily's father, and second from the joy he witnessed in the families he painted. Mothers and fathers told him that they could more easily see their families' happiness in his paintings than they could see it actually standing in the middle of daily family life.

Yet, still, the already prepared canvas for Old Tony no. 2, the laughing, joyful Old Tony, remained blank for all those years up to the very time Gary moved back to Cleveland. Funny how he resisted, as if it were a sacrilege to the memory of Tony whose portrait made him rich beyond any fears of ending up a starving artist. True, he had good excuses over the years: a beautiful daughter to raise, a dream home on Durango Mountain to build with Dianah and contractor Fred, plus scores of patrons willing to pay him big bucks to paint their family portraits.

But, if truth be told, more than the excuses, Gary was actually afraid of the overwhelming task of painting a new *sfumato* Old Tony. After all, it took Gary more effort and time to paint Old Tony — eight years — than it had taken him to paint all those hundreds of family portraits in recent years. It was downright hard work to replicate Leonardo's celebrated *sfumato* techniques. But to paint all those impressionist beach portraits of happy families? To Gary, that was joyful art, more akin to replicating those rapturous, goddess-like images of Dianah in Paris. Sure, Gary could teach the *sfumato* techniques to a studio, but it's a new day, and Gary had no desire to paint his next major project using that painstaking, life-consuming *sfumato* detail work.

"Maybe," Gary said aloud to himself, "Maybe that's why Leonardo left so much of his art unfinished. Too much *sfumato*. Too much OCD!" he quipped. He shook his head thinking how life reinvents itself day by day. And the smoky haze, the *sfumato*, of days gone by graciously resets one's eyes clearly upon the day at hand.

And this day? Is this a day begging to repaint Old Tony?

His mind and his heart agreed. No.

But the laughing Tony painted with joyous impressionist stroke and color? That's what he had always wanted to do with that blank canvas. After all, he still had those two sketches of laughing Old Tony from the day when he was ten and Gary had told Tony his face was carved by the Hand of God, and Tony laughed. "The Hand of God?" he blustered as his face lit up with joy at the thought of God carving his face with deep lines to make him beautiful to Gary. Gary sketched two versions of Tony's lit up face in his sketchbook that day.

He still had them, plus he had an unfinished canvas of laughing Tony he started for Ms. Green. He remembered Ms. Green looking at laughing Old Tony just before she left the second time for a new round of cancer treatments at the James Cancer Center, telling him, "Gary this is delightful. It must be what Moses looked like when he came down the mountain with the tablets of stone, when the Bible says his face shone so brightly that people could hardly look at him. Good grief! What did they expect? Moses had just had 'a moment' with God Almighty. How else would a person look after a moment with God other than impossibly radiant?"

Then she paused. "And you know what else, Gar?" she asked him not expecting an answer. "It reminds me of Leonardo's laughing John the Baptist pointing the way to heaven. I'd love to have that painting hanging in my home with its joyful invitation to heaven."

Gary never did finish that laughing Tony. *Sfumato* consumed him. Well, maybe *sfumato* wasn't to blame. But then, on the day he learned Ms. Green had died, he pitched his unfinished happy Tony in the trash.

"Death sure has taken its toll on my art," Gary ruminated. "Tony and I need to get laughing again!"

That day, when Tony laughed, he looked impossibly beside himself with joy. But in the original Old Tony the first, the award-winning painting, Gary had subdued that joy, like Leonardo had done with the Mona Lisa. So, Gary thought, 'Maybe this is the day to paint that joyous Old Tony, shining with the face of Moses, radiant in splendor, coming down the mountain from God. Or, like Leonardo's John the Baptist, ecstatically pointing his invitation to heaven. Maybe that's what all those joy-filled impressionist portraits of families on the beach have prepared me for, filling that empty canvas with heaven's joy.'

"Yep, it's decided!" Gary declared. "Today is the day to begin to fill that blank canvas with the joy and laughter of my old friend Tony! Get to it, Gar. Just get to it," he admonished himself. "After all, right there is the blank canvas. It's been waiting twelve years." Then channeling his inner cowboy, he sauntered in the way that used to make Dianah laugh, mimicked spitting out his pretend cowboy chew and said, "Jest get 'er done, Gar! Jest get 'er done!"

Pumped up with a vision of a joyous Old Tony in his eyes and a mission to paint it *now* in his heart, Gary called his friends at the Cleveland Museum of Art to share his ideas. They put him on speaker phone and eagerly listened as Gary poured out his ideas.

And they loved his plan. "Yes, yes! Let's do it!" they all cheered.

"Gary, this is Melanie."

"Of course. Dr. Zurkos. Were you cheering me on too?"

"I certainly was. A Joyful Old Tony would make my heart sing!"

"You are forever my encourager," Gary testified. "I will always appreciate how much you encouraged me through Old Tony the first, when I was ready to give up more than once in the midst of years of tedious *sfumato* work. You saved me and my Old Tony MFA final project."

"Yes, I remember your struggles. But you stayed the course. Perseverance is a too little acclaimed character trait of great artists. You had it then, Gary, and I'm certain you have it still.

Artistic talent goes only as far as the tenacity of the artist will allow. With that combination of talent and tenacity you and Old Tony created the very best masters project I had ever seen up until then, and likely ever see in my lifetime. Your mastery of *sfumato* and of Leonardo's journals inspired all of us back then, and you have continued that inspiration with your eight unfinished canvases hanging here in the glass studio."

"Hear! Hear!" cheered the rest of the staff listening in.

Dr. Zurkos continued, "Gary, I love, love, love your idea. Goodness gracious. Every day with you here will be a Master Class. Students and full time professional artists will learn *sfumato* just by watching you mix and apply your glaze, just as we did back in the day. Even if you don't finish your *sfumato studio* painting, Gary, I believe you will inspire us all over again with a new impressionist Joyful Old Tony. Please, will you come in and talk with us about details of your proposal?"

Dr. Zurkos still knew how to set Gary's spirit aflame.

"Absolutely! Dr. Zurkos, I was already enthused to paint Joyful Old Tony, but you have set me on fire! However, right this minute I am in the midst of moving from Colorado, buying a home in Cleveland and sleeping nights at my mom and dad's house, so would two weeks from today be convenient for all of you? Maybe by then I'll feel a little more on top of the moving chaos as well as my emotions. Plus, do you think maybe before then, I could stop by and just walk around the restoration studios to get my bearings?"

"That would be perfect, Gary. Yes to both: two weeks for our next meeting and any time before then. Two weeks will give all of us time to arrange our schedules, because folks here who remember you from your Masters work of Old Tony will love to see you again. And others who don't yet know you personally will love meeting Old Tony's artist, even if they may not

105

get directly involved in your proposed art education outreach project. Because of Old Tony you are a well respected celebrity artist in our Cleveland art world." Then Dr. Zurkos concluded for everyone with, "So, shall we say two weeks from today at 10:00 AM in the art restoration area?" Everyone around her nodded in agreement.

Gary concurred, "Sounds perfect for me."

Dr. Zurkos continued, "Good deal. We can all walk together through the glassed-in areas you're thinking of to get our minds clicking along the same lines. Then, if you are willing, we could all share lunch together in the staff dining room and continue our conversation. Some of our staff may need to leave right after lunch, but you and I can then return to the art restoration studio and re-think our proposal in the new light of the ideas we all share together as a group. How does that sound?

"Wonderful," said Gary, "simply wonderful. I look forward to seeing all of you then. Or sooner."

"Same here. And when you drop in, please let me know."

"Will do. Thank you so very much, Dr. Zurkos."

"Oh, and, Gary, I am so very sorry about your wife's and daughter's passing. You must still be raw with grief."

"Thank you, Dr. Zurkos. I am still pretty raw."

"I hope your broken heart will heal, and your memories will turn from sadness to joy."

"Thank you again."

"And, by the way, I'm Melanie, please. Or Mel. Old Tony trumps any PhD."

"Melanie it is... , thank you, Dr. Zurkos."

They both laughed as they ended their call.

As Gary put his phone down, he said aloud "And, lo, I saw a new heaven and a new earth, for the first heaven and the first earth had passed away," quoting Revelation 21:1 that the pastor read at Dianah's and Lily's funeral. Then he started weeping again at the healing goodness of God, at the blessings that still seemed to emanate from Old Tony, and especially at the thought of moving forward without Dianah, without Lily. "Thank you. Thank you. Thank you," was all Gary could say through tears of amazing grace that were washing away his grief and his fear.

Surely, 'Thank you,' was enough for the Giver of that grace.

Chapter 15

Ms. Green, Leonardo and Dr. Zurkos

G ary was genuinely excited about calling the Methodist Superintendent. He remembered that when he was 10 years old it was the decision of the Methodist superintendent with a vision back then to hire James as a community organizer to work with older boys in the Harbor and Divine neighborhood where Gary and his family lived. It was James who encouraged Gary to show his drawings to Ms. Val Green, the high school art teacher. It was then Ms. Green who taught him perspective, shading, color, painting techniques. She introduced Gary to Leonardo DaVinci's incessant, compulsive curiosity that made him a great artist who saw things that other artists just did not, could not, see. Like the oneness of the portrait subject in the foreground with the Arno River Valley in the background in the Mona Lisa. Before Leonardo artists did not consider the background important to a portrait. Leonardo made backgrounds essential to his paintings. Ms. Green also introduced Gary to Leonardo's incredible notebooks, especially those that portrayed the job of a portrait artist as bringing depth and life to the two dimensional medium of paint on canvas or board or whatever. That, surprisingly quite naturally, led Gary to learn Leonardo's left handed hatching first and then second and perhaps even more importantly the depth, movement and life that *sfumato* gives to a portrait.

In countless retrospective ruminations Gary discovered how a single seemingly insignificant action by one caring person can change the entire course of another person's life. Dianah called them helpers and spirit guides, that, if you have eyes to see and ears to hear, you can see and hear them with every step you take. Some helpers like Dianah and Ms. Green guided him for many years. Others like James only for a few months. Yet in that brief time, when James noticed Gary's sketch book, he totally redirected Gary's life path every bit as completely as had Ms. Green when she introduced him to Leonardo DaVinci, Mona Lisa, left-handed hatch marks and *sfumato* over years of instruction and mentoring.

Left-handed hatch. For crying out loud.

"Try it," she coaxed him, but he resisted.

"Why? I can't draw left handed."

"Ever tried?"

"No. Why would I?"

"Because your non-dominant hand is more sensitive and precise than your dominant hand. Using both sides of your body and your brain makes you a more complete artist. In fact, because I know you like baseball like I do, you'll get this. Are you right-handed?"

"I am."

"Good, me too. But get this: in baseball, both dominant and non-dominant hands must work together to make you a complete hitter, even if you always batted, quote-unquote, 'right handed.' Your bottom, non-dominant, left hand is actually your power hand, your follow-through hand. Right?"

"Yeah, I guess it is," agreed Gary, already amazed that Ms. Green knew even that much about hitting.

Ms. Green went on, "And your top hand directs and snaps your swing at the precise moment the speeding baseball arrives. Batting coaches even have 'top-hand bats' to work that snap to perfection. Your dominant eye sees the strings on the speeding ball. But your non-dominant eye locates that speeding ball in space and time even as it curves, or slides, or hops or sinks. Together both eyes tell both legs, both hips, both shoulders, both arms, both wrists, both sets of fingers exactly when and where to swing the bat to hit the ball.

"Leonardo's hatch marks for shading were all left-handed, as well as his *sfumato* layers of glaze. They are identifying traits on his paintings. But does that mean he was left handed? Left-side dominant? Not necessarily. The sensitive precision of his left-handed hatch and his left-handed glaze layers suggests to me that he may have been right handed, but that he discovered by observation his left hand was more precise and more delicate. So he used it."

Gary listened intently, captivated by Ms. Green, drawn in by her like no teacher ever before to be an apprentice into the mystical cabala of art known only to the masters, Leonardo, Caravaggio, Michelangelo, Rembrandt, Raphael, Rubens and Ms. Green.

"Gary, Leonardo learned everything he knew from observation, from trial and error. It was not formal education that shaped his art, but, rather persistent investigation and hard work. It may take a while for you, but I think learning left-handed hatch will make you an extraordinary painter. What do you say?"

Gary loved Ms. Green. "If you think I should, then I will."

"It will be a little strange at first, like learning to write left-handed, but I think you can do it. Besides, hatch marks are easier than letters."

"Then I'll learn both. Hatch and writing," he announced.

At that, Ms. Green smiled, like she knew more than baseball.

As Gary recalled, just like that, his life changed direction. And, by the way, he did learn to write left handed. Spirit guides. Helpers. So many. Gary remembered in churches he attended pastors called them angels sent by God. Some angels are invisible spirits, they said, and some flesh and blood, real people taken captive by God for an instant, a moment, a season to do good work and change lives. Like the angel who appeared to Mary in the Bible at Christmas time. Spirit? Or the one who wrestled with Jacob all night until Jacob made the angel bless him. Flesh and blood? Maybe this Methodist district super is another one. A spirit guide. An angel sent by God.

"Well, let's find out," Gary said aloud as he picked up his phone and punched in the numbers.

"Hello, Greater Cleveland United Methodist Church, this is Clara, how may I help you?"

"Hello, my name is Gary Siciliano and I'd like to speak with the District Superintendent, but, I'm sorry, I don't know his name."

"Hi, Gary. His name is Rev. Dr. D. Jerry Scott. Can I give him a heads-up about why you're calling?"

"Oh, sure. I'm an artist working with the Cleveland Museum of Art to establish an art outreach on the Near West Side at Harbor and Divine. The folks at the art museum as well as my real estate agent, of all people, suggested I call Dr. Scott."

"That sounds fascinating. We have something like that on the east side right here in this church maybe you'd like to explore."

"Sounds great. Maybe I can pick your brain."

"Probably not my brain, but somebody here will have a brain you'll want to pick." They both laughed. "I'll connect you with Dr. Scott."

"Thank you, Clara."

In a short minute another warm, friendly voice answered.

"Hello, D.J. Scott here. How can I help?"

"Hello, Dr. Scott. My name is Gary Siciliano."

"Oh, yes! You're the Old Tony artist, aren't you?" Dr. Scott surprised Gary with his unexpected enthusiasm.

"I am, but I'm surprised you know."

"My friend, Melanie Zurkos, thought you might be calling, so I've been looking forward to it. In fact, a real estate agent called me to talk about our church and parsonage at Harbor and Divine just yesterday, and said you are her client and might be calling me."

"Annie Dunlop."

"Right. Well, let's talk. And the first thing I want to say is: Gary, you're an amazing artist! Old Tony is a fascinating piece of art. I've seen your eight unfinished canvases along side that high quality photo print of the original in the art museum. It's a marvel to be sure."

"Oh? I didn't know there was a photo print."

"Hmmm. I guess they had an old digital photo to print from years back, and they made a beautiful, full-size print on canvas. Actually I remember seeing it there several years ago when I first moved back to Cleveland. Sounds like you were not aware of that."

"You're right. It is a bit of a surprise. Several years ago you say?"

"Yes. I'm sure I remember seeing all nine together in one of the glassed-in observation studios."

"Huh. I've never seen it. Nor do I remember approving it. I guess I'll have to talk with Dr. Zurkos about that."

Dr. Scott sensed Gary's upset, so he asked, "Are you okay?"

"A little flummoxed I guess."

"Good word. But does that mean we need to postpone our conversation until you can arrange to meet with Melanie and her staff?"

"Yes. I think so...But, on the other hand, how about we still set a date and a time for us to meet maybe one day next week? I hope we'll have this all figured out by then."

They set the date. But as Gary ended the call, he was quite confused by what he had just learned about the high quality photo print of Old Tony. More than confused. Upset, doggone it. It was a monkey wrench of major proportions in an otherwise exciting plan. Had he agreed to that and had a memory lapse or something?

Gary needed to call. Right now. He felt betrayed by Melanie Zurkos, but couldn't quite believe that she would intentionally deceive him. No one in the art world would purposely undercut the artistic ownership of an artist, especially if that artist were an old friend. 'Something I'm not getting,' he thought. He took a few minutes and some slow breaths to calm himself and think clearly before he punched her number into his phone.

"Hello, this is Melanie Zurkos. How can I help you?"

Calm, calm, calm. Phew. "Hi, Melanie, Gary Siciliano here, how are you?"

"Great, Gary. I've been having inspiring day dreams about your proposal. With all the home and business renovations these days on the Near West Side bringing renewed vitality to those neighborhoods, it just seems like the perfect moment to open an art outreach there. You have such an energetic, creative mind, Gary. I'm glad you're back in Cleveland."

'Wow,' Gary thought. 'This does not sound like a Judas, but like a friend, a caring co-worker.' He felt his blood pressure drop precipitously.

Melanie continued. "Did you get a chance yet to call Rev. Scott about the buildings at Harbor and Divine?"

"Just got off the phone with him."

"And how did that go?"

"Really well ... until he told me something that confused me."

"Oh? What was that?"

"We were talking about the eight unfinished Old Tonys that he loves so much, and then he mentioned also seeing a photo print of my original completed Old Tony sold to the folks in Minnesota. And I don't recall seeing that photo print when I walked through the museum with my wife, a few years ago. So it was a bit of a surprise on two counts. One, that it was not on display while I was there. And two, that I don't remember recently agreeing to make such a print."

"Ohhhh. So you're upset that we would not consult you about making that print?"

"Yes, I guess so."

"Well, it was not a recent transaction. When we bought the eight unfinished canvases at auction thirteen years ago, we included two standard art museum riders in the sales contract. The first was permission to include limited modest quality photo prints for publicity purposes and museum shop sales. That was just for the pieces which we own. The second rider was different in that we have never owned the original Old Tony; however, we agreed at auction that, included in the price, we would be allowed a full-size photo print of Old Tony to display along side the unfinished pieces for instructional purposes."

"Oh? Ohhhh." The light was dawning.

"Does that ring a bell?"

"Ding-a-Ding-Dong! Yes, it does! I remember that. It was a package deal with the museum and the Minnesota buyer. In fact didn't I approve the photo at the time of the sales as well?"

"I believe you did. Actually, I think you took the photo. And signed both sales contracts and the riders. Is it all coming back?"

"Sure is. And now I'm a bit embarrassed that I called. I could have looked it up in my files, but all my art sales paper work is still packed and in storage. So when Dr. Scott mentioned that he saw the photo print, I creeped out, remembered nothing and had no way to look up what I had agreed to or not agreed to. I'm sorry. Thank you for your patience with me. I knew I had to call you right away to get it all squared away in my mind. Thank you very much."

"You're very welcome. I can't imagine all that's on your mind and in your heart these days with your wife and daughter passing, your dream house burned to the ground, and now moving back to Cleveland and starting a new chapter in your life. It must be tough."

"Very tough. But with gracious people like you I'm getting through it."

"And Dr. Scott. He called me right away to give me a heads up that you had some concerns over the photo print, so I had time to search through our files, which I finished 20 seconds before you called. Gary, I want you to know this, everybody here is on your side. Everybody."

"Thank, you Melanie. Thank you very much."

He ended the call and wept yet again. Doggone tears.

Setting up Gary's art museum studio adjacent to the restoration area began right away. The museum hired Gary for a modest salary as a part-time instructor and consultant. It was very fair for both Gary and the museum, so all the involved parties signed the contract. Right away Gary and Melanie worked with the maintenance staff to set up an observation studio for Gary and Old Tony. Melanie helped Gary fill out the necessary requisition paperwork for his own painting supplies, extras for prospective students plus easels, stools, racks, shelves, clean up area and extra lighting for six work spaces, a double space for Gary and five single work spaces for apprentices.

The museum put out advertising in **Cleveland Art,** the museum's semi-monthly member magazine that also went to art schools and museums around the country to find post bachelors degree candidates of artistic distinction for the six-week Old Tony Portrait Workshop under Gary Siciliano. Each participant would need to bring one large stretched canvas, sized and ready for work. Gary would teach two masters-level tracks, one leading to a classic *sfumato* finish and the other to an impressionist finish. The subject would be Joyful Old Tony, based on two of Gary's original sketches given freely to the student artists. Gary himself would be painting two canvases, one of each sketch and each one different in artistic style. He had been wanting to paint a Joyful Old Tony for decades, and now, in his own master studio, like Renaissance artists of 500 years ago, including Leonardo, he had the chance to paint his Joyful Old Tony in the joy of collaborative artistry like the old masters. Gary was over-the-moon excited and invested in the project he had worked out in collaboration with the art museum as his patron.

In fact, Gary was so invested in this artistic adventure that he granted anonymously modest rent-free apartments in the

University Circle area plus a livable stipend for six weeks to each one of his apprentices, all renewable for those who made beautiful progress and wanted to continue working with Gary. He had the money to be generous, because he had wisely invested his income from the sale of Old Tony. And now he had the opportunity and the heart to pay forward to others what had been given to him along the way. In that way Old Tony continued to bless him and people in Gary's orbit. It was so clear that Gary had now journeyed full circle from a needy apprentice whom designated angels had helped along the way, to now becoming one of God's helpers himself, lifting up others as he was lifted up right there in Cleveland. In fact, Gary felt more fulfilled now as a card-carrying angel helping others than he had felt finishing Old Tony or his Dancing Bear.

Chapter 16

Homeless

Still, unfortunately, Harbor and Divine did not yet feel like home, especially without Dianah and Lily, and, let it be said, without an actual house to call his home. Even though he had lived his childhood on the Near West Side of Cleveland, neither the high rise apartment building on West 25th Street where his childhood residence was on the ninth floor, nor the intersection of Harbor and Divine where James had introduced him to Old Tony of the God-carved face and the six-foot body odor, felt anything like a home. Not at all. Still, Gary knew, absolutely knew, he was supposed to be there to pay the kindness he had received forward to the next generation of kids from poor, struggling families.

That high rise and the corner of Harbor and Divine were homes to others now, not Gary. Gary's real home had been with Dianah. Now that was also gone to ashes, ashes of aspen trees, ashes of the log walls, ashes of their bed of joy, all mingled, co-mingled with the ashes of the flesh that gave birth and the flesh that was born. And even there, on the site of their dream home they built together with Fred, another family was now building their own dream house above Durango Mountain's East Canyon wall. When he had left those charred remains of his once-charmed life, driving away in that U-Haul truck, Gary knew Durango Mountain was no longer his home either. Nor was Taos where Old Tony was auctioned off for a fortune to provide Gary with all the money he'd ever need. Certainly not the bars on Lorain, where he used to beg quarters from drunks stumbling out of the bar while he waited for his father to do the same. Sure, that was his alcoholic father's second home, but not Gary's. Never. Good thing there was an elevator to their ninth floor government subsidized apartment, where all the families were poor, on welfare and living there on their way to the American Dream. But home? Not really. Not so much different from a homeless shelter, where they had stayed on two occasions when his dad was in rehab and they couldn't pay their rent. Sure, five rooms to themselves in the high rise was better than five beds in a room filled with twenty strangers, but only by degrees. Regardless, other poor families lived there now praying, as had Gary's parents had prayed for early release from their life sentence to poverty. 'Strange,' Gary thought, 'I have a ton of money, but I really don't belong here or anywhere or to anyone. That makes you homeless, Gar. Everything is temporary. Even marriage.' When he and Dianah repeated "Til death do us part" in their marriage vows, it felt so permanent. But now he knows, everything is temporary. Even marriage vows. Even fatherhood.

Since Gary was born on the Near West Side, he still feels he has a claim to being a native son returning to where he began, even if it no longer feels like home. His parents had moved away decades ago when his dad had gotten sober, but that's not his home. Still Harbor and Divine, the Dairy Delight, the church, even the bars seem, if not quite home, at least familiar.

So, maybe. Maybe, he thought, he could settle in. After all he has a brand new life purpose to give back, to pay forward all the favor he had been given when he was a poor kid with holes in his shoes and a few drunks' quarters in his pocket.

James did it. He and his young wife, Lew, just 'showed up' one July. They moved into one small room on the second floor of the parish house and lived, if you could call it that, on $1,800 for the whole year. She played the organ for that church next door. And James? His job was to befriend poor kids like Gary, and bless them any way he could. And as James blessed those kids, somehow Harbor and Divine quickly became home for him and Lew. Of course, they had one another. Two can easily make a home. But can one alone?

While he sorted out the fire-singed threads of his home-less life, Gary absentmindedly called Dr. Scott's office, never even noticing that his ring in had stopped. He couldn't stop thinking about James, and how, in some way, he had become the new James.

James had once told him, "Gary, sometimes it seems as though God puts my feet upon a path He has already charted for me. Not my choice, but His. And He places people along the way for me to love and to love me in return. He puts words in my mouth to encourage them. And all I do is trust God, go with the flow and embrace what is in front of me, most of it nothing I could have thought up on my own. And strangely enough, people help me along the way." James often talked to Gary as if Gary were his equal, and could understand what he was talking about, never mind that James was 22 and Gary was only 10. However, Gary didn't actually understand much of anything James was talking about, though somehow he knew he needed to remember the words so that now, thirty-four years later, he could pluck them from his all-to-confused brain, tap into his inner James, and understand.

"James," Gary said aloud to his new alter ego, "that's exactly what's happening to me. I have no plan, yet my table is set. I have no words, yet my tongue never seems to run dry from fountains of truth or wisdom or love for people I barely know. It's marvelous, and yet unsettling, like sitting at the easel and painting with my eyes even before my brush touches the canvas. I must commit to color and canvas even before I am fully conscious of what I will be painting. Just so, I must commit to speak before I know what I will say, and know, really trust, that the right words will come." Gary paused, took a breath and then declared with steely resolve, "I could do that."

And a voice startled him asking, "You could do what?"

Realizing he had called Dr. Scott, and the voice was Clara's, Gary laughed at himself and said, "Oh, I'm sorry. Clara? I forgot I called you, and I was busy talking to myself."

"Uh-oh."

"Ya, I know. It's crazy time for Gary Siciliano. Crazy. Crazy. Actually I was talking to James the community worker from thirty-four years ago."

"I know. I heard. I'm sorry, but I listened in for a while," Clara confessed.

"That's okay, as long as you didn't call the funny farm to come get me." Gary suddenly realized he needed to think through a thing or two before talking with Dr. Scott.

"Look, Clara, can I call you back in a few?"

"Gonna finish your conversation? It sounded pretty intense." She chuckled.

Gary laughed along with her. "Yes, as a matter of fact it was, and I am. I need to work through what in the world I'm doing here."

"None of my business, but Dr. Scott might be just the person to help you finish that conversation. And you won't feel crazy if there are three of you in the room. Right? You, DJ and that James?"

"You're right. And talking to Rev. Scott is really what I started out to do, until the crazies showed up. I'll call you back in a few."

"Okay. I'll tell DJ you called. Bye."

Gary ended the call and then loudly declared to himself, "She's right!" He looked around to see if anybody heard him shouting at himself. He saw no one, so he finished with a flourish, "It is time to talk with Dr. Scott. He knows what I'm getting into and where I've come from." He settled down, then quietly appreciated what he was walking into: two places to work, two places to serve, to teach, to love: one the Cleveland Museum of Art, the other Harbor and Divine. Already he was dividing his time, his focus between the two. And now it was time to focus on Harbor and Divine. It was all so confusing. He decided to call Dr. Scott back before he really did make himself crazy.

"Hello, Greater Cleveland United Methodist Church, this is Clara, how may I help you?" If Gary ever had an office manager, he hoped it would be Clara, or a clone.

"Hi, Clara. It's Gary again."

"Hi, Gary again. I'm just fine, worried about you, but I did have a thought."

"What?"

"God's in charge. That's all. When I get worried and discombobulated, I just remember, 'God's in charge.'"

"But that's it, Clara!" Gary said marveling as though he had just received the answer of life from the guru on the mountain top.

"What's it?" Clara asked.

"I'm not in charge. Neither are you. And, you know what?" Gary asked with a new brightness in his voice.

"What?"

"If ever I get to have an office manager, I hope it will either be you or your clone.'"

Clara laughed. "Thank you, Gary, that's very nice of you."

"Well, I mean it. Someone to speak truth to me like you just did."

"Thank you again. But I bet you didn't call back to sweet talk me. Would you like to speak with DJ?"

"Is that what you all call him?"

"Sometimes, when I like him. Other times Dr. Scott. But whatever you call him, I'm sure he would like to talk with you."

"Thank you, Clara."

"Just a sec." Click, click.

"Hello, Gary. So are you ready to meet together and get down to business?"

"I sure am, Dr. Scott."

"Excellent. But how about Jerry or DJ instead of Dr. Scott. Let's save that for when we need to impress somebody."

"Okey dokey. Got it. Look, I know this is a whole week before the day we set to meet, but have you got time today?"

"I do. Let's see, it's nine now, how about eleven. Can you do that?"

"I can."

"Do you know where we are on University Circle?"

"I do, and I can be there at eleven."

"Great! See you then, Gary."

As Gary hung up, he started back up the self talk, "Wow. One more step. Then another. Then another. All unplanned, all unanticipated. Creepy. But good creepy. Well, let's go see DJ Jerry. Hah, sounds like a rap artist. Cool. I wonder if DJ Jerry is as much fun as his name. I have a sneaking suspicion he is."

At 10:55 Gary walked into that huge stone church with a 75 foot steeple topped with copper and a forty-foot metal spire making it look exactly like a gigantic oil can on the western edge of University Circle. At the entrance to the circle stands the classic limestone and marble, temple-like Cleveland Museum of Art sitting above a three acre reflecting pond. Two large limestone beautifully landscaped terraces lead the way past Rodin's The Thinker, minus his feet blown off by vandals in the 1970's, to a grand entrance framed by thirty-foot Corinthian columns. The rear of the art museum faces a huge, five hundred foot diameter grassy circle with walkways, park benches and beautiful trees. Surrounding the circle stand the Cleveland Natural History Museum with dinosaurs standing watch, the Institute of Music, the Botanical Gardens including a fabulous three-story atrium filled with tropical plants and free-flying butterflies, Case-Western Reserve University's main campus and fabulous Severance Hall, home of the world famous Cleveland Orchestra.

The Holy Oil Can stands as a sentinel over that cultural hub of a city trying to hold its own over decades of decline, like a dowager who still dresses up and wears her pearls.

Gary walked in through the grand church entrance and there skipping down the steps to meet him was Rev. Dr. DJ Jerry all excited.

"Hey, Gary. Let's hop in my car and drive over to the West Side. We can talk on the way. I want to explore the buildings at Harbor and Divine with you when we get there. Is that all right with you?" he asked like a person in charge, not really expecting an argument.

"That's a great idea, DJ," and talk they did.

They talked as they walked around the building to DJ's parking space. They talked as they hopped into his Camry. They talked as DJ merged into inner city traffic, and they kept talking for the next 25 minutes straight, prompted by DJ's questions like, "Tell me, Gary, why the inner city? Why would a world famous artist move into the Near West Side where, at best, the neighborhoods could be called 'up-and-coming?'"

Then for the whole rest of the trip Gary talked and DJ listened, something only the best in-charge people ever know *how* to do let alone *when* to do it. Actually, everything DJ did impressed Gary, and he felt comfortable telling DJ his life story right up til that minute, the abridged version, of course, but especially including all the people who helped him along the way as well as his tragic loss of Dianah and Lily.

"I want to give back, DJ, especially now with Dianah gone. Now's the time to take what others have given me and pay it forward to some other poor 10-year old kid like I was, who otherwise might not have a chance to grow his God-given abilities. Make sense?"

DJ whistled in admiration and exclaimed, "Does it ever! Gary, I have spent my entire life as a pastor encouraging people to live exactly that way. And —— oh, wow, here we are already."

DJ parked the car at the curb on Harbor Street right in front of the house that Annie Dunlop had shown Gary the week before. Gary just smiled at the coincidence, but he decided to keep mum for now. As they unfolded themselves out of the car DJ added, "Gary you're just the kind of man I admire, and I've concluded that I want to help you spend all your money in all the best places." They both laughed.

"Okay then," Gary smirked, already liking DJ. "I can see there's no pulling punches here."

"No sir." Smiles all around. "Oh, and one more thing. I have some one here in the church I want you to meet. It's not James, but doggone close. His name's Joe, and he's quite a bit older than James was back then. I think he's 51 or 52. Ready?"

"Ready."

They stepped onto Harbor Street each delighted with the other and both excited to see where this nascent partnership was headed. Actually, Gary thought he and DJ and were also close in age, both in their forties, but he soon discovered DJ was also in his early fifties. 'Every step gets curiouser and curiouser,' he thought remembering Alice's words in her Adventures in Wonderland, his favorite book of all time, with it's profound teachings hidden within a delightful children's story. Step by step. Curiouser and curiouser.

Gary and DJ started walking across Harbor Street toward the church and a man bent over working on a bike near the back door. They got about half way across the street when Gary suddenly stopped.

DJ asked, "Gary, what's up, Gar?" But Gary didn't say a word. That's when DJ noticed Gary's eyes were glazed wide open, with the pupils darting back and forth, up and down. DJ gently tried to move Gary forward, but Gary stood fast, said nothing and kept staring, pupils darting. DJ noticed Gary's breathing was shallow and quick, his face looked panicked. Cars stopped. Drivers watched. Five cars back horns started blaring. Still Gary didn't move.

One driver yelled out his car window to the man working near the back door of the church, evidently a friend. "Hey, Joe, do you know these goof balls standing in the middle of the street? If you do, tell them to get a move on, will ya?"

Joe looked up and saw his friend, DJ, with some guy he had never seen before. He got up from his work and walked slowly toward them.

DJ put his finger to his lips to signal 'quiet' to Joe.

"Hey, DJ, you all right?" Joe asked nearly whispering.

"Yeah, but he's not, Joe," DJ said quietly

"I can see. Can I help? Call the squad or something?"

"Not yet. I think I can help him. PTSD."

"Oh, yeah. We've both seen that look before, haven't we?"

"Yep. I think he'll be okay in a minute or two, and, I bet, with a story to tell. If he's not we can call the squad then."

Chapter 17

Gary, DJ and That James

G ary did have a story to tell — a terrible, PTSD story that began with **Alice's Adventures in Wonderland**, and ended with his wife and daughter dying in a mountain fire and Gary unable to help them one bit. The standing in the street time was actually only three or four minutes, but in Gary's tortured memory it was a terribly long time.

Starting with Alice following the well-dressed White Rabbit into his hole, she suddenly found herself falling down a dark, dark shaft she thought would never end. Down, down she fell, telling herself, "I must be getting somewhere near the center of the earth." Eventually she hit rock bottom. Actually Lewis Carroll never used the words "rock bottom." But that's what it must have been, Gary thought, debating the efficacy of how Alice landed after dropping down her dark, dark hole nearly to the center of the earth without hitting rock bottom. 'Not likely,' Gary argued, spellbound in the middle of Harbor Street, 'in real life to land unhurt. Just falling hurts, let alone all the way to the center of the earth. If the story is an allegory meant for me to apply to my own life, how will I know when I have landed? How will I know when I have stopped falling if there's no rock bottom crash?'

Surely falling down an endless hole is exactly what Gary had felt like since Dianah and Lily died. Falling. Falling. Falling. Down a dark hole. Hurting all the way. So, in real time, standing there in traffic on Harbor Street, Gary replayed the whole story of that night eight weeks ago, as if in a movie, when he had panicked not being able to get Dianah on her cell phone. His flight from Columbus, where he had once again won Best of Show, landed at the DRO out in the country meadows of the high desert west of Durango. He literally ran out of the plane, through the small terminal to his SUV, threw his luggage in the back, slammed the lid, paid the parking fees and sped through the country roads, not to the hotel where they should be, but toward their home with a sick feeling in the pit of his stomach that something terrible was happening, and that's why he felt he was already falling, falling, falling. Maybe it was just the smell of the mountain fire smoke filling the air that so rattled him. He shouldn't have been worried, because Dianah and Lily had been evacuated two days earlier. Dianah had called to tell him that they were both safe in Durango at the General Palmer Hotel, their favorite hotel in town. She told him that after all the work it took to move their favorite possessions and art from the house to Gary's Durango studio they were both exhausted and needed some of the hotel's delicious chocolate chip cookies and hot cocoa. That was just last night. So why did he now feel like he was falling? Surely they were still safe and sound. Still, he did not go to the hotel, but headed straight for home. The closer he got to their home, the thicker the smoke became, almost impossible to breathe, and yet he was still miles from their house, from their log cabin dream home.

When it seemed as though he had been driving forever through the smoke, with his spirit falling ever faster into darkness, he got within a mile of home and came to a road block where rangers stopped him.

"Hi," one of them said as Gary rolled down his car window trembling. "There's a mountain forest fire down there. Where are you headed?" he asked through his smoke mask.

"Home," Gary replied choking more on terrified emotion than the terrible smoke.

"Where's home, sir?" the ranger asked quietly.

"185 East Canyon Drive."

Filled with dread, the ranger took a deep breath, steadied himself, then said with sad resolve, "Sir, I hate to tell you this, but twenty minutes ago a wicked updraft drove the flames up the east canyon wall and engulfed that house."

"Were there any people there in the house?"

"There shouldn't have been, since everybody was evacuated day before yesterday."

"Shouldn't have been? What do you mean?"

"Well about 40 minutes ago a woman and her daughter begged the rangers to let them get into the house to retrieve something, I don't know what, something they accidentally left behind day before yesterday. She told them it would take less than five minutes. And since the flames were still a mile away, the rangers fitted them with smoke masks and I let them drive through. Five minutes later, however, a forty, fifty mile per hour up-draft drove those flames the entire mile over the tree tops and engulfed the area around that house in mere minutes. I'm sorry, sir. They did not drive out past me, and right now this is the only way out."

Gary exploded in a blood-curdling cry. "No, no. Dianah, Lily. No, no." And he collapsed on his steering wheel in mammoth sobs.

The ranger gave him a minute, maybe two before he interrupted Gary's weeping. "Sir, sir? I'm terribly sorry. You can't go down there, and the fire is coming this way. We have to get you out of here. Now." Another ranger brought a mask for Gary. "Sir, please put on this mask. Philip here will drive you and your car to a safe ranger outpost several miles back where you can collect yourself and give our rangers your contact information. Where were your wife and daughter staying?

"The General Palmer," Gary sobbed.

"I'll call right now and make sure they will let you into the room. Sir, I am so very sorry. I know it doesn't look good, but, still, there's always hope." The ranger didn't really believe what he was saying about always being hope. Gary could tell, and he didn't believe it either.

Huge stifled sobs broke through Gary's resistance. And down, down, down he went slumping over into unconsciousness. The two rangers jumped into action. "He's down, Phil, help me move him over. Get him to the ER as fast as you can." Phil drove like a maniac. But first he stopped at the ranger outpost minutes away to get Gary some oxygen which did revive him so they took it with them to the ER.

Once at the hospital the ER staff, well-skilled in treating patients suffering from the traumas of mountain fires, took over. Soon they had him stable and talking with the ER staff. ER Dr. Turner later told Gary that Ranger Philip had saved his life by getting him oxygen on the way.

Gary looked around at Phil and Dr. Turner and all the ER staff, and he could only marvel at and be thankful for all the people there who were helping him. The angels. The spirit guides.

So was *this* rock bottom? Gary could not know yet, but his time of falling down the dark rabbit hole had only just begun. And like Alice in Wonderland, Gary would soon wonder if the falling would ever end.

Gary and DJ had still not crossed Harbor Street and Gary still stood stricken, in a trance. DJ, an army combat vet, recognized that look as a PTSD, Post Traumatic Stress Disorder, episode he had seen in dozens of soldiers back from combat still on assignment, or back home after all the combat was long past. He knew better than to agitate Gary, or shout, or even push him. along.

So he called quietly, "Gary, Gary. Are you all right?"

Even as quietly as DJ had spoken, Gary snapped right out of it, but totally unaware that he was standing in the middle of the street blocking traffic.

So DJ quietly told him, "Gary, we're in the middle of the street, We have to walk across now."

Horns blared. Somebody shouted, "Be quiet, you idiots!" The horns stopped.

Gary gradually became aware of his surroundings and said, "Oh. I'm sorry DJ." He let DJ lead him across the street. Gary talked on. "All of a sudden I get these flashbacks, some of them terrible, of the Durango Mountain fire that killed Dianah and Lily and I can't stop them. They consume me."

"I can see that. You look like you could use a break. How 'bout we go back across the street and get an ice cream cone at the Dari Delight. My treat. We can sit down there for a spell.

"That sounds perfect. Thanks for noticing."

"Something I'm good at noticing. I'll tell you why some-time. I do know that 'consume,' is a good word for it. But for now let's consume some ice cream." DJ turned toward Joe and called out, "Hey, Joe! Thanks for being there. We'll get back with you in a few."

"Yes, sir. Sounds good. In a few." They both waved.

DJ turned back to Gary. "Ready?"

"Yeah, let's go. Is that the Joe we came to see?"

"The very one and only."

"Good. But for now, just thinking about ice cream makes me feel better."

"I'm glad." DJ smiled. "What's your choice?"

"Oh, if I remember right from when Dianah, Lily and I stopped here last year..." He choked a sob back, took a breath and resumed his ice cream recommendation, "they have great raspberry chocolate. One scoop in a sugar cone would be per-fect for me."

"On your recommendation I'll have the same."

The young woman inside the window was listening, so she said, "And that is a very good recommendation, if I must say so. Two single scoops of raspberry chocolate in sugar cones. Right?"

"Right," the men said together.

"Coming right up," and she turned to make their order.

They got their cones and headed to a bright blue, round, expanded metal picnic table. By the time they sat down DJ was totally enjoying raspberry chocolate ice cream. "Gary, this stuff is delicious. As the ladies like to say, 'I love, love, love it!' Thanks for putting me onto it, man."

"My pleasure, DJ. Glad you like it."

For a bit they traded talking for slurping ice cream. When Gary had pressed all the remaining ice cream into his cone, he looked intently into DJ's face for a couple of beats until DJ looked back, and then he asked, "So, when we first got here, you quickly recognized the look on my face, and you quietly talked me out of my attack, and then you told me that it's something you're good at recognizing and that you'd tell me about it sometime. So tell me. I think I have a lot to learn from you."

"Okay, but are you in for a long story?"

"As my grandpa used to say, 'In for a nickel, in for a dime.'"

"That's when you could actually buy something for nickel."

"Yeah, certainly not these days. Grandpa lived in the Riverview Apartments when he was a little kid, off Professor and West 7th right on the west bank of the flats above the steel mills and oil refineries."

"Woah, I'll bet that smelled pretty rich."

"No doubt. Gramps used to tell us that usually the winds blew from the west and carried the smells over to the East Side where all the black folks lived. He was a bit of a racist, so his language was much saltier than that. And it wasn't just smells. When his mother hung out the wash on clothes lines, sometimes the wind changed direction, and Grandpa remembered her screaming like a banshee for help getting the clothes off the line, because it wasn't just the smell that blew west. It was also thick, black, oily smoke from the steel mills and oil refineries filled with carbon suet plus purple, green, orange and blue rain along with it. If grandma didn't get the wash down in time she'd have to wash the clothes all over again, maybe twice to get out all the filth from the polluted air. In fact, the air was so foul back then that the workers in the mills and refineries either took the bus to work or bought beater cars to drive, because the acid rain was so strong that it ate off all the paint from the cars right down to bare metal."

"Wow," said DJ, "what a nasty place to live."

"True, but there were lots of jobs, so people came from all over the country — all over the world — to work in Cleveland. But, hey, I took us down a rabbit hole, so to speak, it's your turn now. Tell me how you knew the look on my face."

"First tell me, did your, let's see, your great grandfather migrate here for work?"

"Yes, from Slovakia when Emperor Franz Joseph swept down from the north and conquered all of southeastern Europe, conscripting every able-bodied man to fight for him. Great grandpa was a sharecropper, and had no belongings to speak of, so he packed up his family and, in 1902, they left for America, landing in Cleveland. Your turn."

"Okay. After college and seminary and a couple of years pastoring small country churches, I joined the army reserves as a chaplain with immediate rank of first lieutenant. After my second summer of basic training I also trained to be a medic, so I did not have to fire weapons. I did carry a side arm, but that was it. Almost everyone else learned to be mechanics as well as soldiers. We were part of a mechanized division to drive and service whatever vehicles we were assigned, most of the time supply trucks and personnel carriers in and out of combat zones. I was six or seven years older than most of the guys who were either just out of high school or working dead end jobs or both and needed the extra money. Nobody ever thought we'd actually be deployed into a war zone. But that was wishful thinking, because, amazingly, within eighteen months we got deployed to the Middle East. No one in our group had ever even seen real war. Just being bombarded in our barracks shocked everyone into fear, anger, aggression and reality. It was quite clear that we were sent there as soldiers to fight a war. In fact, that day, the very day we arrived, that very first afternoon, our CO ordered us out on our first mission. No time to get nervous or scared. We drove out eight vehicles, six returned, because two trucks exploded running over i.e.d.'s, seriously wounding four young soldiers. Boys they were. The nearly simultaneous explosions sent soldiers and truck metal flying twenty feet in the air and a hundred feet away. It was terrifying. Everybody helped me tend to the wounded and load them up into the ambulance that our chief radioed in. All four wounded GI's lived, but none would ever be the same, scarred for life. Eventually, after medical care in Germany and then back in the States, all four were medically discharged, crippled, disfigured and constantly afraid.

The truth is, all of us came back from that first deployment shell shocked, with those glazed eyes that had witnessed the horrors of war. PTSD we call it these days. And, every day after that, while we were still deployed, some of our men would shriek at the sounds of gun fire or explosions; some would dive under their beds for cover and shake. My job as chaplain and medic was to talk them down, hold them like a mother until they stopped shaking or crying and love them like a father telling no one of their tears, until the next time we went out.

"The looks on their faces will haunt me the rest of my life. After six months in country and dozens of assignments, all of us returned home suffering from PTSD, myself included. My wife endured way too many of my 3:00 am outbursts, and far too many daytime anger explosions directed at her, for no fault of hers. I got treatment at VA hospitals for years, including weeks of inpatient therapy. When I came home, I brought the war with me. Couldn't help it. But it was all too much for her. She left and divorced me after I returned from my second deployment tight as a drum and more explosive than an i.e.d. Flashbacks were daytime terrors for both of us. I didn't blame her then for leaving me. And after twenty years, I don't blame her now. I loved her, but I brought the hell of war into her home."

DJ took a deep breath to chase away the demons before he said, "So Gary, I know the look. Believe me, I know the look. And I empathize with anyone who has flashbacks of terror. My doctorate is actually not in theology, it is in PTSD counseling from the Gestalt Institute in Cleveland and Cleveland State University. The Gestalt Institute required me as a trainee to undergo three plus years of personal therapy, plus group therapy, plus supervised counseling, plus teaching others under supervision. It has been a long dark journey, even the training, but these days, thank God, I see more light in a day than darkness. Much more."

Gary sat stunned. "DJ, I'm sorry. So sorry. I can see and hear your pain even now. Thank you for telling me. It was brave of you to open up all those wounds just to help me. But my experience is nothing compared to yours."

"Gary, not so. PTSD is PTSD no matter what the source event. The fact that your wife and daughter might have been dying in the fire and smoke that you could see at the very moments you were driving to meet them, and you could do absolutely nothing to help, is a terrible thing to live with. And then not to even get to say good-bye to them before they died is a soul-crushing, catastrophic loss. To live with that, I can see, tears at your heart, and saps your courage in the very same way as my horrific war time experiences tear at mine. There are no gradual degrees of PTSD. The pain is the same. Terrible. The darkness is the same."

Gary cringed in a desperate effort to strengthen himself against the encroaching darkness. DJ intimately knew his pain and his dark hole as Gary now knew DJ's. In a few short moments Gary and DJ had become brothers in loss, grief, suffering, pain and faith. DJ had wept those same tears a hundred times, so he knew the very best things he could do for Gary were to listen and to pray.

"Gary, can I pray for you?"

"Yes, I would love that, DJ."

Like Annie the Realtor had done for him over the phone, DJ lifted Gary's spirit up to God for healing, resolution and forgiveness. Gary had always believed in God, but at that moment, Gary came to believe that God knows, loves and believes in him. And furthermore, Gary discovered that he could trust God, even while falling down his dark rabbit hole of grief, to send him angels like Annie and DJ to care, to listen and, to pray for him, even at a Dairy Delight.

Chapter 18

Athos, Porthos and Aramis

O nce more DJ and Gary started across Harbor Street toward the church. And oddly enough once more DJ stopped in the middle of the street, stared at Gary and asked, "Gary, are you okay?"

"What?" Gary asked pleasantly defensive. "What?"

DJ was smiling this time. "Well, Gary, you've got another funny look on your face, but I'm pretty sure it's not PTSD this time. Although, still, I think I've seen that look on some other people before. What's up now?"

"Not telling," Gary said with a smug smile as they stood in the middle of Harbor Street

DJ chuckled. "What do you mean, you're not telling?"

"You've got to figure this one out too. I think you will. I'll give you three guesses," he added smirking as if they were 9-year-old kids.

"Game time. All right, first guess. Well, let's see, The ice cream was good, but I don't think it was *that* good."

"You're warm. Next guess."

"My next guess," he stopped, shook his head and snorted a laugh then said, "My next guess is that you and God just had moment."

Gary grinned broadly and nodded his head.

"Is that right?"

"Yes, sir, Rev. Dr. D. Jerry Scott. We have indeed had a moment."

A couple of cars honked their horns, and one driver shouted out his window, "Hey you guys, move it. You're blocking traffic — again." And then the same guy saw Joe and shouted at him as if he knew him really well, "Joe, talk to these guys!"

"Sorry, Joachim. Will do." And he did, "Hey you guys."

"Sorry, sorry," they both apologized and moved a few feet to the sidewalk and then saw Joe sitting on the church's side door steps working on a bicycle.

"Hey, DJ, you're lucky those guys didn't just run you down, what, with you standing in the middle of Harbor Street like that again! Come on over here. Look, this is a sidewalk, safety zone for people. Cars in the street; people on the sidewalk. It works out real well that way."

DJ and Gary laughed as DJ said, "Wiseacre Joseph, Joe Whitehorse, this is my new friend Gary Siciliano."

Joe reach out his hand, "Hey, Gary, nice to meet you. But what are you doing hanging around this character?"

"I'm learning stuff, Joe," Gary answered as they shook hands. "Lots of stuff."

"Hah!" DJ chortled. "Whitehorse, what have I been telling you all along. Listen and learn. I am the master."

"Yes, Master Obi Wan."

"Now look, no more horsing around, this is serious stuff. This man right here was all set to buy this here church and that house."

"For real?" Joe asked Gary breaking into a huge grin.

"Yep, for real," Gary confessed.

"Until, that is," DJ broke in, "until he found out who has the real power here."

"Oh, my, here we go. Is that also true, Gary?

"Yes, I'm afraid so," said Gary getting into the swing of the banter. "All true."

"Well, son, you and I need to talk. How 'bout we go inside, sit down and talk about this over a cup of coffee?" When the other two nodded yes, Joe gave the come hither sign and said, "Follow me to the kitchen and the magnificent new coffee maker."

Having no more smack to talk, they followed Joe to the kitchen and straight to a brand new single cup coffee maker. "Have at it, guys. The pods are on the shelf below, three or four kinds of coffee and some tea. It's the only item less than fifty years years old in the whole building, except maybe you, Gary. Plus, unfortunately, three weeks from this very day, I will hit the next old age barrier, break down, join AARP and make peace with all the other antiques in this building." He sighed. "I rue the day."

They all laughed, served themselves, sat down together at one of the eight-foot church fellowship hall tables and then talked for two hours straight, broken by periods of boisterous laughter as if they were long lost friends from the old days. And that's just how it felt to Gary. These guys made it feel, for the very first time, like a homecoming. Not the buildings, not the streets, not even the West Side Market made Harbor and Divine feel like home. But these guys? With DJ and Joe, for the first time Gary felt like he was home. Funny how strangers can become friends in a short minute. No longer strangers, but friends, brothers even. Athos, Porthos and Aramis. All for one and one for all!

When they talked about Gary's experience and DJ praying for him, Joe surprised the heck out of Gary by saying, "Woah! Gary, that very same thing happened when he prayed for me six years ago. He was the pastor at my parents' church. I worshipped there after my wife died of cancer that she had battled since she was a junior in high school. I used to visit her in Columbus when I was a kid in her husband's church. She fended off that cancer, got a teaching job up in Cleveland and convinced her husband to move and serve a church up here."

Gary's ears perked up, he cocked his head like the RCA dog, and listened in utter amazement as his heart began racing. The more Gary listened, the faster his heart raced. As Joe continued Gary could barely take in the wonder of his story. He felt like he was going to burst with curiosity.

Joe continued, "Everything was good for a few more years, but then the cancer came back. They moved back down to Columbus for more treatments. He got his old job back. I started visiting her again, but I wasn't a kid any more, and I was liking our visits more and more each time. Then she beat the cancer again. We all cheered, you know. But when she told her husband that she wanted to move back to Cleveland and get her old job back, which they had left open for her, he balked. She was absolutely sure he would go. For her, you know? But he wouldn't do it. So she moved without him. She was angry; he was heartbroken. Later that year they divorced.

"Wait, wait, wait. I'm sorry to interrupt, but what did she teach?"

"Art. She was the art teacher at Lincoln-West High School."

Gary almost fainted. He gathered himself to ask what was for him the obvious next question. "Was her name Ms. Green?"

"Yes, at that time, Val Green."

"What do you mean, at that time?"

"Even though she was six years older than I was, I fell in love with her and she with me. So I moved up to Cleveland and we got married. She took my name for a summer, but then when she went back to work at Lincoln-West she went back to being Ms. Green, something about health insurance and retirement and the kids knowing her by that name. Besides, she told me that she just felt more comfortable as Ms. Green at school. She had so many struggles, I didn't think she needed another one, so I agreed. Gary, why do you ask? You knew her?"

"Oh my, yes. She was my mentor for years."

"Wait a minute. DJ said you're an artist? Right?"

"Right."

"Are you that Old Tony artist?"

Gary laughed again at being known by Old Tony. "I am."

"Oh, my God. You know she came back to Cleveland because of you, right? And I got to marry her because she came back for you. She told me, 'Only once in a hundred years does God put such an artist on the earth, and I have the privilege to teach him, to mentor him. I can't give that up.' She came back for you, Gary."

A flood of tears streamed down Gary's face. "I never knew that."

"Of course not. She would never have put that burden on you... Of course, I, on the other hand, just did. Sorry."

"Don't be. It's an incredible gift I never knew she gave me. I knew she thought that I could learn to paint like Leonardo. She told me that many times, but I just dismissed it as a mentor's hyperbole. I guess she really meant it more than I ever knew. And she changed her life, gave up her marriage, so she could help me fulfill a dream that we both shared. Wow. I'm honored beyond belief by her sacrifice. Joe, thank you for telling me. Thank you. Thank you."

"You're welcome, Gary. But let me tell you the rest. DJ was our pastor when Val died. He conducted her memorial service six years ago. After the funeral I was a mess, so I went to him for counseling. He counseled me once or even twice a week, for months, and after every session he would pray for me, all good, helpful prayers. But after this one particular session, as he prayed he... he ..." Joe interrupted himself. "Gary have you ever seen Leonardo's painting of John the Baptist?"

"Oh my, yes. Many times. Ms. Green made me study it lots."

"Figures. So you remember what John was doing in that painting besides smiling, laughing?"

"Yes. He was pointing. Upward, toward heaven."

"Yep."

"With heaven's joy on his face," Gary added. "It was that joy I remember most, because I have longed to paint another portrait of Old Tony, this time with his face lit up with the joy of John."

"Gary, Val and I bought a very expensive copy of that painting that we believed to have been painted by one of Leonardo's apprentices in his studio 500 years ago. Other than our house, I've never bought anything that cost even close to that much money. But Val loved it. So we bought it. She loved the joy on John's face so much that we hung the painting in our living room so that every day we would pass it a dozen times. And whenever we would look at it she wanted us—she told me this a hundred times, a thousand times—she wanted us to take up the joy on John's face so that 'John's joy in the Lord would become our joy in the Lord.' Time and again when she felt overwhelmed by her cancer, she would walk past that painting, she would turn to face John, then she would smile like John and point her finger to heaven. Then she would say to me, 'Like John, I know in whom I believe, I know in whom I trust, and I know where I am going when my time comes.' John knew — like Jesus knew, like Val knew, like Leonardo knew — John knew that he would die soon. And yet he kept the joy of the Lord upon his face, and he kept pointing his way to heaven.

"At that counseling session, before he prayed, I told this same story to DJ. Remember?" he asked looking straight at DJ.

DJ nodded, "Oh, yes. I will never forget that day, my friend."

"And when he prayed for me, he finished his prayer paraphrasing Val, saying, 'Like John and like Val, we know in whom we believe, we know in whom we trust, and we know where we are going when our time comes. In the Name of Jesus, our Lord. Amen.' And, I kid you not, when I looked up I saw DJ with his hand raised, pointing heavenward and with the joy of John shining upon his upturned face. Changed my life, that prayer did. Gave me back the hope I thought I had lost when Val died."

DJ tearfully nodded his head, pointed heavenward and prayed in the joy of John. Joe and Gary joined in.

Chapter 19

The Mission at Harbor
and Divine

P erhaps never in the annals of friendship, if there ever
were such a thing, had three men bonded as quickly as
co-workers and friends, with DJ as the prime mover and shaker.
Within a week DJ established a working West Side District
office at Harbor and Divine including workspaces for both
Joe and Gary, plus room for someone yet to be found from the
Cleveland Museum of Art. He also arranged a rental agreement
with the United Methodist Church to rename the building The
Mission at Harbor and Divine. DJ convinced the Methodist
Bishop, his boss in charge of 850 churches and over one thousand pastors in East Ohio, to appoint Joe Whitehorse to be the
pastor in charge of the mission. In addition he enticed Clara,
DJ's office manager in the Holy Oil Can, to agree to organize
and manage the mission office including, she said, keeping "the
boys" on task, meaning, of course, DJ, Joe and Gary. All three
were at the mission at that moment, and playing quite well
together. Clara admired all three of them, but still, she jokingly

146

told everyone who would listen that keeping the boys on task would certainly be her toughest job.

Last on DJ's to-do list was hiring Gary. He knew that Gary was happy to work as a volunteer for the mission, but DJ still wanted to hire him for a modest monthly salary to be a two-day-per-week outreach worker just like James had been thirty-four years earlier. As DJ thought might happen, Gary demurred.

"DJ, before you hire me, how 'bout we wait to see how things pan out at the art museum. After all, The Mission at Harbor and Divine is in part an 'art outreach,' and maybe Dr. Zurkos and I will find someone we'd like to have in the mix at the mission, with a heart for kids and who might need the money a lot more than I do. Truth is, I'm pretty set financially. Who knows? Maybe one of my apprentices may love the idea of mission work with kids *and* actually need the money more than I do. What do you think?"

"You're not opting out altogether, are you?"

"No, no. Just leaving room for unexpected blessings, you know, creative, open-ended planning. It's more of an artsy approach: don't decide 110% on what you're going to paint until you've got the paint on your pallet and the brush in your hand as well as a tentative plan in your head and a sketch on the canvas."

DJ nodded sagely before he spoke. "I don't know, Gary. I'm usually a little more anal about tidying things up, but, then again, I trust you and Melanie enough to keep things open-ended for a little while — not too long though. I don't want to leave Joe hanging out there twisting in the wind. How long do you think?"

"A couple of weeks to a month, maybe sooner."

"I can live with that. You gonna tell Joe?"

"Absolutely. Hey, and as long as you're here, do you want to sit in with us? We still have to decide together when I start and exactly what we're going to do in this mission. Baby steps for both of us, I think."

"Thanks for asking, but I need to hustle back to the Circle and then out to a couple other churches before supper. I've got 48 other churches on my plate. Not complainin', just sayin'. I'm sure you two men will do just fine without me. Better than fine. Just let me know what you come up with."

"You've got it, boss!" They both smiled, DJ left for the East Side and Gary went to find Joe.

Gary was loving this teamwork. As an artist, he'd pretty much always worked alone, in his studio, well, except time with Dianah — lots of time. Now, all of a sudden, he had two teams of people — all of whom he likes — to share ideas, give and take points of view, grow friendships. Plus, just like James had blessed Gary's life, Gary now will be able to pay those blessings forward to other kids in need. Technically Joe would be Gary's supervisor, but realistically the two of them were already working together as a fabulous team, and Gary looked forward to their first test at joint decision making coming right up. When he found Joe, Gary jumped right in.

"So, Joe, I still have lots of work left to do to establish the Old Tony Studio at the art museum and start planning the museum's role in our art outreach mission here at Harbor and Divine. Do you think we can put off my starting date here at the mission?"

Joe thought for just a sec, then said, "How much time do you think you'll need?"

"Hard to tell, but at least two weeks. Of course some of those two weeks I'll spend searching for someone in the Old

Tony Studio who might like to help us in the mission. I'm ready right now to call Dr. Zurkos and get started on that end of our planning. So, yeah, I'm thinking at least two weeks, maybe three. You okay with that?"

"Absolutely. Maybe not more than three though," Joe cautioned.

"Agreed. So how about I call Dr. Zurkos right now and get that ball rolling?"

"Go to it, my friend. This is getting fun!"

They smiled, gave each other a high handshake and went their ways, saying to one another, "See you soon!"

Gary found a quiet corner in the newly renamed mission building near where DJ said the offices would be, and called the Cleveland Museum of Art Education Director Dr. Melanie Zurkos.

Melanie answered, "Hello, art education. This is Melanie Zurkos."

"Hi, Melanie, this is Gary Siciliano."

"Hey, Gary, good to hear your voice. How are things going on the West Side?"

"Fabulous! We have christened our new venture 'The Mission at Harbor and Divine,' and DJ has built a ready to go staff, including me, Joe and Clara, to begin our art outreach mission. Now we're ready to connect Harbor and Divine with the art museum to schedule art education events here on the Near West Side. What do you think? I'm excited, but are you ready for that?"

"Gary, I am, as well as everyone else on the education staff here. We are all simply amazed at what you, DJ and Joe have accomplished in such a short time. When can you be back here at the museum for some extended planning time together?"

"Let's see, this is Friday already, how about Monday morning, 9:00, bright eyed and bushy tailed?"

"Sounds great. By the way, we already have fifteen applicants for your Old Tony Studio."

"Wow! That's even more than Leonardo had! And these guys are *paying me*. Well, somewhat. Somewhere up in heaven Val Green is satisfied, smiling and saying, 'See, Gary, I knew you could paint like Leonardo.' And I'm still saying, 'No way.'"

"Time will tell, Gary. But I think Leonardo daVinci would have been proud to have painted Old Tony himself. Very proud. In fact, have you ever noticed the resemblance between Old Tony and Leonardo's self portrait when he was older?"

"I have. And you know I studied it quite a bit when you mentored me through my MFA painting Old Tony. Except Old Tony has no beard, so I got to paint his whole face, with all the details of character and lots of wrinkles of joy."

"You sure did. Now don't respond to this, Gary, but Old Tony is better because of that face. See you Monday at 9:00."

"See you then. And Melanie, thank you — again."

"Just calling them how I 'sees 'em,' Gar."

Gary ended the call tamping down his pride. Fifteen applicants for his studio and Melanie's compliment were pretty heady endorsements for an artist trying to put his life back together. He chuckled to himself remembering that Dianah had told him the same thing, but said she thought his Paris paintings of her were even better. Hmm. Would he dare donate some of them, say four, to the art museum in gratitude for studio space and joint publicity for places in his studio? He wondered what Dianah would say. Maybe if he chose from the batch she approved in Paris, like the head shots, it would be okay. Yes, he would definitely need to feel he had Dianah's approval, because he would not only be sharing some paintings, but also the love of his life with the whole world. He would always be so very proud of her beauty — and their joy together. Goodness, how he loved her. Still. "Okay. Enough. Don't go down that rabbit hole," he told himself. However much he enjoyed thinking about her, remembering her dancing around their Paris apartment while he painted and lusted, he knew, unfortunately, that when he would recall their joy of those days, the darkness of his grief would inevitably ambush him and threaten to consume any bits of joy with a swirling vortex of darkness for days on end. Yet, even though he knew that would happen, he was still determined, when he could move into his new home on Harbor Street, that he would hungrily explore those paintings, lust after her beauty and relive their *sfumato* of love when the two became one. Gary took a deep breath, then another, and sighed, "Oh, my, I am so undone," then shook his head as if to reset his mind from the past to the present. Of course, first he needed to take care of purchasing and moving into that house before he could even think of letting loose the dogs of secret lust.

So he called Annie. 'Annie the Realtor.' Right.

"Hello, Dunlop Realty. This is Annie Dunlop."

"Hi, Annie. This is Gary Siciliano."

"I know," she said in a sultry voice. 'Whoa. Did I really say that?' asked Annie herself. She wanted to take it back, hang up and start all over again with a cheery voice. But Gary beat her to it. Click.

Chapter 20

Feels Like a Homecoming

With his heart racing a mile a minute Gary knew he had to call her right back. But he needed to take a second or two. He did not want to talk with that voice. Well, yes he did. Just not now. Not yet. Not for a long time. But he did want to talk with Annie, and he needed to be honest, transparent about his fears of jumping into a relationship way too fast. 'So just call,' he told himself. 'Right now. Just call.' He did.

"Hi, this is Gary. We must have gotten disconnected."

"No, we did not. You hung up, and I am really sorry. I must have scared the bejesus out you. It just came out. I am really sorry."

"You're right, I did hang up. And I'm sorry too. Plus you're also right, you did scare the bejesus out of me for sure. Annie, I like you, I like you a lot, but I can't jump into a relationship with you right now. A friendship, absolutely. And who knows what later on. I'm just still very fragile on the romance thing. I sure do want you as a friend, but with both of us on a leash."

Annie laughed. "You are so honest, you make my heart sing. But I will dial it down for as long as you need me to. I can't

152

even conceive of the grief you have, and I want to honor the love that you and Dianah had together for one another. Still have, right?"

"Yes."

"But, to be honest, Gar, that leash on me is going to have to be pit bull strong."

Gary laughed. "Thank you, Annie. Two requests?"

"Anything. I owe you."

"No you don't. You flatter me. Okay, enough. My first request is this: May I speak to Annie the Realtor please?"

"Of course. Just a minute. Hello, this is Annie the Realtor. Annie the love-sick-puppy is on extended leave. How can I help you?"

Gary howled with laughter. 'Holy cow,' Gary said to himself as he settled himself down. 'This woman is a hoot.' "Annie the Realtor, I'm ready to buy that house on Harbor Street. Can we make a deal?"

"Um," Annie stammered, double entendres were so tempting, "Mr. Siciliano, that house is still available, and I actually have paper work all set for you to sign. The home inspection, all taken care of, went very well, and the seller is eager to get it sold."

"Great. Sounds like you did your homework."

"Sure did. I have a buyer who expects the best, and a seller who is eager to sell. Want to meet at the house to sign the offer sheet right now?"

"Yes, that would be great. But just be sure that you leave that other Annie behind."

"Will do, but, admittedly, with reluctance."

"Thirty minutes?"

"I'll be there. See you soon. Oh, but you said you had two requests. What's the other one?" Too late. Gary ended the call.

Thirty minutes later Gary and Annie met at the Harbor Street House, 1965 Harbor Street, Cleveland, Ohio.

First thing Gary said was, "Annie, you're bad, you know."

"Sorry. Not sorry. Sorry. Really, sorry. Annie the Realtor is very sorry, and would like to sell you this house. Ready?"

Gary smiled, nodded, and said, "Ready. Let's go in. Okay if we look around again before I sign, just to make sure?"

"Yes sir." Annie got the key out of the realtor's box, opened the door and they walked in.

Gary looked around with a smile and a nodding head. "This place looks even better than the last time I saw it." He kept on walking and nodding and smiling. Upstairs, outside, down the basement still nodding and smiling. "But do you remember the last time we met for me to sign papers at your office? Remember what happened?"

"I do. I had some bad news. You couldn't buy the parish house or the church. But I did show you this place."

"And reclaimed your status as the World's Best Realtor, if I remember right. So, no surprises this time?"

"None that Annie the Realtor can tell you," she said smirking.

"Good." Gary returned the smirk and turned it into a smile, which turned Annie into mush.

"Okey dokey. Annie the Realtor, please show me where to sign."

"Right here," she said handing Gary a pen, putting it into his hand, then picking up his hand, pausing long enough to gaze into his eyes, and putting his hand on the contract, saying again very softly, "Right here."

"Annie, bad girl." Equally softly.

"That's to pay you back for that smirky smile that you know turns my legs to mush."

"Sorry. Guilty as charged. This is hard, isn't it."

"Very hard. Now just sign the papers," she ordered. "No more funny stuff."

"Yes, ma'am." He did and it did not escape him either that this house now replaces the home he, Dianah and Lily built on Durango Mountain that burned and took the lives of Dianah and Lily. Now he has a new house, new jobs with people he really respects and likes, new friends like Joe, DJ, Annie and Melanie all amounting to a new life. Without Dianah and Lily, true. But, for the moment anyhow, his descent into darkness has been overcome with the brightness of hope, new friendships and a freshness of life that even a few weeks ago he thought would be unreachable for years to come. 'Goodness, goodness, goodness. Feels like a homecoming. Yes it does,' he thought as he signed the papers.

Even though the house purchase was not yet a fully closed deal, Annie told Gary that the former owner gave his okay for Gary to start moving in. So he did. Joe offered to help, so the two of them drove the U-Haul that Gary was still paying rent on from Guy and Phyllis's house all the way down Lorain Avenue and parked it right in front of 1965 Harbor Street. "That's a beautiful house, Gar," marveled Joe who never paid much attention to it, even though it was just across the street from the church where he had been working the last five months. This time he just stared to take it all in. "Wow. And you said Annie Dunlop nailed this down for you?"

"Yep. All Annie."

"That girl just might be a keeper, Gary Siciliano. Just might be."

"Ya, well, you know, we'll see. We'll just have to see."

"Hey, I've seen you two making moon eyes at each other."

"You just made that up! You've never even met her, seen her!"

"True. But still, come on, fess up. You two are getting very friendly, aren't you?"

"We are good friends. But I'm not ready for anything serious yet."

"Who is ever ready for romance? Love comes when thou art loved, Mr. Artiste. Who could ever be ready for that? Just saying."

"Thanks, Dr. Phil, I'll keep that in mind. In the meantime, let's get to work. DJ should be here any minute."

"Is *she* coming to help too."

"Yes, *she* is. Even as we speak."

"Where?"

"Right there up by the The McCafferty Health Center," said Gary pointing to the building on the corner of Harbor and Lorain.

"Oh, yeesss. Look at her why don't ya. She has got her eye on you, my brother. You are toast. Gar, I believe you two have got it bad."

"Thanks, Dr. Phil, for your solid insight."

That triggered Joe's best Dr. Phil impersonation. "What were you thi-i-inking? What *were* you thinking?"

"Shh. She's right here, you idiot."

Annie walked up with a big smile on her face. "Good morning, Gary. And you must be Joe. Great day to move in, isn't it? I'm Annie."

"Nice to meet you, Annie. And, yeppers, it is a great day for moving," agreed Joe.

"By the way, Joe, why was Gary doing all the shushing as I was walking up?"

"Oh, nothing. Just banter."

"Gary?"

"Joe was just teasing me," Gary avoided.

"Really?" She asked with a big flirty grin on her face. "Hmm. Joe were you teasing Gary about me?"

"Could be."

"Well, keep it up."

Joe just about lost his cookies he laughed so hard. All Gary could do was say, "Bad Annie," and laugh right along with them. "I thought you were supposed to leave Annie the LSP behind."

"Wait, wait, wait," Joe interrupted. "Why should Annie the LSP be left behind? And what is an LSP anyway?"

Gary just couldn't let this go any further. It was already out of hand. "Joe, I can't tell you that. National security, you understand." Wink, wink.

"Ahh. I get it. I'll weasel it out of you later."

Annie jumped in Joe's face, "Oh, no you won't. Right, Gar?"

"Right," Gary said, laughing at Annie. "All right, now you know what I was shushing him about. So let's get to work, okay?"

"Yes, Boss."

DJ joined them five minutes later, and in three hours and ten minutes the four of them had totally emptied the truck putting nearly everything in the right places. Much of it was the art, both Dianah's and Gary's, that Dianah had saved following the 48-hour evacuation order. DJ, Joe and Annie had never seen much of Gary's work in person, and they loved seeing the Dancing Bear and a few of his other painted canvases ready to be framed and sold. But when they dug out Diana's blankets, rugs and sealed sand paintings they were awestruck.

DJ was already unrolling the largest of Dianah's hand tied rugs on the beautiful hardwood living room floor totally amazed. "Gary, Gary, Dianah did this? Wow. Look at this. This is so beautiful I would never want to walk on it. You need to hang this on a big wall someplace. It is just magnificent. Look at this." He whistled in admiration.

"Gary, what's with all the bears? I mean, I know that's part of her name, but what do they mean?" Annie asked.

Gary took a deep breath and decided to tell Annie all about Dianah Springer Brownbear. "Dianah Springer Brownbear's Dine` Navajo birth parents died in an auto accident on their way home from the hospital the night she was born. She was adopted and raised by loving Anglo parents, Bill and Della Springer. But as she got older and studied her Dine` heritage and learned traditional Dine` art, she chose a native American sounding artist last name Brownbear to honor her birth parents, but kept Springer as her legal name to honor her loving mom and dad. Most people, including her mom and dad called her Dianah Brownbear. And the brown grizzly bear became her signature motif for most of her art, as well as her spirit guide. She sold almost all the work she did, but the pieces she kept all have the Brownbear motif, like that rug on the floor with the running brown bears around the edges."

"Oh," marveled Annie, "that rug is beautiful, Gary. It's the work of an artist, to be sure." Annie paused, then said, "And, Gary, thank you very much for sharing her with me, with all of us."

"Thanks for listening. All of what I told you also explains why I painted that oversized picture of the joyful Dancing Bear. As petite and beautiful as Dianah was, she was also full of joy and wonderfully playful. So I called her my Dancing Bear. I won best in show in San Francisco with the Dancing Bear and was offered $350,000 for the painting. By that time I had already sold paintings for a lot of money, and the Dancing Bear, well, I just couldn't sell her. She was *my* Dancing Bear.

So I turned down the offer, and, especially now, I'm glad I did. I have it hanging in my bedroom, if you'd like to take a peek."

They all got up to take a quick look, but they stayed to take quite a long peek. Joe turned to Gary and said, "She makes me want to laugh, Gar. Puts a smile on my face."

DJ and Annie agreed.

"Thank you," Gary said. "She makes me smile too. And thanks again for listening." With that, Gary glanced over at Annie whose face glistened with tears. They locked glistening eyes, and smiled at each other. Joe noticed their beautiful chemistry, but he didn't say a thing. This was their moment. Joe admired them both: Gary for sharing so beautifully his love for Dianah, his Dancing Bear; and Annie for her sweet empathy for the man she, obviously, loves.

"Thank *you*, Gary," DJ said. "It seems like every time we get together tears fall."

Joe chimed in, "I'm proud of you, my brother. But I think we better get going and leave you to figure things out here."

"Good plan," added DJ. "Gary, if the Lord had told me I could designate any man to be my new friend, I would choose you. Have a good two weeks at the art museum. I'm looking forward to the ideas Dr. Zurkos and her staff will have for us at Harbor and Divine."

Suddenly Joe perked up with an idea. "Say, maybe the two of us could have supper together a couple times this week. You think?"

"That'd be great, Joe," Gary agreed. "How about DJ and Annie too, Tuesday, here at my house, say 6:30? DJ, Annie?

They all chimed in, "Perfect" "Great" "I'll be there."

"I'll make barbecue beef on buns and a salad. If any of you want to bring something to share, that'd be even better. Thanks again for all your help. See you Tuesday."

Joe and DJ walked out, but Annie stayed behind. "Do I have to leave too?"

"Annie the Realtor can stay."

"How about Annie the Hybrid? Mostly Annie the Realtor."

He chuckled. "Annie the Hybrid, I'd like that. Let's give it a try."

However, Gary didn't recognize the power of playing house.

Chapter 21

1965 Harbor Street

Annie dug right in. "I love a clean house, so is it okay if I wash the kitchen and bathrooms?"

"Whoa! That would be excellent, Annie. But before you start, I just want to tell you that this feels so awesome, you here. I still want each of us to be on a leash, though. And Annie?"

"Yes?"

"You handled my story about Dianah Springer Brownbear just perfectly, you know. And if that was as difficult for you to hear as it was for me to tell, you were stellar."

Annie nodded her head. "It was tough to hear. But only a sweet, sweet man could tell that story the way you did. And, Gary, I can share that sweet man for quite a while with Dianah."

Oh boy, that did it. Gary rushed to Annie and they embraced.

"Ten seconds," he said and they both laughed. "Actually ten seconds is a long time. Maybe we should start with three. What do you think?"

Annie was catching her breath from the ten. "Yeah, I think ten seconds is much too much even for Annie the LSP. Besides, I need to keep on my pit bull leash. From now on, three seconds sounds way more doable. And maybe not more than two a day. What do you think?"

"Two a day at three seconds sounds — still scary, Annie, I have to confess. I know how vulnerable I am, especially with you. How about adding no more often than two days in a week? It'd be a little bit like getting to know each other in high school, but it might work."

"I agree it's pretty goofy. But it does sound safe and good. All we need to add is an overprotective father in the house to keep us on track." They both laughed.

"Maybe not that far. Anyway, how 'bout we get to work?"

"Let's do that," she said with enthusiasm. And work they did until they were both exhausted, collapsing to the floor.

"Gary, I'm totally done. Maybe I better get going."

"Okay. Annie, thank you very much for your help as well as for your patience with me."

Three seconds later Annie was out the door as Gary watched her walk to her car. She turned to wave, got in the car and drove off.

Gary, on the other hand went back into the house and suddenly realized just how empty it felt. Annie had filled it up, even without much furniture. His parents and new friends have warned him not to jump into a relationship too fast lest he slide a new woman into the Dianah spot and then be disappointed that she couldn't be Dianah after all. It made sense for sure. But still, how can you be friends in the meantime? He really did need to talk with Dr. Phil. Hmm. Maybe DJ? DJ counseled Joe years ago and it seemed to work out well. Suddenly decisive, Gary proclaimed to himself, "That's great idea, Gar. Let's call DJ right now."

"Hello, University Circle United Methodist Church, this is Clara. How may I help you?"

"Golly, you're good."

"Thank you, Gary. And you're smooth, maybe too smooth for your own good."

"Whoa. Where'd that come from. Felt like a two-by-four upside my head. What's up?"

Clara stood up in her 'lecture pose,' even though she was just on speaker phone. "I'm sorry, Gary, but I overheard the boys talking about the sparks between you and a certain young lady named Annie. I know you didn't ask, but here's what I think. You are dying of thirst in the desert of grief and loneliness, and this lovely, sweet lady is a pitcher of ice water, and you are ready to gulp the whole thing down to slack your thirst. She on the other hand has been fasting from chocolate for way too long, and here you come like a two-pound Whitman's Sampler on Valentine's Day, all sweet and chocolatey smooth. And she wants to eat the whole box, every bit. And she'll scarf it down so fast, she'll end up barfing with a belly ache (and don't miss the metaphor.) And you'll get cramps and the shivers from all that cold water. You'll use each other in a heart beat to get your own needs met, and in the end you'll both feel used, disappointed and unloved. That's what I think."

At that she sat down with an angry look on her face. Good thing Gary couldn't see it, but he could feel the chill even over the phone.

"Holy cow, Clara."

"I'm sorry. I hardly know you. But I'm old and I've seen it too many times. Haste makes waste and breaks hearts. You've gotta wait until you know who she is as a woman in her own right, and not just as a patch over the hole in your heart. You may think you can't go any slower 'cause you're hotter than a bull in the cow barn. But if you don't cool down you are going to break that girl's heart and your own as well."

"Holy cow, Clara."

"You said that already."

"Yeah, but you sorta blew a gasket and what you don't know is that the reason I called was to set up an appointment to talk with DJ exactly about what you just said, about Annie and me. I thought I needed to talk with Dr. Phil, or at least Dr. Scott, but, evidently, what I also needed was to listen to Dr. Clara."

"No, listen to Rev. Dr. Scott. Anyway, good for you, Gary. I'm sorry to interfere, happy to set up that appointment for you, but why don't you include Annie in on the discussion. A lot of couples come in a year or even two before they even think about marriage just to sort things out between them — their values, their goals, what they are looking for in a mate, and what would be the best time line for them. DJ is a wonderful couples counselor even if marriage is never even thought about let alone mentioned."

Gary quietly considered Clara's Annie idea, a new one for him, and maybe too, too soon. So he said, "How about we set a couple of tentative dates, so I can talk with Annie first, see what she thinks. In fact, Tuesday DJ and Annie and Joe will be here for dinner. What if Annie and I meet with DJ an hour or so before Joe comes? Based on his and Annie's okays, of course."

"We can do that." And they did. DJ liked the idea and so did Annie when Gary called her right away at her office. In fact, she got all emotional just talking about it over the phone. It sounded like it could be a winner all the way around. But still, pretty scary. Lots of scary first steps in this new life.

His mind shifted, and Gary realized he needed to straighten up the house, set up his bed and plan a bit for his meeting with

Melanie Monday morning, all of which would get his mind off Clara and Annie.

There wasn't a whole lot of straightening up to do, because, truth be told, Gary didn't have much stuff. The fire burned up nearly all that Gary and Dianah had collected over the years. The little bit of furniture he brought to Cleveland came from his studio in Durango where he used to do nearly all of his artistic work. So he had a bed and linens, two large book shelves, one dining table and four chairs he had just picked up at the used furniture store at West 45th Street and Lorain, along with a large desk and a small couch from Durango. Plus he had his studio supplies — easels, two drying racks, some paints and pallets, canvas, stretchers, studio paintings plus the paintings that Dianah had saved when she and Lily were evacuated, like The Dancing Bear. Gary thought he might take a few sample paintings to his morning meeting at the art museum, because all they knew of his work at CMA was Old Tony. So he planned to show them several styles of portraits, especially the impressionist beach paintings that his patrons loved the most. Often Gary would paint three versions of beach portraits for folks to choose from. Some clients bought all three, but others left one or two behind, and he saved those to decorate his studio. If there was room at the museum studio, he just might do the same for his apprentices and students to study and imitate.

After Gary had set four paintings aside, his heart suddenly started racing a mile a minute as he found, then picked up the Paris folio and just held it. He was uncertain that he even wanted to open it up as he remembered painting Dianah's lush beauty as she joyfully modeled for him, and then teased him until he would throw down his paint brush and chase

165

her around their Paris apartment giggling until he caught her and they fell into each other's arms. Quiet tears welled and streamed down his face, until he realized that the folio was not thick enough to hold all of the paintings. In a panic he shouted, "Oh, no. No!" and began flipping through the folio realizing that not even half of his paintings of Dianah were there. Frantically he began searching everywhere, hastily tossing aside other marvelous paintings, shouting, moaning, totally out of control. It felt like he had lost Dianah all over again, and was falling into that terrible darkness, helplessly sobbing just as he had that night of the fire. Eventually, rendered immobile by shock and grief, Gary just sat in the middle of his scattered art work yelling viciously at the dark, when from what seemed to be a far distance away he heard his name. "Gary. Gary." A soft, gentle woman's voice called him. "Gary, Gary. Oh, you poor baby." The voice sat on the floor next to him and put her arms around his trembling frame and drew him to herself. Only then did he look to see Annie's face, the front door open behind her. Confused, dumbfounded, he said her name, "Annie," and let her pull him to her.

"I've lost her all over again. All over again."

Annie scanned the strewn paintings and in the middle, closest to Gary, saw exquisite impressionist paintings of a most beautiful dark haired woman, who she instantly knew must be Dianah. "Gary, she's right here. Right here. Look, my love. Here she is." Making herself smile, Annie picked up and handed Gary one of the paintings. "Here's Dianah. Right here. Here she is."

"Thank you. But you're here. How...?" Gary was so befuddled he couldn't finish his thought.

Annie, dismayed by Gary's pitiful struggle and wanting to calm his aching heart, gently moved paintings aside to allow her to put her arms all the way around him and hug away his trembling as if he were a child.

Gary let her. His trembling calmed. His mind began to clear.

He understood Annie was there to help him, but he didn't understand how she knew to come. "Annie, I'm so glad that you're here. But how did you know to come? How did you know I needed you?"

"I was napping on my couch. And, believe it or not, I was dreaming of a bear, and the bear told me you needed me because you were in trouble. So I ran to my car, drove here like a maniac, parked in the street, knocked on your door at first. But then I heard you crying, yelling, shouting, so I just walked in. Was that okay?"

"Okay? Yes. Very okay. Annie, you're an angel." They embraced again casting aside both the three and the ten second rules without a thought. His trembling calmed. In dismay, he surveyed all the art work he had, like a mad man, thrown around him on the floor, and sadly said, "I'm afraid I've made quite a mess." He looked from Annie to Dianah's picture and back again, then said through more sobs, "Annie, this is Dianah."

Instantly Annie knew what to say. "Hello, Dianah," she choked out. "I'm very pleased to meet you. I'm here to take care of Gary. I hope you don't mind."

As Annie was talking to Dianah's picture, Gary's eyes and mouth opened in amazement. His grieving tears dried, but new ones came again, not frantic tears, but the soft tears of someone who has just been given an inestimable gift. The Gift-Giver spoke, "Gary, if you're feeling better, how about I help you straighten up a bit? All right?"

"Yes. Thank you, Annie. *Thank you.* But this is a heckuva way for you and Dianah to meet." He chuckled, eyes still wet.

Smiling, Annie responded, "You can say that again."

In fifteen minutes Annie and Gary restored order to a dazzling sample of Gary's art.

Pleased with their progress, Annie judged, "There, that's better."

"It sure is. Thank you for coming to help me. I guess that's a PTSD episode at its finest."

"You're welcome, and, yes, I agree, that was quite an event. But, Gary, I don't think you should be alone tonight. I'm not suggesting we take off the leashes. I'm just worried...about you. And it's after midnight."

"What?" Gary cried out. "Midnight? Holy cow, I had no idea."

"Well, you were pretty much out of it, Gar. Look, here's my idea.

Your couch is just the right size for me. How about you clean up and go to your bed. And I'll clean up and sleep on the couch. I'll keep my pit bull leash on tight, and you keep yours tight on you. Sound like a good plan? You okay now?"

"Sounds perfect. And, yes, I'm okay now, thanks to you. Annie, you're such a good person. Thank you. Oh, and I have a meeting with folks at the art museum tomorrow morning."

"Early?"

"Not too bad. 9:00."

"Any breakfast food in the house yet?"

"Coffee."

"Well, while you're getting yourself ready tomorrow morning, I'll go to the Pick-n-Pay and buy a few things for breakfast. Got any favorites?"

"Instant oatmeal with cinnamon and raisins. Please."

"Will do. And Gary, how about a three-second good night hug?"

"Okay," Gary said compliantly.

Three seconds felt way too short this time, though necessary for sure. So Annie lightly kissed his cheek. He loved it.

"Good night, Gary."

"Good night, Annie. And, thank you again."

"You're welcome."

After a good night's sleep, an oatmeal and coffee breakfast and another three-second hug, Gary was off to the Art Museum and Annie was thumbing through Dianah's pictures saying, 'That must have been a fabulous six weeks in Paris.' Then she packed away the pictures and drove herself home.

Chapter 22

Four Unexpected Lessons

Gary decided not to take any Paris paintings of Dianah to the museum, not after last night. Just some portraits of other people. While he fell asleep up in his bedroom with his Dancing Bear on the wall and Annie downstairs sleeping on the couch in the living room Gary felt a deep, inner peace he had been missing since the fire. He had to smile remembering two of the chaotic night's totally unexpected lessons: one, how looking at his Paris paintings of Dianah's radiant beauty brought him such utter distress; and two, how Annie's arrival brought him such peace out of the distress. Oh, and three, how much he loved Annie's three-second bed time hug topped off with a sweet kiss on his cheek. Oh, yeah, and four, how Annie said she dreamed a bear told her to go help him. A bear.

Once he hopped into his car, Gary, almost immediately, started talking out loud again, no tears though. "So, let me get this straight. Reliving our Paris past, those paintings in particular, brought me dark, turbulent, chaotic distress. Was all that chaos Dianah telling me not to live in the past, no matter how very beautiful it was for both of us, because it will only cause you to live in darkness, grief and distress? Is that possible? And if so, was Dianah the Bear in Annie's dream sending her to help me? If so, is Dianah telling me she approves, even delights in Annie's caring for me? And if so, was that like a handoff? Was that Dianah's love setting me free for Annie?" Gary smiled a crooked smile. "This is so weird. Wonderful, but chaotic and weird. I have got to run this by DJ Tuesday night. I am one messed up puppy."

By then he was already on Superior Avenue five minutes away from University Circle. He took a deep breath, slowly shook his head, smiled a satisfied grin and redirected his thinking to Dr. Melanie Zurkos, his one time mentor and now ... now, a museum curator, supervisor and friend. And plus now what? Colleague? Gary marveled at all the helpers like Melanie Zurkos who helped him on his twisted life journey at just the right moments — James an age ago, Ms. Green, Annie, DJ, Joe, Clara, and now Melanie again? Spirit Guides, Dianah called them. Angels, Gary's pastors said, sent by God. Maybe both describe the very same wonder. His Catholic friends used to tell him it's all a mystery, not for us to know or understand, but only to be grateful and amazed with God. Gary was both — grateful and amazed. And now that Melanie was back in his life, he felt excited to see new things unfold.

"Yep, we'll find out more in a minute or two," he said quietly to himself as he turned into the art museum parking garage. Melanie had already sent him a parking pass, his very first piece of mail at 1965 Harbor Street, and today he was using it for the very first time. He chuckled at how having an employee parking pass made him feel like he already belonged. It felt good. But what a crazy roller coaster ride his life had become. He drove to the lower level parking area with a locked entrance that led to the cleaning and restoration studios, display areas as well as the glassed-in studio that housed his very own spot in the art universe. When his pass got him through the locked doors right up to Melanie's office-studio Gary realized that he was pretty excited, although he had no idea just how over the moon he was about to become.

With all the glass walls and doors in the studio area, Melanie saw Gary arrive way before Gary saw her. No sneaking up on people in this place. She opened her door to greet Gary with a cheery, "Hi, Gary, so good to see you."

"Good to see you too, Melanie. And this place. I just love it. And today even more so. It always looks sparkling fresh and inviting. Must be good management," he said with a grin and wink at Melanie.

She took Gary's compliment in stride and told him, "This is a glorious place to work, especially for a basement. Plus there are so many high character people here that I just know you'll love working here as much as I do."

"Thank you. You've been here, what, twenty-eight years now?"

Melanie nodded, "Sure have."

"Wow. That's amazing. You must love it. Twenty-eight years is a long time. Twenty-eight years from now I'll be seventy-two. Holy cow. I can't even imagine what that kind of stability must feel like."

"It feels good, Gary. Feels very, very good. But come with me. Let's look at the progress of your studio area. Then we can sit down in there and study your fifteen applicants. Lots of high quality people in that mix, Gary. I already recognize quite a few of them by their return addresses on the envelopes. Believe me, I wanted to tear open every single envelope, but

I was a good girl and waited for you. Can you tell I'm pretty pumped up for this?"

"Yes, I can. I am too. Where are those applications, by the way?"

"In your studio. Let's go." Melanie was really excited for Gary to see the studio and open up the applications, but even more excited for him to see the surprise she had cooked up with lots of generous help. She could barely contain herself anticipating the look on Gary's face. "Come on, let's go," she said again as she lightly grabbed his arm to hurry him along.

Gary chuckled at her enthusiasm. "All right, all right, I'm coming. Hold your horses," which made her tug him all the harder toward Gary's new studio and her marvelous secret.

"Move it then," she commanded with a girly giggle even though she was twelve years older than Gary. When they turned the last corner, Melanie stepped ahead, dramatically threw out her arms and exclaimed in her very best French, "Voila!"

Gary turned and stood stunned speechless. He scanned the immense brand new studio space, much larger than the last time he saw it. "Wow, Melanie. Goodness, goodness. This is beautiful! And look at all this space. Where did it all come from?"

"We got rid of a couple of walls. Had to. The people whose return addresses I saw are accomplished in their field, and deserve good artistic space. You too, Gary. That's your lair over there."

Gary looked past the eight twelve by fifteen foot studios partly partitioned from one another toward the twenty by fifteen foot master studio, all of them surrounded by glass observation walls which were in turn surrounded by a small gallery of seats. Gary entertained a brief moment of trepidation that maybe he had overstepped his abilities, but he quickly

overcame that when his eyes went to the Old Tony photo print
he expected to see next to the lineup of eight unfinished Old
Tony canvases. As he surveyed the scene his eyes returned to
Old Tony, thinking something was odd about that print. So he
squinted and squinted again and finally cheered with amazed
joy, "No way! No way! Melanie, no freaking way, Melanie! Is
that for real?" he asked as he rushed to Old Tony.

"Go look."

He was already there. He wanted to hug the painting, but
settled for caressing the frame. "This is really him. You stinky
old Slovenian, how-r-ya doing?!" He hadn't seen the original
Old Tony for fourteen years. "This is *really* him."

"Yes, it's really him," Melanie said smiling that Gary's
excitement matched her hopes for the surprise. "We explained
what we are doing to the owner, and asked him for an extended
museum loan and he loved the idea. He even plans to come
visit you himself. He agreed in a heartbeat to the loan, but on
one condition. He wanted to swap us for our fancy Old Tony
photo print. We jumped at it, packed the copy and sent it with
our restoration team to make the switch. So we now have Old
Tony for at least a year. And once we choose your apprentices
and they start their own canvases, we will sell tickets for artists
and art lovers alike to come view Old Tony and watch you and
your studio artists in master classes. It will be the hit of the art
world. And I do mean world. Even some of your applicants are
from other countries, in particular, two from France."

"France? No way! Paris probably. Old friends." Gary could
hardly take it all in and struggled for words through his red-
dening eyes and choking throat. "Can you imagine that?
Goodness gracious. All this and Paris too! Melanie, you are
amazing. This place is amazing. I am flabbergasted! And, I

admit, I am also intimidated by it all, you know. Now I've got to pull it off, make it right for everyone."

"Gary, you're not alone in this. We're all behind you, the whole staff. This is a big deal for all of us here as well. And now with Paris added in, you have more glam than I ever imagined."

Gary smiled, blushed and said, "Thank you Melanie. Right now I feel like a kid at Christmas. And let me tell you, in some ways I still feel like that little ten-year-old kid who was afraid that the high school art teacher was going to laugh at his drawings. Which included Old Tony. Actually, in my sketchbooks, I drew three of Old Tony. Did I ever show you the other two?"

"No, I don't think so," Melanie said caught a little off guard.

"I'll show them to you when we sit down to chat, because I thought I'd make at least one of them available to the studio so all the artists might have more of an actual original Old Tony to their credit."

Now it was Melanie's time to be speechless. "Wow, Gary, that's quite a gift to your studio."

"I hope they'll feel that way, especially my colleagues from Paris. Your visitors will be able to watch the progress of wonderful works of art taking form right before their eyes. Then, at the right time, whenever that might be, we can all have a public art show of the work we will have completed. Maybe up in the beautiful atrium. How does that sound, Melanie?"

"Wonderful. But, Gary, colleagues from Paris?"

"I'm thinking those are the applications from France."

"You are amazing, Gary, replete with creative surprise that I just love. I think we're off to a great start working together. I never expected you to be such a promoter as well as an artist of renown. When you're ready we can sit around your desk and explore the applications, and get even more excited, if that's at all possible."

"Give me ten more minutes, Melanie, and I'll be ready."

"Perfect. I'll excuse myself then and meet you at your desk in ten minutes."

"Okay, see you soon." Gary then sat in every studio chair to get a feel for the perspective his colleagues and students of Old Tony would have as they painted. He anticipated that with differing sight lines to Old Tony every artist would have a unique perspective, almost as if the live Old Tony sat right there right in front of them, each artist painting him from a slightly different angle. As he hopped from chair to chair Gary got more excited imagining how that might work, even producing a marvelous collaborative effect with the paintings displayed to viewers at the very angles from which the artists painted and applied the life-giving effect of *sfumato glaze*. "It might just work!" Gary said aloud to himself. "Goodness gracious, it could turn out to be a dazzling effect. Dazzling! Cool. We'll surely plant that idea in their minds."

At that, he moved a chair right next to Old Tony, as if he were about to talk with an old friend in a nursing home. Gary just looked. He studied Old Tony's eyes, and hair, and eyebrows; his nose, ears, and that not-quite-a-smile that had pushed all Tony's God-carved wrinkles to create a pleasant, peaceful countenance. He studied every stroke he had painted, trying to deconstruct the layers of glaze in his mind, critiquing his method of *sfumato* so, in remembering, he could explain, teach and guide others in Leonardo's most sublime technique. Unfortunately, Gary was also dismayed to find dozens of places that needed a layer or two or three or more of *sfumato* glaze, lightening or darkening the smoky haze to obfuscate any unnatural lines that would artificially separate one part of Tony's cheek from another, or even Tony's hair from the background building behind him. Leonardo despised dividing lines in a painting that did not exist in what human eyes actually saw. With *sfumato* glaze Leonardo waged war against all the line painters of his age.

Then Gary suddenly caught what he was doing and laughed aloud at himself, thinking, 'That's exactly what Leonardo would have done right then and there, on the spot. Leonardo would have pulled out his brushes and paints and made the corrections. Of course,' he grieved, 'Leonardo could do that with the Mona Lisa, because he never sold her. He carried the Mona Lisa with him for years from patron to patron making minute alterations in what some art historians call the most perfect portrait ever painted, keeping her close at hand until the day he died. I, on the other hand, auctioned off my best friend for tons of money, so the painting is no longer mine to perfect. Still, it's pretty doggone good!'

"But I guess that's what it feels like when the creator gives over control of his creations," Gary concluded aloud. And then he added quietly, "Little bits of helplessness, spiced with anger, regret, frustration, longing and love all blended together in *sfumato* style. Oh, and maybe a bit of grief on top." He slowly backed away from Old Tony as a courtier would from his king, and walked to his desk. Melanie was already there watching him study Old Tony. It had been way longer than ten minutes.

She spoke first. "So what do you think?"

"He needs more work." They both laughed out loud.

"Of course. Just like Leonardo, you know," Melanie grinned.

"Yes, I know." He shook his head remembering Ms. Green.

"You realize you have become just exactly what your teacher, Ms. Green, prophesied you would become."

"I do. I wish she could be here. She would love all of this. And Dianah would too."

"In equal parts they would both love the art, the teaching and you."

At that Melanie pulled out the applications and said, "Shall we get to work?" Gary nodded, and they spent the next three hours perusing fifteen outstanding applications for Gary's studio. It never escaped him that he was in a dream actually in the process of coming true. If only we lived every day always aware that we live in the middle of dreams that are coming true.

Chapter 23

Living the Dream

G ary was somewhat disappointed when the applications from Paris were from two students of the master artists he and Dianah had come to know during those six weeks in Paris, instead of from the master artist friends themselves. Of course, he could still contact his friends and invite them to visit, critique his Old Tony studio, maybe lead a master class or two and enjoy Cleveland restaurants and clubs together after hours. They might love the freedom of such an opportunity, and Gary knew he would enjoy them being in Cleveland, even with Dianah missing from the mix. "I'll send them invitations today," he vowed.

In every way, Gary and Melanie worked wonderfully well together. They easily picked their top three candidates, and equally easily picked the bottom four. Not that those bottom four were slouches by any means. All four were master artists themselves looking to gain teaching tips from Gary, making them a category all their own that could easily upgrade the Old Tony Studio. So, why not, thought both Gary and Melanie, invite them all to be observers, at their own expense, of course?

Or each teach a master class? They could stay for as long as they wanted and move in and out of the classes choosing which sessions interested them most. Gary could even offer, if he thought it warranted, a weekly Q and A designed just for the observers to give and take. Maybe, with a little advertising, others in the art world would also like to be observers, plugging into a high quality studio experience with no expectations or obligations. That kind of observing might appeal to the gadfly mentality of many artists, including his Parisian colleagues. Could work. Who knows? Both Gary and Melanie agreed it was worth their effort to explore.

That left eight candidates for the three or four remaining full time spots, all of them excellent prospects. However, none fulfilled Gary's secret hope to teach a ten to twelve year old prodigy from a poor family. They would have to keep looking.

"Except," interjected Melanie, "for Angelina Anderson."

"What do you mean?" asked a surprised Gary.

"I know Angelina. She has been very active in our East Side museum outreach program, taking all the classes she could afford and spending countless days sitting, sketchbook on her lap, learning by mimicking the best art in the world for the last four years. And even though, like you, she can draw whatever she sees, she is definitely no longer ten years old."

"How old is she?" Gary asked.

"Nineteen. But she is hardworking and easy to teach."

"She sure sounds intriguing, but it will take us a lot of time to talk through what would be best for her. And since we've been at this for hours already, maybe we should save Angelina Anderson for next time. I'm tired right now."

"Good idea, I'm tired too. How about we put off Angelina until next Wednesday? Want to check calendars?"

Gary and Melanie agreed to meet the next Wednesday morning to discuss Angelina, rank their final eight candidates and then invite them in order of preference.

That left Gary free on Tuesday to prepare for both his 6:30 dinner party and his 4:00 counseling session with Annie and DJ. Actually he was looking forward to both events anticipating good times with his three new best friends. In a very short time Gary had gathered a dream team of friends and colleagues from the art museum, the Holy Oil Can and the Near West Side. When people asked him, "How ya doin?" Gary had actually taken to responding with what he used to decry as the era's most trite pop response, "Living the Dream!" But in his case he felt it was really true, he was 'living the dream.' One time when he gave that response to a museum co-worker she said, "That's what everybody says these days." To which Gary defensively responded, "No, no. It's really true. So many good things are happening to me right now that it really does feel like I'm living the dream." He received a smirk for his open honesty and decided he would save that testimony for only closest friends and family. Of course, they would also know that the dark side to that dream sometimes crippled Gary with the sadness, tears, grief and regret in his version of PTSD. But that is exactly what made them his closest, most valued friends, and he was looking forward to spending the whole evening with them that day starting at 4:00.

Gary decided not to plan or script out anything he had to talk about with Annie and DJ. He didn't want a hidden agenda that could undermine his friendship with either Annie or DJ, or derail DJ from drawing out from Annie and him the most important issues for their relationship. Besides, Gary thought DJ should be the one guiding their conversation. After all he's

181

the trained counselor. "That's settled, and with no extra work. Huzzah!" Gary cheered aloud. "Now let's go buy food!"

And off he went to the Pick-n-Pay to get beef already cooked and pulled, an eight-pack of buns, potato salad from the deli, chips, Sweet Baby Ray's barbecue sauce, a six pack of, oops, no drinkers here. Hmm. And, oh yes, vanilla ice cream and chocolate sauce for dessert, some decaf pods, Vitamin Water, Rooibos tea and napkins. And that about does it. Planned like a true man who rarely cooks anything from scratch. No, make that *never* cooks anything from scratch.

As he began shopping Gary realized this was the very same grocery store about which he had heard a story from his little brother 34 years ago. The story went that a little five-year-old kid stole food Saturday mornings for his own meals while his mother wasted away her child support money on drugs and booze. Gary thought, 'I wonder whatever happened to that little kid? Hmmpf. He'd be like 39 years old by now. Heavens, probably married with five kids of his own.' Back to shopping he went. By the time he paid for his food, Gary was whistling, singing and altogether happy. So when he walked in the door of 1965 Harbor Street at 3:00 whistling and singing, his joy swept any remnants of sadness right out of his mind. "Hmmm. Maybe the house fills itself with the mood of the one who enters. Happy heart, happy house; weeping heart, weeping house." And with that he kept whistling as he set the table, "prepared" the food, set out pods for coffee and put the Vitamin Water and the potato salad in the fridge. He'd nuke the beef in the Sweet Baby Ray's at the last minute when they all got together. "Sounds like a plan, Stan. Just Living the Dream, team."

Just before four Annie and DJ knocked and walked through the front door right into joyous whistling and singing. They looked at each other with surprised raised eyebrows, broad smiles and Annie said what they both thought, "Wow! That's different."

"Hi, Annie. Hi DJ. Come on in. What's different?" Gary asked.

"Huh?" Annie didn't realize Gary heard what she said.

"You said, 'Wow! That's different.' And I asked 'What's different?'"

"You. You sound happy. Lots different than the last time I was here."

Gary nodded his head vigorously. "Boy, Annie, that's for sure. I am happy. The house is happy. You're here. DJ's here. And I'm preparing dinner for my three new best friends. I'm stoked." And then he added reflectively, "Happier than I remember being in a long time. Come on into the living room. As you may remember so well, I've only got the couch and four dining room chairs, so the dining chairs get double duty today," he explained pointing to three chairs and a small end table next to his desk, which housed the fourth chair. "Come on in and have a seat."

They sat down, and Gary offered proudly, "I've got tap water, Vitamin Water, coffee, decaf and Rooibos tea. What's your pleasure?"

Annie's heart sang with the joy coming from Gary and his house. To answer Gary's question, she quietly thought, 'My pleasure is seeing you so happy.' At first she decided not to say that out loud, but then she just had to tell him, "Gary, my pleasure is seeing you so happy."

"It's the house, Annie. This is a happy house. Thanks to you and DJ, this is a happy house."

DJ saw Annie's eyes begin to redden, so he quickly jumped in. "I'd like high test coffee, please, Gar. How about you, Annie?"

Annie took a sobering breath so she could answer. "Decaf for me, please, Gary. Thank you."

Gary ran two pods through the coffee maker, gave DJ the high test and Annie the decaf. Then he got a Vitamin Water out of the fridge for himself.

"We all set?" he asked.

"I am, thank you, Gar," answered DJ.

"Me too, Gary. Thanks." With her eyes now dry, Annie was all beautiful with smiles.

"You're welcome, for sure. So, DJ, what's next?"

"Well, let's pray to start. And then I'd love for you both to tell me what happened Sunday night. Is that okay with both of you?" Annie and Gary both agreed. DJ prayed for them. And then Gary told him about his Sunday night darkness that started out with admiring his paintings of Dianah. When he finished, Annie recalled her part, worked hard to hold back tears that sometimes overcame her.

When Annie was done, Gary looked straight into her teary eyes and declared with, in DJ's mind, unmistakable love, "You were my angel, Annie."

DJ let some silence settle in as he smiled at them both. He then bowed his head and took a few deep breaths for himself struggling over what he should say to his two new friends, what would help them the most. He silently prayed for God to lead him, listened for a beat and then began, "So, Gary, what are you going to do with those pictures? And Annie, you've seen them, what do you think? They seem to have been the catalyst for a very serious post-trauma episode, wouldn't you both agree?"

Surprisingly, Annie spoke first, successfully battling back all but a few of her tears. "I think they were, DJ, but it was the bear who knew Gary needed help. Gary, it was a big brown bear. And it had a *woman's* voice. Do you think it was Dianah? I mean, it sounds a little off the wall, but the more I retell the story to myself, the more I think Dianah was the brown bear. After all, when you say those two words together, brown bear, it's Dianah's name. I'm just absolutely certain she is the one who woke me up and sent me to you."

DJ responded. "Gary, what do you think?"

"Honestly, DJ," Gary answered, "I think the same thing. Plus I've come to three conclusions. Maybe four," he chuckled. "The first is that Dianah did choose the brown bear as her spirit guide even before she adopted Brownbear as her artistic name. Spirit guides are sacred realities to the Dine` people. And they believe bears heal and lead a person to decisive, deliberate action with soul-searching insight. For a brown bear to appear in a dream with a warning call to action fits what Dianah taught me about her spirit guide. So yes, DJ, I totally agree with Annie. Annie, I do believe with you that the brown bear of your dream was Dianah. My second conclusion is this: since the brown bear appeared to Annie, who never met Dianah, and not to me, means she trusts Annie with my life. And my third conclusion is that Dianah was warning me that I must not live in the past, neither in that catastrophic fire nor even in the wonderful days we enjoyed together in Paris. Such hanging onto the past will only result in my falling into darkness, and missing out on the blessings right in front of me. DJ, I'm afraid that the Paris paintings will always lead me to lust after Dianah when I can never love her again, and therefore keep me from welcoming another woman into my life. Like Annie. It was almost as if Dianah brought Annie into my house of darkness, not..." Gary struggled for words, "to be Dianah's replacement, but to bring to us both a new day of healing and hope."

Now all three were drying their eyes, but DJ seized the moment to return to his original question, which he thought would become a crucial decision in Gary's recovery from PTSD. "So, Gary, what about those paintings? What are you going to do with them?"

"Well, I believe that Dianah went back into the house with Lily to retrieve the rest of those paintings. And that's when the fire fell down upon them. Not that the pictures themselves are darkness or evil or anything like that. But Dianah was going back also to retrieve our past joy together."

"Gary," Annie started, "I'm sorry to interrupt, but I see it the same way. As I sat on the floor with you Sunday night in the middle of those paintings and your chaos, and then Monday morning again after you left for the art museum I looked over your paintings again, and I saw her beauty and your memories right there in your art. And Gary, I realized first off, that I cannot compete with your memory of Dianah. I can live *with* her memory in you, yes. But compete? No way. And, second, I am sure that the brown bear of my dream does not want to compete with me either, but wants to let me into a new, separate place in your life."

With that, Gary lost his composure, but not with dark tears, rather with smiling tears that actually enhanced his joy. "That's exactly, that's exactly it, Annie. That's why I have been whistling and singing all day." He jumped out of his chair and moved to embrace Annie, as she got up to welcome him with eager arms. "Ten seconds?" she asked knowing the power of a ten second hug.

"No less," Gary affirmed. "DJ, count ten seconds. Slow."

DJ laughed but obeyed. "One, two..."

"Slower, DJ," Annie pleaded.

"Thrrrrreeeeeeeee… fourrrrrrrrrrrr…

Gary started to say, "Much betterrrrrrrrr…" but Annie interrupted him planting not a peck on his cheek, but an impassioned kiss fully on his talking lips.

DJ stopped counting, smiled and enjoyed every second.

"Ten."

Following that they couldn't discuss much else, except to suggest that Gary donate the paintings of Dianah to the Paris Academie, the idea being out of sight, out of mind, but not destroyed. However, he would keep his painting of the Dancing Bear, since both Annie and Gary had now experienced Dianah's Spirit Guide themselves. They came to no final conclusion, so they decided to meet together again in a few weeks. DJ prayed for them, and at 'amen' Joe knocked at the door, and the dinner began.

DJ, Annie and Joe raved so boisterously over Gary's barbecued beef on warmed buns, that a visitor might have thought he had prepared scallops and lobster served with a chunky seafood bisque and potatoes au gratin. But Gary's concoction actually tasted better to them. No lie. The guys even had seconds, warming more buns and cleaning out the pan of barbecued beef. Then, amazingly, they still had room for ice cream with chocolate sauce. No four friends ever had a better dinner together, or enjoyed each other's company more.

Joe hadn't yet heard about Gary's meltdown Sunday night or Annie's rescue until he asked what the three of them were confabbing over when he knocked at the door. After they told him about Gary's meltdown that began with the paintings, Joe responded with his typical brash humor, "All I've got to say is show me one of those paintings!" Gary nodded and mouthed,

"Okay," but he wasn't going to touch them. So Annie got the folder and showed Joe the picture on top.

"Holy cannoli, Gary. She's gorgeous, and your painting is steaming, bro. I can see your point, and I think you need to send them back to France like *right now!* OR... You could, you know," he said grinned snidely, "just give them to me." At that everybody booed. "Hey, hey, just kidding. Hold on. It's a tease." Then when Annie snatched the painting out of Joe's hand and made a big deal of hiding the folio from him, the whole table devolved into laughter, including Gary.

Once they settled down they chatted like long time friends, cleaned up together and shortly after 7:30 left for home. DJ was the last to leave because he wanted to talk a little more with Gary. "Gary, I know Joe was teasing, maybe tastelessly so, but he had a point when he said, "Send them back to France, like right now." How about we pack them up right now, label them fine art, and I'll ship them out tomorrow for you. What do you say?"

"You're forcing my hand, DJ."

"Yes, I am."

And Gary already knew that when the stakes are high, DJ is not one to pull punches. He is straightforward, honest and caring.

"DJ, I'm just not ready to let her go, not even the Paris paintings. Annie fills a big hole in my life, and I appreciate her for it, but I'm not ready to take a next step with her and forget Dianah."

"Well then, be careful with Annie. I understand what you're saying. Grieving takes a long time to work through. But I believe that Annie wants to help you work through your PTSD, and she is ready right now to commit to it — to you. There's no doubt in my mind that the two of you care deeply for one another, but there's some danger in working out a volatile problem like PTSD compounded by grief, compounded by growing, can I say, love. Can you see that?"

"Yes, I can see that, DJ. Are you saying I like Annie too much?"

"More than that. I think you're past 'like.' And you're in the danger zone of chaotic PTSD with Annie, until you deal with your loss of and love for Dianah. Annie's love for you tells her that she can save you. My experience says she cannot. It's something only you can do for yourself. Look, there is some similarity between PTSD and drug addiction. Both consume your thinking, and both demand your life. In addition, you have no control over when the drug or PTSD makes its demands, knocks you down into a black hole and hurts the people closest to you. I know an old guy who had come back from `Nam emotionally damaged by war and physically crippled by agent orange. When he got home, looking for healing and love, he burned right through two marriages. Not because he didn't love the women he married or was unfaithful, or that they didn't love him, but because he couldn't control the PTSD, the flashbacks, the days of total darkness and the anger at being held hostage by terrors of the past. He went down too many dark holes too many times, and visited his war upon the women he loved. You remember my story, don't you? It's not so different. We take our wives right into the war zone and make them live there with us. It crushes them.

"Look, Gary, as fragile as you are now, if you continue to build a relationship with Annie that you cannot emotionally sustain, not only will you be inviting Annie to live with you and Dianah, which she says she is willing to do, but you will also be inviting her to live with you in the charred ruins of your Durango Mountain dream and your subsequent overwhelming grief. She will see the fire through your eyes again and again. Gary, Annie deserves to live her own dream with you. But, my brother, you are not even ready yet to send off those paintings, let alone give that wonderful woman a healed man and a fresh dream."

"Wow. That's sure laying it on the line, DJ."

"Yes, it cuts to the chase, doesn't it?"

"So, what do I do? Just cut her out of my life because I'm too risky. I don't want to do that either. She's a wonderful woman."

"I know, and I think that cutting ties is too drastic for both of you. But, Gary, you need to make a commitment to leave what's lost behind. Understand, there is no cold turkey with PTSD. It's all up here, in your head, and it takes a lot of time and a strong will. You are addicted to the memory of loss and pain. You can't let it go, because when you do, you fear Dianah will go with it. And to be honest, some of that will surely happen, but not nearly as much as you fear. The fear for you to overcome is no longer the fear of the fire, but your fear of living *without* the fire and therefore *without* Dianah. Gary, Dianah will never be farther away from you than she is is right now. Or closer. So, no amount of dwelling upon her or grieving that life-snuffing fire can bring Dianah or Lily back into your life any more than they are. Yet that's what you attempted to do with those pictures. When you focused upon your loss by dwelling upon her pictures, you thrust yourself helplessly down a treacherous dark hole. It's not a matter of giving up Dianah, because the living-with-her or living-without-her choice was irrevocably taken out of your hands three months ago. No, your real choice now is to believe that you can take a next step without her."

Gary simply nodded his tear-streaked head. "I know. But that's hard, DJ."

"Yes, it is. But I think you can, and I know you must. And, Gary?"

"Hmm?"

"Right here, on the Near West Side of Cleveland, you have everything you need to take that next step. Your parents live 15 minutes away. You have the foundations of a new career at the museum with Mel, including dozens of museum staff plus your Old Tony Studio. You already have close friends in Joe, Annie and me. And you've got faith in the Lord God who gives fresh starts and new life. We're all with you, every single one of us. All you have to do is take that first step."

"And you're not talking about with Annie?"

"No. The first step is in your own heart. Will you trust God, who said, 'Behold, I make all things new?' Like that old Thomas A. Dorsey song goes," and DJ softly sang,

" 'Precious Lord, take my hand, lead me on,
let me stand;
I am tired, I am weak, I am worn.
Through the storm, through the night
lead me on to the light,
Take my hand, precious Lord, lead me home.' "

Neither friend said a word, until DJ lifted his right hand, bowed his head and started praying. When he finished, he refocused upon Gary and simply asked, "Gary, are you ready?"

Gary slowly nodded his head. "Yes, I am."

"Good. Then, how about you and I package up those paintings right now, and you let me take them home with me for safe keeping. And when you're ready, together we'll send them away to Paris." It was DJ's hard sell, but they both knew that at some point overcoming PTSD takes a caring friend to put things plainly on the line and give his friend a chance to choose a new life. "What do you say, Gar? Deal?"

"Deal."

Gary went to bed that night realizing what a life-changing gift DJ had given him that day. Not only had his friend helped Annie and him connect the dots between Gary's struggles with PTSD, his love and grief for Dianah, the darkness trap of the Paris paintings and his growing affection for Annie, but DJ also named the Paris paintings as the barometer for Gary's willingness to reshape the broken pieces of his life without Dianah. DJ's counsel and prayer blew away the smoke of fear, and blew in crystal clear insight. Truth and confidence took up residence in Gary's healing heart, and that night he slept like a baby.

Chapter 24

Paying It Forward

When Gary's alarm woke him at 7:30, he sat bolt upright and said aloud, "I owe DJ a steak dinner!" Why a steak dinner in particular? Who knows. Any dreamscape reasoning was lost to Gary in the tail end of a rather pleasant dream about his new friends. So perhaps it could be something else equal in value for the hope DJ had given him the night before. And something else. The Paris paintings were gone. DJ took them when he went home last night, and it surprised Gary how their absence already lifted a heavy load off of him. He was surprised that he felt so bright, hopeful, even victorious and ready for a day at the Cleveland Museum of Art. Melanie expected him at 9:00 and it pleased him that he was on time and eager to get started. So he hopped in the shower, started soaping up and began singing. Fifteen minutes later, showered, shaved and dressed, he sat down for his breakfast of coffee and oatmeal with raisins thinking about the candidates Melanie and he would consider for the remaining four or five spots in his studio. As he left his house and drove away in his SUV he reached to turn on the radio and suddenly realized he had not thought for even two seconds about Dianah or Lily or the fire or even Annie. "Hmphf," he puffed aloud. "That's different. First singing. Then whistling. And now a cleared mind." He grinned and chuckled. "Forget the steak. I owe DJ a two- inch filet mignon!"

Gary still loved arriving at the art museum and using his key card to navigate his way through the locked doors and down to Melanie's office. When he got there, Mel was seated at a small conference table already reading the studio applications. When through the clear glass wall she saw Gary smiling, she smiled back and motioned him in.

"Good morning, Gary," she crooned.

"Good morning Melanie," Gary smiled. "Good to see you this morning. Looks like you've already gotten a head start on the applications."

"I just got started five minutes ago. I've been thumbing through them to refresh my memory." And she passed the files to Gary. "Gary, remember last time we talked we realized that there are no child prodigies here. They're mostly college and graduate school age, which is good, but, like I told you last time we met, there is no disadvantaged youngster like you had hoped so you could 'pay it forward.' But right there on top is the application of Angelina Anderson. Still want to look at her application first? I had her in my top three anyhow."

"Absolutely," Gary agreed. "I would like to explore Angelina's application first. But still, thanks for pulling that dream of mine into our conversation first thing. Our talk last week prompted me to think that maybe the studio and the prodigy are two related but separate endeavors. But, on the other hand, it could be that Angelina Anderson bridges the gap between the two, gives us someone we didn't expect, but who might be even better for our outreach mission. What do you think?"

"Agreed. So let's get started with Angelina."

"Onward and upward! Excelsior!" Gary joked.

"Here you go," Melanie offered, "I have duplicates of everything."

"Melanie, you're so good."

"Hey, Gary, my close friends and family call me Mel. I'd love you to call me Mel."

"Thanks, Mel. And sometimes I'm Gar. Let's dig in."

And they did. For the next hour and a half they read aloud every word of the top three candidates' applications, Angelina being first, and then they searched online for corroborating due diligence. For two of those first three Gary and Mel found so much on line that they ended their search satisfied with their choices. Not so with Angelina. In fact, there was absolutely nothing on line about her. *Nada.*

"Strange, isn't it?" asked Mel. "Over the years I have known her, I never felt the need to run due diligence on her. After all, she was just a kid. This is different. Let's start with her college references, shall we. Maybe we're missing something here."

"I'll call." Gary dialed the number listed on the application, but got a 'not a working number' message. "Whoa. There's a red flag. Any speculations, Mel?"

"None that match the high quality of her 12-page essay on *sfumato,* or what I have come to know of her during the last several years. We do have her home phone number there. Her address is East 51st Street.

"I know that area, Mel."

"I do too. Pretty poor neighborhood, but I've known about Angelina's poverty. In fact, I worked hard to get her in free classes or in scholarship programs over the years. And, of course, that *sfumato* essay just blew me away, so I never took time to read much else on her application."

"I want to call," said Gary excitedly. "She's a maybe, huh?"

"I've talked with her and her mother on the phone to sign her up for classes. Maybe you should be the one to call this time and use the art museum line. I can't recall if they have caller i.d., but if they do, it will give you instant credibility."

"Okay. Here goes."

Somebody did pick up. "Hello, Anderson residence. To whom am I speaking?" The woman had an interesting accent Gary couldn't place plus she had wonderful, practiced politeness.

"Hello, Ms. Anderson, my name is Gary Siciliano from the Cleveland Museum of Art. May I speak to Angelina."

"She just got home from work, I'll get her." Ms. Anderson took a beat and then shot back with, "Is this *really* the art museum?"

"Yes ma'm. Angelina applied for one of our programs."

"I told that girl she was just dreamin' and not to apply."

"Dreams sometimes come true, Ms. Anderson."

"Whoa. I'll get her. Just a minute. Don't go away. Angel! Telephone."

A girl's voice shouted back, "In a minute, Mama."

"You best make it a short minute, girl."

"I'm coming." Angelina took the phone from her mother. "Hello, this is Angelina."

"Hello, Angelina, my name is Gary Siciliano."

"No. No you're not. Who are you really? Rafa, is that you? If that's you, I'm gonna kill you good."

Gary lost it laughing. "No, I'm not Rafa. And I don't want to die." Angelina's turn to burst out laughing. And Melanie could not contain herself from laughing along with her.

"Who's that woman laughing? I hear a woman."

"That's Dr. Melanie Zurkos, curator and director of art education at the museum. She and I are working together to find artists for my Old Tony Studio. We're calling you, because both of us were totally impressed with what you wrote about *sfumato* for your application. Angelina, that was outstanding work, the very best essay on *sfumato* of all our applicants, some with masters degrees in art history. Yours was better. Much better."

"So you really are Gary Siciliano? Old Tony Gary Siciliano?"

Gary chuckled at the Old Tony reference. "Yes, I really am. And Dr. Zurkos and I would like to meet with you. Would you be willing to come to the art museum and meet with us tomorrow when you're off work?"

"I'm off all day tomorrow. I can come any time. And I'll bring some art. I already know Dr. Zurkos from kids' summer art programs I was in. Hi, Dr. Zurkos."

"Hi, Angelina!"

Gary grabbed back the lead. "Wonderful," he said. "So you already know how to get here?"

"I sure do. I've been to the art museum hundreds of times. It's my favorite place in the whole world."

"One of mine too. So, how about 10:00 tomorrow morning at the main rear entry upstairs by the welcome desk? Does that sound good? Know where I'm talking about?"

"I sure do know where you're talking about. And it sounds very good." Angelina took a beat and then shyly added, "Oh, and Mr. Siciliano, I'm, I'm really excited to meet you."

"I'm excited to meet you as well, Angelina. See you then."

"See you then."

When Gary hung up the phone, he and Melanie just stared at one another, both saying, "Wow!"

Mel spoke first, "She could be the real deal, Gar. She sounds so much more mature than she was even last summer."

"And we just 'connected' on the phone, didn't we?"

Mel smiled and said, "I know. You were both fun to listen to."

Gary spent all evening thinking about Angelina. She wasn't as young a prodigy as he had hoped to find. In fact, he hasn't seen any of her art yet, so he didn't even know if she was an artist of any kind, let alone a prodigy. And then there were the 'false' statements on her application. Gary had been trying to ignore them, giving her an ethical pass, because he himself knew the temptation a poor kid has to lie, cheat and even steal to escape the stranglehold that poverty held upon the hopes of inner city kids.

The truth is, though, that lots of kids who 'make it' never ever feel compelled to lie or cheat in order to succeed. After all, Gary himself was one of those kids. Definitely he would gently confront her about her false statements and hold her accountable. Secretly, he now even questioned her authorship of that wonderful *sfumato* essay.

Still, he couldn't deny how she won him over with her excitement over the phone, excitement, he hoped, borne of her love of painting and her eagerness to learn.

"Well," he said aloud, "we'll find out soon enough."

He fell asleep that night excited about his meeting that morning and eager for the morning to come. And instead of counting sheep, Gary counted all the human angels who have helped him along the way. *Zzzzzzz.*

Morning came on time and Gary found himself confidently flowing with the current of the day. Some days are meant for traveling on the appointed path toward the promised land, and this felt like one of those, prompting Gary to whistle and sing all the way to the Cleveland Museum of Art to meet young

Angelina Anderson. He was especially looking forward to his new assigned parking space that Melanie arranged for him in addition to his key pass. And as he pulled into the parking garage he even perked up his whistling and singing a notch. Then, when he actually drove into his own private parking space, he let out a giant "Wahoooo!" followed by a quiet "Thank you." He wasn't exactly sure whom he was thanking — Melanie, the art museum, God — but in the last few days he had just taken to smiling and saying "Thank you" out loud for everything from a green traffic light to a sunny day to a special parking space. He had never done that before in his life. But these days he had such a thankful heart filled with such joy that the thank-you's just naturally flowed out of him. It was different being so thankful, kinda weird, but Gary liked it. Actually, he liked it a lot.

He arrived at the CMA Welcome Desk at five minutes til ten still humming a tune as he looked around. The museum guard sitting behind the desk had already gotten to know Gary, so noticing he was looking around the guard greeted Gary, "Good morning, Mr. Siciliano. Looking for someone?"

"Good morning, Larry. Yes, I am. I'm looking for Dr. Zurkos and a young lady I've never seen before."

"I can't help you with the young lady, but here comes Dr. Zurkos now."

"Yep, there she is. Thanks, Larry."

"Oh, and Mr. Siciliano, there is a young woman been standing over there by the coat check counter. See her?"

"Yes, I do. Thanks, Larry."

"Lucky guy," Larry added. "She's quite a looker."

Gary snickered and said, "Yeah, Larry. And young enough to be my kid." Larry just shrugged and grinned.

As Gary turned toward Melanie, that beautiful young woman leaning against the coat check counter holding a fairly large folio watched him. Her light caramel skin was actually a shade lighter than his own swarthy eastern European complexion, and her large eyes topped a lovely, peaceful face. Could be her, Gary thought, but he'd wait for Mel so they could walk together to meet her.

"Good morning, Gary. I think that's our girl. She looks more grownup every time I see her."

"Shall we go meet her?"

"Let's."

Then just as they turned, the young woman began walking toward them. So they kept moving toward one another and met half way.

"Hi!" she greeted them. "I'm Angelina Anderson."

Melanie took the lead. "Hi, Angelina. Good to see you again. You know, we have known each other for a long time already. I remember you in those summer classes years ago when you were just a little girl" They smiled at each other with good-to-see-you-again kind of smiles. "And now, every time I see you, you look less and less like that little girl and more and more the beautiful young woman you have become."

"Thank you, Dr. Zurkos. I remember all those years too, fondly, I might add. It's always great to see you too."

"Thank you."

"And this gentleman, as you may have already guessed, is Old Tony's artist, Gary Siciliano."

"Hello, Angelina. I'm not often introduced referencing Old Tony these days, but it is nice to meet you."

Melanie jumped in, "Gary, I've seen Angelina in the museum many times before, and particularly, as of late, studying the Old Tony photo print and unfinished canvases, so I thought she might like the confirmation that you are indeed the Old Tony artist."

"That's true," Angelina said. "And even though when you two met at the Welcome Desk, I was pretty sure that he would be Mr. Siciliano, I still liked the formal introduction."

Gary missed the second smile that passed between Angelina and Melanie because he was trying to peek into Angelina's slightly opened folio. He couldn't see a thing, so he confessed, "Angelina, I'm trying to sneak a peek at your art, but I can't see a thing."

"Oh, here take it," she said offering him the whole folio.

"No, I can wait. But I'm just sorry I was so rude. Why don't you hang onto it and let's head down to the studio, talk a bit and find a large work table where you can tell us all about your work. Okay?"

"Sure, that's okay with me."

Melanie agreed. "Let's head on down."

They made small talk on the way until Gary went right to the red flag on the application. "Angelina, you had a college reference on your application. We tried calling, but the number didn't work."

"Oh, I'm terribly sorry for that. There was a small art program in Boehecker's, a local two-year business school. I applied because I was pretty sure I could afford the tuition, and I did get accepted. But then Boehecker's closed the art program. So I signed up for a computer graphics class, applied for a part-time job through the school and got hired. Anyhow, I'm sorry I didn't let you know."

Gary was both relieved there was no deceit and proud of Angelina for taking a business class instead and getting herself a part-time job. So he told her, "No problem, and good for you for taking a computer class and getting that job."

Melanie was just a little surprised that Gary hit on a sticky issue before they even sat down. However, she was grateful in the end how they both handled it and that there was no deceit whatsoever on Angelina's part. Still Melanie decided she needed to take the lead back from Gary.

"Ahhh," Melanie said. "Here's the best big work table. How 'bout we claim it and get right to your art?"

"Dr. Zurkos, that sounds good to me. I'm much more comfortable talking about my art than anything else."

Gary chimed in, "Great, because your art is exactly what I'm looking forward to the most."

They settled around the table as Angelina opened her folder and pulled out the four pieces on the top.

"Okay if we start with these?" she asked as she put out four renditions of Old Tony similar to four of Gary's unfinished canvases displayed right in front of them, a sketch, a charcoal cartoon, a wash in the color palette, and a very nicely, unfinished painted portrait with the beginnings of *sfumato*. Gary almost gasped as he broke into a giant smile, and Angelina smiled in return, obviously very proud of her work.

"Whoa! It's Old Tony himself!" Gary crowed. "And, Angelina, this is excellent work. Absolutely excellent." Gary took some time to study closely each one of Angelina's Old Tonys, all of which impressed him immensely. "Did you get some help with these, or did you figure this all out on your own?"

"Mostly on my own, but I had a little help."

"Oh? You got very good help. Who was it, if I may ask?"

"Dr. Zurkos."

"Whaaaat? Melanie! You fox, you!" Gary's smile exceeded the width of his face, or seemed to anyhow. "You said you knew Angelina from the kids' summer classes, but this...this is impressive."

"It's all her, Gary. Angelina was here so often, that one day last summer when she had her sketch book I walked over to see what she was doing, and there was Old Tony in a fabulous sketch. In fact, Angelina, is this the one that you were working on that day?"

"Yes, that's him."

"Gary, she can sketch whatever she sees. Angelina has that ability, like you did." Gary and Mel exchanged knowing smiles, each thinking the same thought: 'Angelina surely is the one.'

The three of them spent the next hour or so studying all of Angelina's art, with Gary giving Angelina encouraging comments piece by piece, just as Ms. Green had encouraged him the first time they met looking over his fabulous sketchbook, which, he remembered not only included three Old Tonys, but also many perspectives of the long-legged fly plus anything else that caught young Gary's sketch-crazy attention. Gary was now as impressed with Angelina's art as Ms. Green must have been with his art thirty-four years ago. And he laughed to see how giddy Angelina was over all the richly deserved encouragement Gary was lavishing upon her. They both enjoyed the moment and got even happier when Gary turned toward Angelina and simply said, "Angelina, these are outstanding pieces of art, many of them worthy of framing and selling right now. You are such a talented artist and a quick study to boot, that I would love for you to be part of my Old Tony Studio. What do you say?"

"I say that's awesome! Thank you! I would love to. I don't know what else to say, Mr. Siciliano. I can't wait to tell Mama. Oh, but I have to help her with the rent. Can I still keep my job?" Her youthful bubbling was infectious, and Gary just chuckled, thinking what a wonderful addition she would be to a studio probably populated with more introverted artistic personalities.

"Sure, I think a part-time job would be great; however, there is a stipend attached to your studio position granted year by year for a maximum of three years."

"You mean money? I actually get *paid* to learn from you?" Gary nodded his head and smiled. Angelina continued, "Mr. Siciliano, that would be wonderful. I would love to be part of your Old Tony Studio."

"Good, I'm glad. But still I want you to take a few days to think it over and talk about it with your mother. Then if you still want to proceed, and I hope you will, we'll meet again for you to sign some paper work and make it all official. Sound like a plan?" Gary smiled.

Angelina beamed. "It sounds like a great plan!"

"An awesome plan!" Melanie added.

"So, Angelina, let's give ourselves a couple of days to think things over, Melanie and me and you and your mother. Then we can talk again — maybe Friday? What if I call you and your mother 10:00 Friday morning? I mean, even though you and I both know that at 19 you're old enough and capable enough to make your own decisions, I'd still like to know what your mother thinks. That's important to us, and to you as well, I bet. And maybe she'd even like to come in with you when you sign the agreement? You think?"

"Oh, she'd love it. She'd be over the moon!"

"All righty then. Friday morning it is, when your mother gets back to earth, we'll talk on the phone."

Angelina giggled as she packed up her art. "Okay. Thank you again, Mr. Siciliano. Talk with you soon!" Angelina packed up her art and off she floated to the bus stop.

Meanwhile Gary and Melanie left for Mel's office. On the way, Melanie, a big smile on her face said, "I think that went well. Don't you?"

"I sure do. You knew I was going to ask her, didn't you?"

"Well, it's a little late to ask me now. But yes, I just knew you would. And, I'll tell you this, if you hadn't asked her I would have been sorely disappointed."

"Good." Gary took a breath, then asked, "She's quite a find, isn't she?"

"The best."

"And you, Dr. Zurkos, did a great job tutoring her. How long did you actually work with her? And wherever did she get such a wonderful understanding of *sfumato*?"

"Well, as for your first question, I began working with her nearly five months ago, way before you and I even talked about your studio. In fact, when you put out your applications, I encouraged her to fill one out"

"Amazing. And *sfumato*? Did you help her with *sfumato*?"

"Not with the essay, but I served as her librarian to get her, for example, an English translation of Leonardo's notes on painting, which, by the way, she simply devoured. Devoured."

"I'm impressed, not surprised, just very impressed. But how about actually painting those microscopic thin layers of glaze in just the right places, which for the most part she did quite well?"

"That's all on Paulo."

"Who's Paulo?"

"Paulo Ringetti is a fabulous art restoration specialist on staff who knows Leonardo and *sfumato* intimately. He agreed to tutor her, and is still working with her. Plus he helped her understand Leonardo's studies of light and how it reflects off different surfaces from different angles determining what glaze goes where and how it should be applied and how it brings a painting to life. Together they studied Mona Lisa and Old Tony, especially when we got the original Old Tony. By the way, Paulo was thrilled with the Old Tony trade, almost as thrilled as you were. As for the essay, if Angelina got any help with her *sfumato* essay, it came from Paulo, but I made sure he understood that Angelina needed to be the sole author of that essay. They are both ready for you to take over the tutelage, though. Ready and excited."

"That sounds awesome, Mel. But maybe we need to keep Paulo involved, I mean, if he's willing. What do you think?"

"Like team teaching? Planning together?"

"Yeah, the whole nine yards. Would he be available for that? Could he, you know, team teach the whole studio with me? It sounds like he would have a lot to offer."

"Gary, my brain is exploding at the possibilities of the two of you working together, improvising, creating art, shaping artists. Let me think about it. He's already got a pretty full work load, but if he likes the idea, and I think he will *love* it, maybe we can tweak staff assignments just a little to free him up for you. Let me think about it for a day or two and then we can revisit it. Is that okay with you?"

"Yes, ma'am. And thanks... especially for the Paulo idea. Wow. So now we need to offer positions to the two others in the top three, and then we can determine the next four or five, maybe tomorrow?"

"Tomorrow sounds great. And Gary, I love working with you. You welcome new ideas. You appreciated my initiatives with Angelina. You even welcomed Paulo into your vision of the Old Tony Studio, trusting my judgment without ever having met him. It's wonderful to work with somebody I don't ever have to worry about as a colleague. I just appreciate how positive you are with me. We are a great team, Mr. Siciliano. I can't wait to see this studio at work."

"Me too, Mel. Me too."

Chapter 25

Dinner at Houdka's

I t was still early afternoon when Gary left the art museum, certainly early enough to call Annie and ask her to go to dinner with him. He had lots to tell her and get her take on, especially concerning Angelina. So as soon as he got home and into his house he called and got to hear Annie's wonderful voice: "Hello, Dunlop Realty, this is Annie."

"Hi, Annie."

"Hi, Gary. Good to hear your voice, big guy. What's up?"

"I just want to talk with you and catch up on things. So much has happened in just the last five days, you know?"

"Yes, I sure do, Gar. Anything in particular?"

"Well, you, Annie, are at the top of my list. And then there's this 19-year-old applicant for the Old Tony Studio, Angelina Anderson. She has amazing talent and drive. I was hoping I could bounce some things off of you."

"Of course. But Gary, that name sounds really familiar. Maybe she and her mother came looking at houses a few years ago. I'll think about it. Is she Latina?"

"She is. Definitely mixed race. But that's not a concern to me as much as how fast I offered her a spot in the studio. Would you go to dinner with me? We could go to Houdka's out in West Park near my mom and dad's? Would that be okay?"

"Perfect. I love Slovenian food, especially theirs. I'm already salivating for their chicken paprikash. Yum. You want to pick me up at my house on your way?"

"Love to. How about 5:30?"

"Sounds perfect." Annie said. Then turning on the charm Annie added, "If I leave work early I can be cleaned up and beautiful by 5:30."

"Whoa, cleaned up and beautiful. Mmmm, mmm. You really know how to change a guy's agenda. See you in a little bit."

"Don't be late now," Annie teased playing up the vamp.

"Not a chance. See you soon."

"Bye."

Gary ended the call and said aloud to himself, "It's just dinner, Gary. Right? Everything in my life seems to be layered with twists, turns and innuendo. Annie, Annie, Annie. Bad Annie! I need your help, not more confusion from Annie the LSP." He'd never say that to her, but goodness, goodness, goodness, she sure could let loose with Annie the LSP in a flash. And it sent him swirling way too fast. What he needed was a cool shower. "How in the world does she send the heat over a phone call?" he asked out loud.

So he showered and shaved and put on casual, working man's clothes befitting dinner at Houdka's Slovenian Family Restaurant...comfy fit blue jeans, a light weight, sweater-shirt kinda thingy and his Nikes. It's only dinner at Houdka's for crying out loud. "Settle down, Gar," he warned himself. Annie's vampy charm got him pretty rattled and off his game. Trouble is he liked that a lot. "Slow down, Gar, just slow, slow, slow. Deep breath."

He decided to sit down at his all-purpose table with some Rooibos tea and the <u>Cleveland Plain Dealer's</u> funny pages to settle down a notch by seeing Sarge beat up on Beetle Bailey again, Dagwood fall asleep on his desk at work and Snoopy 'dogfight' the Red Baron. He liked the funnies mainly because even Sarge's fisticuffs got settled in one four-frame strip, and other matters took, at the most, a week of four-frame strips. That's why the funnies settled him down, because, unlike life, they were predictable, that is to say, nobody dies in a mountain fire, unless the comic strip becomes a soap opera, in which case he'd just stop reading it for a while, so he could hide ... from goodness knows what. "Humphf," he said aloud. "So, Gar, hiding now, are ya? From what? Or is it from whom? Yeah. Yeah." He could feel a dark wave washing over him. Not depression. No, he wouldn't call it that. Battle fatigue maybe, even though he had never been in a war. He was just tired of battling. Battling what, though? The day? Yeah, but not every day. No, not every day. Who? Ah, yes. Who indeed. Annie. He drifted back to the funnies, scanned "Marmaduke," read "Pearls Before Swine" and started to doze. Before Pig and Goat and Rat could finish their lines, Gary was out like a light.

He woke with a start at ten after five almost falling off his chair. "Cutting it close, Gar," he admonished himself. "Getta move on."

A splash of cold water, a comb through the hair, a stick of gum and he was out the door, wondering again who in the world *was* Annie? Gift? Problem? Angel? Destroyer of a golden past? Giver of new dreams? "Huh," he said aloud. "All the above. How did that song go in the Sound of Music? 'How do you solve a problem like Maria?' That old nun sang it out of her frustration with a novice nun who probably shouldn't have been a nun in the first place. Too cute. Too lively. Too sexy. She needed a home, a husband, a family, not a convent. Movie goers could see that in the first twenty minutes. I wonder what movie goers would see in a movie of my life?"

He pulled his car up to Maria's door — right, and out stepped Annie. Too cute. Too lively. Too sexy. Anybody would see that in the first twenty minutes. Check that, in the first two minutes. But this is more than a two and a half hour movie with an intermission. This is days, weeks, months, maybe years and no intermissions.

Annie opened up the passenger door, and his heart thumped a mile a minute. "She is all that," he told himself out loud, maybe too loud.

"Hi Gary!" Annie half sang with a Julie Andrews smile. "What did you just say? 'She is all that?'" She grabbed his hand, looked at his suddenly stricken face and asked smiling, "You okay?"

"Yeah," Gary said. "Just day dreaming."

"About me?"

Oh, good Lord, how does she know stuff? Embarrassed that she was spot onto him, he half-fibbed. "Actually about 'The Sound of Music.' Long story. How did your day go?"

"Just okay, until you called. Then much better."

"I'm glad to be on the much better side. Ready for Houdka's?"

"I'm starving! I even skipped my cookies and milk after school so I wouldn't spoil my appetite."

"You're such a good girl."

"Oh, that reminds me. I'm sorry about when you called? I sorta let Annie the LSP sneak in. Your fault, though."

"Oh?"

"A spontaneous dinner invitation to a girl? Mister, that's a turn on, and an invitation for visions of joy and, well, fun times."

"That bad, huh? I didn't know. Honestly, I thought it was just dinner."

"Now you know."

"Now I know." Gary couldn't help smiling. Annie smiled back.

"Not that I'm complaining, though."

"That's a relief," Gary fudged the truth again. There's no relief when there she is sitting so close that he can hear her every breath. Smitten he was by this problem called Maria. "Ready?" he asked.

"Absolutely. And may I say it again, 'I'm hungry.'?"

"Got it. Let's go."

Seven minutes later they pulled into Houdka's parking lot, flew out of Gary's SUV and into the just-as-they-advertised delicious aroma of Houdka's Old Country Slovenian cooking. Because the waitress saw they were still youngish and 'obviously in love,' something Gary struggled to hide, though not Annie, she seated them by the cozy fireplace at a table for two in the most romantic spot in the restaurant. Gary and Annie smiled at one another and Gary shook his head, thinking every minute is a battle with lust — honest lust, but still.

So he asked, only half joking, "You *are* wearing that strong pit bull chain, aren't you?"

"Yes, I am. However, no guarantees, what with a romantic table for two, by the fireplace, nobody close enough to hear us and a chicken paprikash dinner on the way. Poor Annie the LSP is already straining at her leash. Down, girl."

Gary couldn't help laughing. She was all three of those things that disqualified Maria for the nunnery.

They both ordered chicken paprikash with Rooibos tea and an appetizer of small cabbage rolls plus cheesecake for dessert.

"All this and cheesecake too? Whoa, girl, settle down," Annie gushed pretending to calm the pit bull sitting next to her.

A few minutes of relaxed chit-chat did settle them down from the ribald humor that sprung from pent-up desires like a hot-and-ready pop tart springing from the toaster. Then, calmed-down, but against her better judgement, Annie asked, "So, Gar, what is it about this Angelina that you want to run by me?" Instantly she regretted bringing it up right off the bat. If this were a sticky problem in a business discussion, she knew that the one who brings up the sticky issue usually has the upper hand in negotiations. But this was so different. She wanted romance, Gary wanted business. Well, maybe, to cut him a break, not one hundred per cent business. But she wanted him one hundred per cent. Really wanted him. And yet she's the one who brought up this Angelina thing, whatever it is. What a screw up, she chastised herself. Oh well. She tried to get off her high horse and just settle back and listen as Gary talked.

"Well, mostly it's about how fast I made the decision that she is the prodigy I'm looking for, and that she should take a spot in my Old Tony Studio." Gary went on to explain a little more, then asked, "So what do you think?"

"That's it?" she asked more snippy than she wanted.

"What do you mean, 'That's it?'" Gary asked picking up an angry vibe from his date.

"Gary, two things. Number one: This is a great romantic dinner. You have outdone yourself. If your goal is to wine and dine me to get me 'in the mood,' you don't even need the wine. Get it? Gary, you have no idea what a catch you are...for me." She sipped her tea.

"Oh. Oh my. I've let the other Annie off the leash, haven't I?"

Annie laughed so loud she sprayed her Rooibos tea all over Gary causing him to join her in crazy laughter that filled the restaurant and caused heads to turn.

"Yes, you have." She tried to look serious, but she couldn't stop laughing. "And number two: Gary, — stop laughing!"

"Yes, ma'am."

"I'm serious!" But she was still laughing. The hard shell business woman she thought she needed to be, crashed like Humpty Dumpty, and all she had was love for this man. "Look, Gar, this Angelina thing is a simple business decision about something you are very good at. You already know how to make good business decisions about art and artists, in a snap. Plus you have Dr. Zurkos backing you up. What did she say?"

"She thinks it's great. She's already spent five months working with her. Melanie says Angelina draws just like I used to, anything she sees, spot on representation, all the time."

"Then, Gar, there you go. It's a slam dunk. You and your business partner are in total agreement. Seal the deal and get on with it."

"Wow. You see it all so clearly."

Annie sighed, settling down her upset. "And so should you. End of story, Gary. Don't belabor your decisions once you make them. You're a business man now. You can't flourish in your business if you constantly re-decide a good business decision you and your partner have already made. Once you make a well-thought-through decision together, get the contract signed and move onto the next step or the next deal. If problems arise, which they may even in a good decision, you'll handle them. You will."

"Wow, Annie. That's terrific. That's exactly the kind of advice I was hoping for. Thank you."

"You're welcome, Gar. I'm glad to help. But I have one more bit of advice you didn't ask for. Please don't overlook the wonderful possibilities you have with the person sitting at the table across from you. I'd rather not spend this wonderful romantic dinner reviewing what seems to me to be a slam dunk work decision. I came to be with you."

Gary sat speechless studying her moist eyes, marveling at a new discovery: Annie is quite a catch herself. This time he reached over for her hand. On purpose. With intention. They just sat there and gazed into one another's eyes, with Gary silently admonishing himself, 'Don't toy with her, Gar. You might lose her, and she is way too special.'

The food arrived. They "ooed" and "aahed" and dug in.

Dinner was outstanding, especially the chicken paprikash. And though neither one of them ever drank much alcohol, they ordered a split of Eastern European white wine to go with the main course and the fabulous cheesecake that wrapped up the evening with a grand huzzah!

This was actually the first intimate meal they had shared together without either overwhelming stress, real estate decisions or counseling. And it was delightful. More than that, it was revelatory in that they spoke transparently about everything that came up.

"Gary, you're quite a celebrity in the American art world, and so I was just wondering, when you first started winning art shows with Old Tony, like that first big show in Columbus you told me about, what did that feel like having people chant cheers for your painting *in an art show?* I never heard of anything like that, and it amazes me. How did you feel?"

"Annie, just like you said, it was amazing. After my dad and I hung up the Old Tony painting on my exhibition wall I just faded into the woodwork. I was so young and unknown that I didn't think anybody would recognize me, and they didn't. So I just got to watch how people related to Old Tony. Of course, some just walked up to Old Tony, paused long enough to say, "That's nice," and moved on. But some people walked up to the felt rope and just started talking to him, like Tony was a friend from the old country or the old neighborhood they used to live in — one actually spoke in Slovenian to him. Others, with thick Cleveland accents would say things like, 'Hey, Tony, remember how hot those steel mills were? Yeah, we'd finish our shift and get on the bus with skin so red we looked like we'd been sitting on the beach all day — har, har — except that we were filthy dirty.' Or 'Hey, Tony, did you ever see Feller pitch? My God, he was fast. Rapid Robert they called him in the papers. Struck out 20 that one game. Remember? More than 300 every season. Too bad he lost those years to the war. He would have been the greatest pitcher ever.' Or 'Hey, Tony, you really look great, you know that? That hot shot artist did one helluva job painting you, like you could just walk out of that picture frame and go for a beer with us at Mahoney's.'

"And then there was the old Italian man who walked up to the rope in front of Old Tony and just started weeping. I remember reading how that happened to Leonardo and Michelangelo. People would stand in line for hours just to get into their studios to watch one of them sketch out the cartoon, or add a few touches of *sfumato* glaze. And then when they got to see the masters actually apply color they would weep or cheer. I understand that. Because that was Leonardo, that was Michelangelo. They were the best ever. But for people to do that for Old Tony? Wow. That humbled me. I admit, I just lost it. I wasn't quite the detached observer I thought I would be. Had to walk away and reclaim my composure. But I will remember those days forever."

"You amaze me, Gary. With all your incredible accomplishments you are humble, not arrogant. You are kind and so selfless that you would move back here to inner city Cleveland to find kids to help like you were helped. Are you really going to let your students copy your masterpiece, sign their names to their copies and sell them?"

Gary chuckled. "Yes. But it will be their masterpiece once they paint it and sign it. It won't really look just like mine. And I'll love helping them do it. It's a privilege, Annie. A gift I can give. Like you help people find or build or renovate a home for families where they can make friends and grow up together. You don't just sell a house, you offer them a new life. It's a gift you give. And it makes a difference in people's lives."

"Thank you," Annie said with glistening eyes. "Gar, there's so much about you I admire and love."

"Annie, I feel the very same way about you."

They sat quietly for long stretches, just looking at each other, studying as if it were the day before a big exam in school on remembering each other's face. Then they smiled and held hands, nibbled at the cheesecake.

"Maybe it's time to go," he said, unsettled by his growing feelings for Annie, loving every word, every glance, every touch.

"I think it is too," she agreed.

Gary picked up the guest check. "I've got this."

"Thank you, Gary."

"No. Thank *you*." More smiling with moist eyes. "Ready?"

"Yes, but I don't really want to leave and break the spell."

"Let's take the spell outside with us then."

Annie smiled at the thought. "Okay," she said as she took his hand. Gary didn't mind. He smiled, paid the hostess, adding a generous tip, and they took the spell of a growing friendship into the night.

When they got to Annie's house, Gary walked her to her door, and said to her with a grin, "This better be a three second hug, because I'm afraid a ten second hug would do me in."

"Me too, Gar," Annie said, yearning for much, much more. "But maybe one day?"

"Maybe one day. Never know."

She stood up on her toes and softly kissed his lips. He returned her kiss and said, "Thank you, Annie. That was sweet. Good night."

"Good night, Gary."

Chapter 26

Clueless in Cleveland

Gary divided that sleepless night in half. From 11:00 p.m. to 3:00 a.m. he couldn't stop thinking about what to do with a problem named Annie. Such a problem. She's perfect and he's falling in love with her, but he is scared to pieces to let go of Dianah's memory. For crying out loud, is it even possible to love Annie while he still aches for Dianah? "Sometimes I am so clueless," he told himself around 3:00 a.m. Then from 3:00 a.m. to 7:00 a.m. he switched over to worry about making good choices for the Old Tony Studio. It's not as big a problem for him as Annie, but it was plain he wasn't going to sleep anyhow, so he traded one worry for another but actually did fall asleep about 5:00 am. Of course, he still woke up groggy when the alarm buzzed at 7:00. "Oy, Gar," he said as he shook his head. He tried cheering himself on, "Up and at 'em, buddy," he prodded himself. Slowly he rolled out of bed, plodded to the bathroom, showered, shaved, put on some clean clothes and made himself oatmeal and raisins with coffee, lots of coffee. "I better make double the coffee at double the strength for the trip into the art museum. No falling asleep during rush hour allowed." By the time he pulled into his fancy-dancy parking space he had a caffeine buzz that would surely carry him through the morning, and maybe the next three mornings. "Hopefully I won't chatter like an idiot with Melanie and make a fool of myself." Talking to himself had become his *modus operandi* in dealing with his clueless befuddlement. But it seemed to help him keep his thinking straight and his libido in check. It had worked so far.

Dr. Zurkos saw Gary through her office windows and went to the door to let him in with a bright, cheery, "Good morning, Gary. Good to see you. All ready to make some great choices?"

"Good morning, Mel. I am operating on caffeine, so I can only hope I'll be of some help in making 'okay' choices," he answered sardonically.

"No sleep?"

"Well, I did fall asleep around 5:00 a.m."

"Annie?"

"How'd you guess?"

"Just a hunch. You did say you were going out to dinner with her. And, honestly, you can't possibly be healed enough from your loss to build a serious relationship with Annie. What's it been, three months since Dianah and Lily passed?"

"About."

"Maybe you need to chat with Rev. Dr. DJ again."

"By myself, you mean, without Annie?"

"I think that would be best this time. Just be sure to tell her about it. A woman can get pretty paranoid when she finds out that two men she knows have been talking about her."

"Yeah. But I wouldn't blame her a bit. I am pretty wonky these days, if you know what I mean."

"Gary, you're the most level headed guy I know and quite a catch for Annie. But it's going to take more than three months to work through your grief and PTSD issues. You've got to be patient with yourself — and Annie does as well."

"Are these billable minutes, Doctor Zurkos?"

"Smart aleck." They both chuckled. "Why not call DJ and see if he can work you in this afternoon after you and I have lunch together?"

"That's a good idea, Mel. Oh, and you know what else is a good idea?"

"What?"

"That I call applicant numbers two and three."

"That would be nice. Why don't you tend to that right now. I've got to prepare for my staff meeting this afternoon, including texting reminders. That should take me about 40 minutes. Want to meet back here at quarter till ten?"

"Perfect."

Gary had reviewed the work of the two best candidates after Angelina. Actually, they were both much more qualified than Angelina in every way imaginable except one: inborn, God-given talent. Yes, they had professional success, life experience and age that would make them more like colleagues for Gary than students, and Gary was looking forward to that. In fact, he was downright eager to talk with them. So he set out their papers on his desk, and tapped in the number of Raphael Vicente, age 37, Associate Professor of art in oils at UCLA. Someone picked up on the second ring. "Hello, this is Rafa."

"Hello. My name is Gary Siciliano."

"Oh, super. I was hoping to hear from you soon. I'm getting my paperwork together for the sabbatical I'll need if you want me in Cleveland."

"Well, I do. For sure. Only I figured we'd dance around for a little bit before I'd have to say 'I do.'"

They both laughed. "Yeah, I'm sorry. I did put you in a bit of an awkward position, didn't I?"

"Yes, you did; however, we've got that behind us. I said 'I do' and you're making arrangements for the honeymoon." More laughter.

"Gary, I've got a hunch this is going to be fun."

"Me too. But first let me tell you some things I loved about your application." And he did, and they talked, and Gary was absolutely right, this guy was going to be a great colleague. In fifteen minutes Gary and Rafa had come to basic understandings. Gary would send him the agreement papers, his request for housing, and his financial needs. His wife and three children would remain in California, and he would take two long weekends a month to be with them.

"How long do you think you can keep up the two weekends a month routine, Rafa? That sounds like it might be quite a strain on all of you."

"Yeah, we'll see, Gary. My wife and I both worked on advanced degrees involving weeks apart, but never for a full semester let alone a year, and not with kids. But, Gary, we both feel as though my studying with you will be worth the sacrifices we will have to make."

"Wow. No pressure there! Rafa, I'll do my best to make it worth your sacrifices."

"Thank you, Gary. I'll tell her you said that."

"And meant it."

Next Gary called Michael Krumrei, an artist in residence at Pitt.

"Hello, this is Mike."

"Hi, Mike. This is Gary Siciliano."

"Gary! Great to hear from you, with good news, I hope. "

"Absolutely. Dr. Zurkos and I thoroughly enjoyed reading your application, and you were one of our three no-doubters, especially after we took an on-line tour of your art. You are a fabulous artist, and I only hope our time in Cleveland will give you what you're looking for."

"Gary, as a student, I saw Old Tony in person when you were in San Francisco, and I've got to say, I have never seen a portrait more splendidly alive and vibrant than your Old Tony. Your *sfumato* techniques are angelic, and I am looking forward to your instruction."

"And, Mike, I am looking forward to working with you in the Old Tony studio. I see you more as a colleague, and, therefore, I'm looking forward to learning from you as well."

They dove into the business end of things, and Gary found that Mike's circumstances were far less complex than Rafa's. Still, Gary promised to send him all the necessary papers, and when he ended the call Gary was elated with his first three draws in the Old Tony Draft Lottery.

A few minutes later Melanie walked in and cheered when Gary shared all his good news about Rafa and Mike.

"Gary, that is simply outstanding!"

"You're right, and I already like these guys!"

Mel smiled at her colleague, and said, "Gary, you are just too, too much! So now, before your caffeine buzz wears off, I'm ready for us to get on with the remaining applications, except for one thing."

"Oh?"

"Before we dive into those, did you call DJ to see if he has time for you this afternoon?"

Chapter 27

Such Good Friends

"Oh, nuts. I had such a good time talking with Rafa and Mike I totally forgot that I'm stressed out."

Mel laughed, and said, "Well, that's a good thing, isn't it?"

"Absolutely. I feel great, and caffeinated, ready to go! So, do you think I can just let DJ slide for now, or should I still call for an appointment?"

"Still call. Just because you aren't in the middle of a PTSD meltdown doesn't mean you are beyond needing regular help, especially with Annie."

"I thought you might say that. Okay, I'll call right now."

So he did, chatted with Clara, DJ's office manager, who then connected him to her boss.

"Gary, great to hear your voice. What's happening, and how can I help?"

"DJ, good to hear your voice as well. Have you got some time for me this afternoon? I really need to talk with you."

"Actually, I do. How does right after lunch, say 1:30, sound? Are we talking about Annie?"

"Thanks, DJ, 1:30 is great, and yes, it's Annie. But the whole business is all tied together, and I'm just a big hot mess. Not this minute, actually. But typically I am a hot mess."

"I get it, Gar. Glad you called. See you at 1:30."

"See you then. And, DJ, thanks again."

After Gary ended the call he said aloud, "I have such good friends. What in the world would I do without them? Thank you, Lord."

Gary walked back to his office to rejoin Melanie who asked, "Did you get an appointment to see DJ this afternoon?"

"Yep. And know what, Mel?"

"What?"

"I have such good friends. And in such a short time. You, DJ, Joe and Annie. Plus Clara, have to include her. She's a good listener and gives great advice too. I'm a lucky guy."

"Blessed."

"Yes, blessed. And thankful."

"Gary, you're a good friend to us too. But I've been thinking about the Old Tony Studio and adding up the number of people you already have in line to work with you. Angelina, Paulo, Rafa, Michael to start. Add to that your friends from France and their proteges. That's two more, plus two (or more) if your friends come as well. Then include the four master painters looking for tips rather than a full-time commitment and you're already up to thirteen not counting those who might sign up for your weekly master classes. Gary, that sounds like a very full load, maybe too full when you throw in your Harbor and Divine job along with Annie, DJ and Joe plus Dianah's memory plus moving cross country."

"Holy cow, when you put it that way, I guess I am getting in pretty deep already."

"A bit overextended, I'd say."

"Same thing DJ said. Hey, do you and DJ consult together?"

"We do, and have for many years."

"Huh. So, have you got some ideas on all that for me?"

"I do."

"Shoot."

"Gary, I think that's enough. Let's tell the other eight applicants the studio is full, but when there is a new opening you will call. In the meantime invite them to come as observers and attend your weekly master classes. And, Gary, after a year or so you'll get used to your schedule here, you'll know what you're doing at Harbor and Divine plus you'll have a full year of healing. Oh, yeah, you're certainly going to want time to paint your own work. Right? What do you think?"

"I think you are dead on. My mother used to say, when we took too much food, 'Your eyes are bigger than your tummy.'"

"Good way to put it."

"Yes, ma'am." Gary just sat quietly, nodding his head letting what Mel had said sink in. "Applies here as well doesn't it?"

"It does. And if you'll let me, I'll send letters to the eight and take that off your plate, while you reply to your friends in France, get started preparing for your studio, prepare for your first master class and set your own personal painting goals. Sound like enough for now?"

"It sounds like plenty, but doable. And you're right, any more and I'd have been in way over my head. Mel, I'm learning a lot from you. And from DJ. Thank you very much. You have lifted quite a load off my shoulders."

"My pleasure, Gar. Are you ready for lunch in the cafeteria?"

"Yes, indeedy. Let's go."

It was a short five minute stroll up the steps, through the utterly spacious and beautiful art museum atrium and into the main course cafeteria line. They both chose chilled baked salmon with lemon glaze and capers along with Rooibos hot tea and New York style cheesecake.

Somehow the conversation drifted, and Mel told Gary she was no longer married, having divorced five years ago. Gary then asked if she had any prospects, and Mel laid out quite a bombshell. "Well, now that you ask, DJ has asked me out a couple of times."

"No way! My Rev. Dr. DJ?"

"The very same."

"Well, that is just amazing. A couple times, you say?"

"Maybe a few times," She grinned mischievously.

"Son...of...a...gun! Mel and DJ. Mmm, mmm, mmmmm. Am I allowed to mention this to him? That I know?"

"Feel free. We don't want to hide a good thing from our friends. Besides, we thought you and Annie might like to double date some time. You think?"

"Well, I never thought about it, of course. But, you know what? That sounds like fun."

"He might mention something to you today."

"Huh. Well, I'll be," Gary concluded with a Cheshire cat grin.

"Oh, don't look so smug. Besides, I've got one more something. I was looking over the applications again, and, I don't know how we both missed it, but one application is from a Kinliah Lahcheen in New Mexico." She saw Gary smile broadly. "Does that name ring a bell by any chance?"

"Wow. It sure does. Kinliah was one of Dianah's dine` mentors in Shiprock. I can't believe I didn't put two and two together the first time through the applications. I'd at least like to talk with her. Is that okay with you?"

"Of course. Did you ever meet her?"

"Oh, several times. Kinliah and Dianah drifted apart when we moved to Colorado, but they were very close for a number of years before we were married. Okay if I just play this one by ear?"

"Sure. But, Gar, the studio is still full."

"Right. I was thinking more of an invitation as an observer and a master class. Do you think that would be all right?"

"As long as it doesn't pull you down into the pits again."

"I'll talk with her on the phone for a while before I suggest anything."

"Maybe even wait, and then, after you have a chance to mull it over you can call her back and extend an invitation...or not."

"Good idea. Well, I better be off. It's a good day for a walk over to the Holy Oil Can. Talk to you tomorrow."

Chapter 28

Sfumato: Great Art, Hard Life

T hen Gary was off on the ten-minute walk to talk with Rev. Dr. DJ Scott while he continued to be astounded about DJ and Mel dating. "Goodness, goodness," he said aloud. He figured they were old enough they could date anyone they want. But in his mind that was a bit of a game changer. He wasn't sure exactly why, it just felt like it. Still he said out loud, "Next dinner we'll have to set another place for Mel. Son of a gun."

Gary walked into the church through a door off the visitor parking lot — less by choice and more by force of habit, since he usually drove his car to talk with DJ. All the same, he still got himself buzzed in at the door to the offices. Clara saw him first and shouted out, "Well, look what the cat dragged in. Hi Gar. Good to see you."

Clara had a way of making Gary smile. "Good to see you too, Clara. I'm here for DJ?"

"He's waiting for you. Just knock and walk right in."

"Yes, ma'am." He knocked and called, "DJ, you there?"

"Right here Gary. Come on in." He stood up and thrust out his right hand. "Great to see you, my brother. Have a seat and let's talk."

"Thanks."

"Tea? Coffee? Water? Soda?"

"Coffee sounds great. Not much sleep last night, and I think the morning joe has lost its punch."

"Gotcha. Medium roast?"

"Perfect."

In less than a minute DJ was handing Gary his cup of fresh coffee. "Black?" He asked.

"Definitely black for today."

"All righty then. Let's pray." They bowed. DJ prayed. Amen. Then DJ jumped right in and said, "So tell me what's up. Why no sleep?"

Gary took a deep breath and launched into it, starting with Angelina, then asking Annie out to eat so they could talk, and so forth. The more he talked, the more he realized how Annie must have understood his dinner invitation as much more romantic than he meant it and with very, very little business. Even when she talked brassy, Gary still didn't get that she was sorely disappointed at his "un-romantic" conversation about Angelina, even though Annie was actually the one to open up the topic at the restaurant. And when DJ raised his eyebrows and grinned down his nose at Gary like the cat that swallowed the canary, it creeped out Gary, so he just had to ask, "What? DJ, what?"

DJ grinned even more broadly, shook his head and said, "You have to ask? Really?"

"I was a jerk, huh?"

"You could say that. Clueless for sure. Or you could say it in many other even less flattering ways."

"What should I have said?"

"That's not the issue, brother."

"What do you mean?"

"*That's* the issue."

"Huh?"

"Gar, from your point of view the purpose for the whole evening was what?"

"Getting Annie's advice about asking 19-year-old Angelina to be part of the Old Tony Studio. And then spending time with Annie."

"Right, you and your business problem were first, and then quality time with Annie was, what, a throw-in? How do you suppose Annie felt about that?"

"Oh...Yeah...Cheated? She thought it was a date, just her and me from beginning to end with the Angelina thing a very minor, oh-by-the-way bit of chit chat."

"Right. She went out to eat with you expecting the 'girl-first treatment' right from the beginning."

"So I'm discovering."

"Look Gar, Annie's a good person, so she was willing to help you with your little business problem, and eventually it sounds like you righted the ship and had a wonderful evening. But, Gar, she wanted to be first in your mind for dinner right from the get-go, not second to a 19-year-old art student. Make sense?"

"Phew. Boy, sure does putting it that way. That's exactly what happened. But I wasn't thinking about Dianah."

DJ laughed. "Okay. But you weren't thinking about Annie either, at least not first, not about her needs or her wants, both of which are you. Gar, she wants a love relationship with you. But your grief, your hanging on to your love for Dianah prevent you from needing or even wanting Annie's love. That's the message you first gave her at dinner."

Gary's face fell. "Needing or wanting her love?"

"Right. One word that describes you right now, and many people with PTSD, is *schizoid*, avoiding close relationships, mostly out of fear. Fear to give and receive love because the last time you did it was tragically ripped away from you. It's easier, less risky, to hang on to a memory of past love rather than risk your soul again on loving someone new."

"And losing it all again."

"Right. And that fear can sneak even into a dinner date and blind you to what it means to care about the person you're with."

"Ya, but, DJ, I'm falling for her — way too hard. That's really what kept me up all night."

"Falling. Want to love her. But can't. Does that about sum it up?

"Yeah. I guess."

"Fear is still the issue. Loss, grief, anger, guilt, regret — all the issues tied up with PTSD all leading to one thing that prevents life change, and that's fear. It takes a long time, but people do overcome it, and you can too."

"Thank you, DJ. That's a lot to chew on. But tell me this: How do I overcome it? I mean, like you. Mel told me you and she are dating. And, if I remember correctly, you had that fear, after the war and after your divorce. Right?"

"Right."

"So, how did you overcome that fear."

"I didn't. I'm still in the process of overcoming my fear. Of course, it didn't help that for years I didn't even know I needed to. Gary, Mel is not the first woman I have dated since the divorce. Not even the second or the third. I failed each time to let in even an ember of love that could have had the power to overcome my fear. The women I dated were willing. Not just willing, they welcomed me as a life-long love project, actually loving me somewhat because of my neediness. Willing to love, they were, but they also expected me to love them in return. But like with my ex-wife, I never did keep my end of the love bargain with them either. My fear stopped me."

"So what makes you and Mel different?"

"Me, I hope. Trust in the love God gives us. Welcoming a new life. Mel still wants to help save me like the others I dated. But she has more understanding of the obstacles ahead for us."

"Why do you think that is?"

"Gary, Mel's PhD is not in art. She has a masters in art history like you do. But her PhD is, like mine, in counseling from the Gestalt Institute in Cleveland and Case Western Reserve University. Actually, that's where we met — the Gestalt Institute. We were students in groups and classes together at the same time, both working through our own problems while training to help others with theirs. Counseling succeeds, just like love, when one flawed person helps another, not fixes another or saves another.

"Her widowed father abused her when she was a child. It went on for years. Not forced. Not violent. Not mean. Actually, she loved her father, and he loved her. It was tender, however tragic. Akin to being married in a warped way, they never sought counseling. Her father thought of Mel as if she were her mother. Treated her as her mother. Loved her as his wife. And little Mel fell into the role he had created for her, loving him as she had seen her mother love him. Unfortunately, her father had never dealt with his anger and guilt over his wife's death — she died in a car accident with him driving — and so now after years of loving his own daughter as his wife, he had to deal with a new generation of self guilt and anger in his own mind, in his own life, over what he had now done to his daughter. Every day his fear of real love crippled his heart. His double dose of guilt was that he had killed his wife and now he had destroyed their daughter. Helpless he was to change. Afraid. So in his mind, the next best thing was to kill himself. He used a gun in the bathroom. Mel discovered him. That left Mel without a father, without a 'husband' and traumatized for life. She was left to grieve as his child and as his wife, unable to trust anyone with that knowledge, and unwilling to follow his lead and take her own life."

"That is terrible, DJ," Gary said entranced at the most tragic love story he had ever heard. "I assume she knows you're telling me this."

"Actually, her idea. We both know that it takes time, Gar. You are still young in your journey of healing from your loss and the guilt you have that Dianah died in the fire and you did not, that you could not save her. It will take you years to process that, to heal. But you can still learn how to love again along the way. You can still learn to be less and less afraid."

DJ took a breath and went on, "Mel and I have counseled dozens and dozens of people and couples with their own tragic life stories, while still working through our own healing and learning how to love and trust each other. We have found that self-disclosure, personal transparency and straight-up honesty and decency are love's partners in the process of healing and building the hope that leads to new life. We both want that healing love for you and Annie, and would actually like to help, couple to couple. Mel suspects that Annie has her own story to tell and needs a chance to tell it to someone, or someones, who will still love her unconditionally. We thought dinner together might get that started. It would give both you and Annie support to overcome your fears and take a chance on love."

"Wow. DJ, thank you for trusting me with your life stories. You know, I've spent my entire art life celebrating the wonders of *sfumato*, the art of obscuring the lines so that art looks more like life. *Sfumato* covers up the harsh realities of line art, smooths out the sharp edges making a portrait softer on one hand and more alive on the other hand. However, in real life, I've discovered that smoothing over the harsh realities of living hides the wounds that actually need to be healed."

"That's a great analogy, Gar, especially for an artist. I'll bet Mel would love to hear your take on *sfumato* as great art but hard life."

"I'd love to share that again, because for the first time I see Annie as no less vulnerable, no less hurting than I am. If Mel invites Annie, I'm in."

"Oh my, Gar, Mel will do more than invite her to dinner. Mel plans to invite Annie to lunch so they can share life stories with one another. That way our dinner together won't come off as an ambush for Annie. We'll all be fully transparent. Nothing hidden in smoke. That goes for all of us. It's the only soil in which love can freely grow. How about you pray for us, Gar?"

"I can't pray, DJ. I don't know how."

DJ rummaged in his desk drawer, pulled out a small piece of paper and gave it to Gary. "Here's a simple outline for prayer. Follow it, and you can't go wrong."

They read it aloud together like a Sunday school lesson:

"1. Call on God. 'Dear God' or something like that.

2. Praise God. Tell God why God is good. One thing.

3. Thank God. One thing will do. More are good too.

4. Ask a blessing from God. Usually for someone else.

5. Close 'In Jesus' Name, Amen.'"

"Think you can now?"

"I think so. Thank's, DJ."

"Your welcome. Go on, give it a shot."

"Okay, here goes. Dear God, You are the Author of love and friendship. Thank you. Thank you for my friends, DJ, Annie, Mel and Joe. Please bless them with healing and love. In Jesus' Name. Amen."

"Amen. Thank you, Gary."

Chapter 29

Sfumato: When the Smoke Clears

W hen Gary got home from talking with DJ at the Holy Oil Can, there was a letter from LaPlata County, Colorado waiting for him.

"That's strange," he said as he turned the letter over and over trying to guess what was inside. "Hmmm. Looks very official. Ah! Like a ticket or something. Oh, no. Not old speeding tickets I didn't pay. I thought I paid them all before I left. I guess I better open it." He poked his finger in the corner opening of the flap and slit open the envelope, where he discovered a very official looking letter addressed to Garret Siciliano. "How in the world...?" He never, ever introduced himself by his full given name. "Ahh. Property tax. That's where they got the name. But, still, this isn't a tax bill." It was a letter from the county commissioners of LaPlata County. "Whaaaat?" He read aloud to himself, and was glad he did, so he could hear it too.

"Dear Mr. Siciliano,

On behalf of the Commissioners of LaPlata County, Colorado, we request your presence at the dedication of the Dianah Brownbear Parkway portion of U.S. Rt. 160 overlooking the East Canyon of Durango Mountain as well as the Dianah Brownbear Ridge Park also located on U.S. Rt. 160 between Durango and Mancos overlooking the East Canyon."

Gary had to catch his breath as his heart raced. He kept reading aloud even though his throat tightened with emotion.

"This dedication is in response to a request from the Navajo Nation to honor the life and work of the late Mrs. Dianah Siciliano also known as Dianah Brownbear, for the outstanding contributions she made in teaching, celebrating and promoting traditional Dine` culture of the Navajo People through art and mutual respect. We anticipate a large contingent representing the Navajo Nation from New Mexico, Arizona and Colorado to join in our celebration of her life and work.

The keynote speaker for the day will be Kinliah Lahcheen, President of the Shiprock Chapter of the Navajo Nation. Ms. Lahcheen signed the original request from the Navajo Nation to honor Dianah Brownbear. Ms. Lahcheen also personally requests your presence.

The date for the celebration is July 27 at 1:00 p.m. MST. We will gladly provide airfare for you and one guest on Frontier Airlines plus paid rooms for you and ten guests at the General Palmer Hotel in Durango.

We do hope you will accept our invitation. Please notify us at your earliest convenience.

Sincerely yours,
Matthew Chawka
County Commissioners, Ch.
LaPlata County, Colorado

Gary sat at his all-purpose table feeling every kind of emotion known to man, minus dark sadness. It was a glorious surprise and filled him with pride for Dianah, with awe that her body of work would be so honored and with delight at the honor itself. He was also fearful of returning so close to the site of the fire, although it was still some months away. But, by golly, he determined immediately, he will go, come hell or high water. Celebrating her life would be so uplifting compared to the terrible grief at the funeral service. And he would invite his parents and friends, especially Joe, DJ, Mel and Annie. Yes, especially Annie. "I'll pay for all of them," he announced to the heavens. It would be incredibly exciting, and not morose at all. The Dianah Brownbear Park and Parkway? What an honor! And well-deserved. As he sat and imagined the trip together with his friends, joyful energy coursed through his body, and a proud smile filled his face. The pastor's words from Revelation 20 at the funeral, which at that time seemed so unreal, so unattainable through the fire's smoke, now became real and imminent, so much so that Gary actually cheered, "Huzzah!" and quoted the Bible verses from memory:

> "Then I saw a new heaven and a new earth, for the first heaven and the first earth had passed away." "He who was seated on the throne said, 'Behold, I am making all things new.'"

And Gary bowed his head in his hands and prayed prayers of utter joy and thanksgiving. He felt his life turning a one-eighty in an instant, a nano-second, from darkness to light, from grief to hope.

He called his mother and father first, then DJ, Melanie, Joe and lastly, but, he felt, most importantly, Annie.

"Hello, Dunlop Realty, this is Annie. How can I help you?"

"Annie!" Gary said with off-the-charts enthusiasm. "Annie!"

"Gary, what's up? I've never heard you so excited. Ever."

And he told her about the letter, and asked her to go with him on July 27. "Please say yes."

After she answered, "Yes, Gar! Absolutely!" and they ended their call, Annie sat stunned, mind racing. She said aloud to herself, 'Was that a proposal? 'Please say yes???' He was positively ecstatic, but about what exactly? Me? Dianah? Surely it was about Dianah, but more than the awards, although they are beyond awesome. Does he see it as another chance to love her? No. He's gone that route and it was way too dark. No, he was giddy, absolutely happy, and that's why he called me. He called *me*. Or ... and this is a stretch, and a hope, for sure ... does he see in this a fabulous opportunity for closure that he never saw coming and never could have ever figured out for himself? Just dropped in his lap. Huh... That was a call to celebrate good fortune all around. Posthumously for Dianah to be sure. But for him too. And for us? Whoa. Hold that thought, Annie.'

And while she replayed the phone call in her head again and again, she closed up for the day knowing she was lost to work for sure. She locked up the office, climbed in her car and drove home, still thinking. 'This is a beautiful gift-wrapped opportunity to honor Dianah, celebrate her life and their marriage, and what? To put it to rest? To let it slide peacefully into the past and still feel good about it? No, feel more than good. Fulfilled. Completed in his saga with Dianah. Set loose, even, by a wonderful celebration planned by other people who admired her. Liberated from the darkness of one tragic day, he might now be set free to both cherish the joy of their life together and move on. Hmmm. Maybe I should have been happier for him, and not so confounded by his over the top rejoicing. I'm sure he sees an 'us' in the picture now. After all, he wants me to be there with him on July 27th. "Please say yes," he begged me.'

She got out of the car, walked into her home just as her phone rang. She didn't recognize the number, but she answered it anyhow.

"Hello, this is Annie."

"Hi, Annie, this is Melanie Zurkos, a co-worker of Gary's."

"Oh, yes. Dr. Zurkos, right?"

"Yes, but Melanie or Mel is better."

"Okay. Thank you, Mel. Gary has mentioned you often, mostly how much he likes working with you. How can I help you?"

"I called to invite you and Gary as well as my friend DJ to my home for Saturday night dinner, just the four of us. And since we both know Gary and DJ but you and I have never met, I was wondering if you would like to have lunch with me tomorrow, maybe at Cracker Barrel there in West Park around 11:30? Just the two of us to chat?"

Delighted at the two invitations, Annie replied enthusiastically, "Yes, both invitations sound wonderful. Thank you."

"You're welcome. See you at 11:30."

"See you then."

Once again stunned by a phone call into a cloud of wonderment, Annie set down her phone. "Oh, my goodness," Annie said aloud to herself. "Two crazy cool phone calls. I wonder..." But she didn't finish the thought, because the phone rang again. Gary. Eagerly, she answered.

"Hi, Gar. I'm glad you called again. What's up?"

"Hi, Annie. Two things. First, I wondered how you're doing with my last phone call. And second, Melanie Zurkos is going to call you to invite us to dinner at her place."

Annie smiled that she had the drop on Gary. "Thanks for the heads up, but she just called. We're going out to lunch tomorrow!"

"Great! So, the second thing is, how are you doing with my first call. I was pretty hyper, I know, but when I got that letter I felt like the weight of the world had just been taken off my shoulders. It's indescribable, confusing and wonderful all at the same time. Would you be free for dinner with me, like for right now? At Houdka's? I really want to talk with you, face to face."

"Gary, I'd love to. Pick me up in twenty minutes at home?"

"Yes, I'll be there. See you in twenty. And Annie?"

"Yes?"

"You're the best. Bye."

"Bye," she said to Gary. And then to herself, "The best. Huh."

Twenty minutes later Annie hopped into the passenger seat of Gary's SUV. "Gary, just so you know, I love last minute dinner invitations from you. Don't ever stop."

"Okay then. And I'm glad you're spontaneous. Don't ever stop."

They smiled and Annie leaned over and they kissed.

"Thank you, Annie. That was a nice hello, for sure."

"You're welcome. Let's go eat."

"Yes, ma'am."

They arrived at Houdka's before the dinner rush, so they got seated in a flash, ordered a cabbage roll appetizer to share, two plates of chicken paprikash, Rooibus tea for two and one cheese cake dessert to share since the last time the cheese cake pieces were so huge neither one of them could finish.

"So, Gar," she said jokingly, "long time no talk. What's up?"

"Well, to be honest, that kiss we just had answered just about every question I had in mind."

"Funny. I was thinking the same thing."

"I guess, you could say, we have graduated to light kissing."

"You're right, and I'm glad. Tell me, Gar, about the burden you said that's been lifted. I made up things in a woman's mind, but I want to hear the real truth from you." And she smiled that killer smile.

"You remember two Sunday nights ago, don't you?"

"Vividly!"

"*That* was the burden. I have felt that I never had a chance to finish loving Dianah, to complete our love before she died. It's more than saying good-bye, but that's the sense. If our love were a portrait, I would have to add more glaze, more light, more shadow — more life to it so that it would seem to jump right off the canvas. Compulsively, like OCD, I would add to my painted memory of her. But I could not, so how could I say good-bye when our love, our life is not complete?"

"Oh, Gary," she whispered ever so softly as her heart ached for him. "I think I understand that."

"I'm glad, because that letter helped me to understand what has been missing — a completion. More than a last good-bye, but, rather, a tender and joyful celebration of her life and our love, Lily's life and our love. Without that completion, that resolution, all I can do is remain helplessly stuck in time shrouded in grief and remorse that I was not there."

"There for what, Gar?"

"To save them. To kiss them good-bye."

"Awww, Gary, Sweetie, but you did." Annie said as she touched his cheek.

"What do you mean?"

"Didn't you kiss them good-bye when you left for Columbus?"

Gary thought, and thought. "Funny, I've never thought about that. But, you're right, yes, I did. I kissed them both. And waved. Silly waves. And blew kisses and more kisses until I was swallowed up by the plane. Annie, I did. I did kiss them good-bye. Oh, good. Remembering that helps. A lot." A single tear slid down his cheek. Annie took her napkin, reached across the table to dab it away.

"Thank you, Annie."

She blew a kiss off one finger to say, "You're welcome."

"Now July 27th seems even more like it will be the final joyful act of our beautiful, tragic love story. Almost Shakespearean, you know, satisfyingly complete with tears of passionate love commingled with tears of tragic loss, everything remembered, but, and this is important to me, *nothing more to be added.*" Gary sat still with a quiet smile on his face. "She completed me, Annie, and I her. And Lily was the proof of our wondrous love." More quiet. "The July 27th celebration will make it all complete."

Annie knew to say nothing. Gary was making peace in his soul, and she could tell that it was good — very good. In fact, it was a miracle to behold, a bookend moment to the emotional chaos she had helped Gary endure two weeks earlier. As she matched Gary's quiet smile a single tear escaped down her cheek. Gary reached over and brushed it away. He was right. Complete for Gary and Dianah. And, she hoped, a glorious new beginning for Gary and Annie.

When their waitress brought their food they ate together in a wondrous peace enhanced by joy and smiles — and glances with eyes seeing things as if for the first time ever. New life. Not like rebirth or being born again. No. Brand new, never before seen smiles that had never before been smiled. Faces that never before glowed with radiance like Moses coming down from the mountain top after a 'Moment' with God. Surely this was a moment with God.

As befits a moment in the Presence of the Divine, they hardly spoke at all. Yet they whispered every word that needed to be said. When their waitress brought the cheesecake for dessert, they suddenly realized their dinner was almost over. So they took turns, very slowly taking small bite by small bite until, sadly, the cheesecake was gone. Then they held hands, got up from their table and smiled their way out the door.

Chapter 30

Miracle Smiles

Annie and Gary wore their quiet smiles to the car checking every foot or two to be sure the same peaceful smile was still glowing on the face of the other. It was. On both of them. Gary grabbed the passenger door handle to let Annie in, but he paused first, turned to Annie and asked, "Annie, is something happening to us? I mean a magical sort of something. Or is it just me? Do you sense it too?"

"I see in you a miracle happening right before my very eyes."

"A miracle? In me?"

Annie nodded and softy said, "Yes."

"What does that miracle look like?"

"Like peace in your face, in your eyes, in your smile."

"It feels like peace, yes. What else does the miracle look like?"

"Like joy from a load taken off of your shoulders."

"Yes, exactly, Annie. That's exactly how it feels. What else?"

"Like love has re-entered your heart."

"Yes. You're right again. Since the fire I thought I was carrying around love for Dianah, but it was not love. It was the empty spot in here where love used to be." He tapped his chest.

"It ached in here. And love doesn't ache. Grief aches. Loss aches. Loneliness aches. Emptiness aches. But love? Love anoints the achey, lonely, empty places with healing and hope and possibilities, don't you think?"

"Yes, I do. It heals the aches. Takes away fear. That's the miracle, Gary. That's the miracle I see happening in you right before my eyes."

"Yes, you're right. It's not magic, it's a miracle. I can feel it. And I'm so glad you can see it. Annie, do you think it will go away? Because I don't want it too."

"Me either, Gar. It's a gift from God, don't you think?"

"I do. Thank you. Thank you. Thank you, God. Hmm. Maybe I better open the door." And he did.

"Thank you," she whispered. Then on tip toes she gently kissed his lips. He kissed her back, and they both got in Gary's SUV, checked again for their peaceful, miracle smiles. Yes, there they were.

They held hands as Gary drove Annie home. He walked her to her door for a three second hug. Ten would have been way too risky. They said good byes, but on the way to his car Gary turned around. Annie was still watching him, so he waved, and Annie blew him a two-finger kiss. Gary returned her two-finger kiss with a cowboy 'back-atcha' finger point. Both smiled their miracle smiles, and Gary drove home.

Annie floated into her house on the miracle cloud. 'Yes,' she thought, 'miracles are happening indeed.' She wasn't sure if Christmas miracles were allowed to happen before Christmas, but there it was, and she found herself singing, "Joy to the World, the Lord is come, let earth receive her King." She laughed at herself, stopped floating and danced instead to the hall closet, took off her coat and hat. And tears fell. Miracle tears. No sadness, just tears of deep joy as she whispered a prayer.

"Thank you, God. Thank you, thank you, thank you, God."

Book Club
Discussion Questions

Sfumato
A Story of Love, Loss and Hope

1. Name the people who most helped Gary on his journey out of poverty. What was their role? What was the role, if any, of their faith in God?

Chapters 2, 7, 11, 15

2. Outside of your immediate family, what three people have helped you the most along your life journey? How did they help?
3. Discuss what event(s) most adjusted the nature of Gary's life journey. What event(s) have most altered the direction of your life? How has your faith in God impacted those changes?
4. If you did not include Tony in your discussions of #1-3, consider all the ways Gary's friendship with Tony, the old Slovenian/American man, directed and redirected Gary's life.

Chapter 7

5. Why, for years and years, did Gary take the unfinished painting to art shows? How was that similar to Leonardo's finishing of the Mona Lisa? Who helped Gary persist until Old Tony was finished?

Chapter 7

6. Describe the circumstances leading to Dianah and Lily dying in the mountain fire. Gary arrived 30 minutes after rangers closed the road to their home. List everything that changed in Gary's life as a result.

Chapter 1

7. Describe the role faith in God played in the lives of main characters: Gary, Dianah, DJ, Joe and Annie.

Chapters 18, 22, 23, 24, 27

8. Who were Dianah's helpers along her life journey. How did they help her?

Chapters 4, 5

9. Were Gary and Dianah well-suited to be married? Why or why not? Give some reasoning to back up your answers.

Chapters 1, 3, 5, 13,

10. Describe Gary's friendship with DJ and Joe in light of Galatians 5:13-26. What does PTSD have to do with their friendship?

Chapters 18, 20, 27

11. Describe Gary's friendship with Annie. What do you think are the crucial issues in their friendship? How did they deal with those issues?

Chapters 11, 12, 16, 19, 20, 21, 22, 29, 30. (and those in between!)

12. What significance is July 27 for Gary? For Gary and Annie?

Chapters 29, 30

This section previews Book 2 of the Harbor and Divine series:

Hope at Harbor and Divine
by T.W. Poremba

Chapter 1

Annie and Dr. Zurkos

A nnie Dunlop got up early the next morning for work at her real estate agency so that she could take an extra long lunch hour at Cracker Barrel with Dr. Melanie Zurkos, a friend of a friend. Still, even with the early start, the morning flew by. While yesterday she was actually dreading this lunch date, today she was cheerfully looking forward to it. Go figure. After she had taken care of her on-line listings, returned a few calls, chatted with other agents when they stopped in, scheduled several home showings she was ready to make her way to Cracker Barrel.

Annie knew precious little about Dr. Zurkos. She did know, however, that she was fourteen years older than Annie, that she had a very responsible job at the Cleveland Museum of Art (CMA) where she worked with famed artist, Gary Siciliano, Annie's special friend. She also knew that Dr. Zurkos knew Gary from way back helping him work through his Master of Fine Arts (MFA) degree. Annie knew that it was Dr. Zurkos who helped Gary perfect Leonardo da Vinci's *sfumato* techniques and guided him in completing his award winning painting, 'Old Tony.' And that's it. That's really all Annie knew about Dr. Melanie Zurkos.

Plus, get this: even though Gary had all that history with her, he never shared anything personal about Dr. Zurkos with Annie. Zilch. Nada. Dr. Zurkos was a mystery woman, and Annie felt a little bit of excitement meeting her, as if Annie were a private detective on a due diligence assignment scoping out Dr. Zurkos. So now lunch with Dr. Zurkos filled Annie with the thrill of a detective on the hunt. "This should be fun," she told herself aloud. At 11:00 she closed up the office, zipped out the door, hopped in her car and headed for Cracker Barrel.

Dr. Zurkos was waiting for her at the hostess station. They shared smiles, said "Good mornings, I'm Melanie; I'm Annie; Glad to meet you," etc. and followed the hostess to a booth by the windows.

After they settled in, Melanie started off the conversation. "Annie, I am so happy to meet you. Gary and I have such a long history together, that, right or wrong, I feel like I have a stake in his happiness, which has taken quite a wallop since the fire that killed his wife and daughter. That's just to say, I'm so happy he found you. By the way, how did he get lucky enough to find you? Mind sharing?"

Annie didn't mind a bit, especially since Dr. Zurkos was smiling, seemed sincere and was light-hearted. Why not?

"I'd be happy to put my head on the block first, Dr. Zurkos," Annie said playfully. "But, actually, I feel like I'm the lucky one."

"Annie, it sounds like you're both lucky."

"We are," Annie agreed.

"Oh, and by the way, before you start, would you please call me Mel or Melanie instead of Dr. Zurkos? That title makes me sound like such a stuffed shirt, which is okay at the museum, but maybe not while I'm having a pleasant lunch with you. Is that okay?" Melanie asked sounding way more like a girlfriend than a stuffed shirt.

"Of course, it's absolutely okay. Melanie it is!" agreed Annie with a big smile on her face.

"Thanks, Annie. Sorry to interrupt."

"Not a problem...So, I grew up here on Cleveland's Near West Side, and I actually knew Gary from a distance in high school. He was a senior when I was a freshman at Lincoln-West. A couple of weeks ago when he and I talked about high school once, he told me he remembered 'cute little Annie Rogalsky.' I took that to mean he noticed, but didn't care. Usually high school guys don't notice the scrawny girls, if you know what I mean."

Melanie chuckled, "I think I do."

"Of course. But I really never even talked with him until a few months ago when he called my reality office from Colorado asking for help purchasing a house here in Cleveland after that tragic fire. I own Dunlop Realty. Got my license and business degree at Cuyahoga Community College. I felt lucky to latch onto a great guy who wanted to build his own real estate company. We got married, and I helped him build Dunlop Reality. Pretty good, considering where I came from."

"Whatever do you mean by 'considering where you came from?'"

"I grew up in a very dysfunctional alcoholic family."

"I'm so sorry, Annie. Your father?"

"Thank you. But no, my mother. She actually abused my father. She hit him with pots and pans. Ouch! And me, especially when Dad was at work she smacked me with wooden spoons.

"Spoons? As in more than one at a time?"

"Oh, yeah. She was ambidextrous in her violence, including her fists. But Dad, he was a great father, and I loved him, so naturally my mother resented him for that too. Resented both of us, actually."

"Was she drunk every day?"

"Just about... except for the times neighbors called Children's Services on her, and the judge sent her to rehab."

"Oh, my, I'm so sorry."

"Don't be, because the times when she was out of the house and in rehab were the most wonderful times for Dad and me. Sorry to say, when my mother wasn't around I actually had a very good home life. Finally Dad divorced her."

"Did that help?"

"Oh yeah. Big time. My grades went up. I actually made friends. I never went to school any more with bruises on my face or in places nobody else could see. But even divorced with a restraining order, she still snuck around to hound Dad for money, beating on him when she could and then trying to get to me. But Dad stopped her, wouldn't let her hit me any more. Finally the courts sent her to prison in Marysville for armed robbery and assault. I never saw her again. Not much of a role model for girl growing up, huh? Know what I mean?"

"Actually, I do."

"You grew up in an alcoholic family?"

"No, but I had no role model. My mother died in an automobile accident. My father was driving. After that, my father was not the saint your father was. Not bruising violent abuse, but..."

"Sexual abuse?"

Melanie nodded her head, "Yes, for many years."

"I am so sorry."

"Me too. But that life drove me in two directions. The first was art, which I dearly loved and into which I escaped at every opportunity. Fortunately, or unfortunately, my father died while I was still in school, and that's when I threw myself wholeheartedly into painting. I got pretty good at it too, even won a few prizes, thanks to school art teachers. No big prizes like Gary won, but good enough to get scholarships to Cleveland State where I earned an MFA and got a job at the art museum. That's when I met Gary."

"Holy cow, Melanie. That's a heck of a life story, and I have a hunch you're leaving out a ton of details."

"You're right. Maybe I'll tell you more sometime. But let me tell you about the second life direction I gained because of my abuse and all the counseling I needed to get my life straightened out. I guess I was pretty messed up. The silver lining was that, as a teenager, I got free counseling at the Gestalt Institute in Cleveland through Medicaid. Those wonderful people at the Institute both helped me and inspired me. And because of them I fell in love with the whole idea of helping people work through life's disasters. My masters degree, even though it was in art history, actually qualified me to study Gestalt counseling, and learn to help people the way the Gestalt counselors had helped me. So, Annie, my PhD is actually not in art, but in counseling from the Institute and Case Western Reserve.

"Along the way I also got married and divorced. Not a surprise, given the lessons I learned from my dysfunctional family life. However, Gestalt training, including more than ten years of one on one counseling and group therapy as well as a growing faith in God, helped me overcome my grief, anger, and general distrust and fear of men. New life was not easy to come by because I kept falling back into dark holes. So if you ever get a chance to look at my art, you can tell the periods with the deepest darkness. I met DJ during Gestalt training. While his story involves wartime PTSD, we still hit it off as two lonely people struggling to avoid falling back into darkness. We have become a team counseling couples, which is the best part of my new life. In fact, we are actually dating now, which is a huge step for both of us."

"Wow. How cool for you both! Melanie, thank you for trusting me with your story. You know, we do have some things in common: we are both scarred women, both survivors and both hungry for new life."

"Yes, ma'am! You hit the nail right on the head. And you can expand that to include Gary and DJ as well. That's the real reason I have invited you, Gary and DJ to a holiday dinner at my house. Together we would be four wounded people with wonderful chances at new life. Still want to come?"

"Now more than ever. Melanie, we can throw out life lines to each other, wipe away tears, and celebrate victories. Is that it?"

"That's exactly it, exactly what I have in mind."

⟢

To continue reading Book 2 of the Harbor and Divine series read:

Hope at Harbor and Divine
by T.W. Poremba
Coming early in 2022

Acknowledgements

Cathy Poremba, my wife and best friend, who endured all my conversations about my 'new best friends' in this book of fiction. She also read everything at least three times to find mistakes, come up with better ideas and hand me enough "atta boys" to keep me going.

Everett Stoddard, long time good friend, brother in faith, newspaper editor, pastor, counselor and encourager who gave generously of his time, effort, advice and counsel about what makes sense and what does not.

Robert Capes, illustrator, confidant, encourager, brother in faith, friend and one-time fighter pilot who has the encouragement gene from Barnabas.

Gerald Lewis, friend, brother in faith, who gives criticism wrapped in humor and tied up with ribbons of Christ's love.

Walter Isaacson, whose book, **Leonardo da Vinci,** introduced me to the mind, soul and art of the quintessential Renaissance Man. Dr. Isaacson's admiration of Leonardo's *sfumato* techniques inspired my creative thinking about artificial lines that divide us one from another and what it is that brings us together.

Joseph Campbell and his transformational book, **Hero with a Thousand Faces**, which taught me that heroes, men and women of all nations and races, change their world by traveling boldly upon the path set before them, relying upon angels and spirit guides along the way and then returning home to bless those once left behind.

Micah Poremba, the son who taught the father how to write a good fiction prologue. Thanks, Micah!

Jesus Christ, my Hero and Savior, as well as those who follow Him: **Mary His Mother, Paul of Tarsus, the Apostle John, sisters Mary and Martha, Francis of Assisi, Dr. Martin Luther King, Jr.,** friends of the Sea Islands Rural Ministry, who taught me the meaning of love across the artificial boundary lines of class, race and ethnicity, and lastly the real life missionaries of Cleveland's Near West Side, **Gary, Jack, Doug and Charles.**

All my helpers at Xulon Press.

And to all my readers, thank you all from the bottom of my heart for finding and then actually reading this book! I hope you fell in love with my characters as much as I did.

For Further Reading

Carroll, Lewis. **Alice's Adventures in Wonderland**. Deep wisdom wrapped in wonderful fantasy. If you haven't read it you need to before you fall down the rabbit hole yourself.

Campbell, Joseph. **The Hero with a Thousand Faces**. New York: Meridian Books, 1956. This is a creative mix of comparative religion, psychology and cultural anthropology. The Hero Myth has been a template for countless students, authors and film writers.

Isaacson, Walter. **Leonardo Da Vinci**. Simon and Schuster, New York, NY. Copyright 2017 by Walter Isaacson. Especially pp. 474-524. An engaging, enjoyable, enlightening, informative and inspiring biography written by a wise story teller.

What Life Was Like at the Rebirth of Genius, by the editors of Time-Life Books, Alexandria Virginia, p. 127, 'Assault Vehicle,' illustration. ISBN 0-7835-5461-3. A great summation of the Renaissance with Leonardo da Vinci as the ultimate Renaissance Man.

The Mona Lisa Foundation, Bellerive 29–8008 Zurich, Switzerland. Their website is fascinating and includes discussions of *sfumato* and excerpts from the journal of Antonio de Beatis. I found it all enjoyable to read and explore. It informed my prologue above.

The Holy Bible Pick it up and read it every chance you get.